Readers love The Haffling series
by CALEB JAMES

Haffling

"If you love fantasy and like to escape into secret lands with mysteries at every turn, if you love strong young men putting all they have on the line for love… then this is the book for you."

—Gay List Book Reviews

"I thoroughly enjoyed this dark and colorful adventure. *Haffling* really captured the essence of a modern fairy-tale, but it was so much more than that."

—Fabulous Fictions

"I was really enthralled by this Young Adult novel…"

—Reviews and Ramblings

Exile

"Caleb James has arrived—and his work is more polished, fascinating and truly top notch."

—Joyfully Jay

"Mr. James… weaves an incredible tale of fantasy in the modern world that, for me, makes it all work wonderfully."

—OJ He Say!

By CALEB JAMES

Dark Blood

THE HAFFLING
Haffling
Exile
Hound

Published by DSP PUBLICATIONS
www.dsppublications.com

Hound

CALEB JAMES

DSP PUBLICATIONS

Published by
Dreamspinner Press

5032 Capital Circle SW, Suite 2, PMB# 279, Tallahassee, FL 32305-7886 USA
www.dreamspinnerpress.com

Hound
© 2017 Caleb James.

Cover Art
© 2017 Alan M. Clark.
http://www.alanmclark.com
Cover Design
© 2017 Paul Richmond
http://www.paulrichmondstudio.com
Cover content is for illustrative purposes only and any person depicted on the cover is a model.

ISBN: 978-1-63533-921-5
Digital ISBN: 978-1-63533-922-2
Library of Congress Control Number: 2017950123
Published November 2017
v. 1.0

Printed in the United States of America
∞
This paper meets the requirements of
ANSI/NISO Z39.48-1992 (Permanence of Paper).

Veritas ex Cineribus.
Truth from the Ashes

One

DR. REDMOND Fall, the Unsee's leading criminal psychiatrist's head pounded. He fought the urge to scream. *Everything I have worked for, all that I've built, she would destroy.* His resolve faltered as he gazed on Queen Lizbeta, one of the fabled three sisters. She was beyond lovely, like someone had dipped the ethereal brunette in sapphires and mirrored obsidian. *I cannot listen to this. I should never have let her through the gates.*

"Redmond…. Dr. Fall." She gently laid a hand on his shoulder. He flinched.

"Please, there is no one else. There is nowhere else."

He felt the tentacles of her magic, a nuanced mix of glamour and persuasion, tap at his brain like the big, bad wolf encouraging three tasty little pigs to come out and play. He let out a stream of breath. On it he floated a silent defense ward so well practiced that not even Lizbeta Summer, queen of the Mist, would notice.

"I would not have come," she continued, "if there was another way. My sister May is too strong for me to hold."

He regretted his words as they left his mouth. The queens were not to be trifled with, even Lizbeta, whose magic was predicated on peace. "She is your sister. She is your responsibility."

Lizbeta pulled back. She gazed on him and then looked out the window of his turreted study hundreds of feet in the air. It was the highest remaining structure in the Unsee. He watched as she took in the view, the grounds of the Center… his Center, a gleaming white marble city, the one place in the realm that Lizbeta's power-mad sister May had never conquered, though she had tried. Beyond the Center's high walls was a ring of meadow ablaze with the purples and golds of spring. Then came the moat, as broad as a lake, which encircled all with its deep waters and scaly inhabitants ever eager to munch on the unwary and unwise. Beyond that was forest to the east and, should she look out the opposite window, the sea to the west. On clear days even her realm, the Mist, like a giant curtain from sky to sea, could be glimpsed, proof positive that their world was not the only one, though all sentient creatures on this side of the Mist knew of the three realms and had heard legends of more.

Her silence distracted him and pricked his anxiety. *This is all bad.* He again questioned the wisdom of agreeing to meet. But he could not deny his curiosity… *which killed the questling*, he mused.

"Yes." She broke the silence. "May is my sister, and if I could control her, I would. But I cannot."

Redmond snorted. "And you think I can. That's absurd."

She held his gaze. "It is not. In the centuries since you constructed the Center, it has never been breached. Though she has tried."

"'Tis true."

"And you have learned from her failed attempts."

"Correct… though I am not fool enough to tempt the fates."

"Your wards are unparalleled."

She flatters me. She tries to use my ego to draw me in. "So you say. But what you ask is reckless. I will not agree to it. I cannot put those who seek safety within these walls at such risk." He braced for her response. Her proximity was a distraction, her movements imbued with subtle magic as the afternoon sun glittered in the jewels of her gown and the strands of faceted black volcanic glass laced through her hair. *I cannot let her glamour me. What she asks is suicide.*

Lizbeta's hands played at her temples. With stooped shoulders she stared at the floor and then at him. "I have failed." She was about to say more when a frantic knock sounded at his study door.

"Enter," he said. The door flew open to reveal two wide-eyed and winded sprites, one forest green and the other sky blue. "Luluba, Seamus, tell me what brings you to my door."

His two students looked from Redmond to his royal visitor, whose graceful presence heightened their obvious panic.

"A giant fire-breathing salamander is on a rampage in the east," Luluba blurted. "It shoots fairy fire!" Seamus added as his hand sought Luluba's.

Redmond's breath caught. He looked from his terrified students to the window behind them and then to Lizbeta. *I knew she could not be trusted…. Cool your temper. It will do no good.* In a calm low voice, he spoke to Luluba. "Tell me everything."

Luluba, who always sat in the left corner of Redmond's lectures in front of his podium, let go of Seamus's hand. Her voice faltered. "A group of pixies from the east came to the gate. They're there now. They said that a massive white salamander burned their village. They woke to houses on fire." Tears tracked down her cheek. Her pointed chin trembled. "It ate them. Mothers, little babies. I don't understand."

Redmond felt the room close in. Brutal memories nipped at him. The murder of his parents by Queen May and the deaths of all those who had opposed her. Her reign of terror was the impetus for the Center's existence. And like the beating of a butterfly's wing that caused earthquakes millennia in the future, this moment felt surreal and all too familiar.

He turned on Lizbeta. "You've not been honest."

She looked at the two young sprites. "I've not lied."

Redmond's early life at the court of the three queens hit him like a train off its tracks. He gritted his teeth. "No, of course not a lie. We don't lie, and you know better than most how to twist and bend the truth. Queen Lizbeta, now is not the time for your mist and your charms. If you want my help, if you mean to bring danger to those I love and all I have built, tell me in clear words what has happened. Tell me the truth of your sister May and stop trying to glamour and persuade me. Tell me." His words tumbled out harsh and fast. But just the mention of fairy fire sent ice through his veins. For him, like so many others, many of them in treatment at the Center, fairy fire had ramifications far beyond its destructive burn. Because after fairy fire came the horrible and enslaving intoxication of fairy dust. Even now, if he let himself, he could smell that delicious reek, like cookies fresh from the oven. *Don't go there.* With an effort he blocked the memories of his addiction, of decades shrouded by the drug and the unending cycle of hunger and oblivion. *Don't think about it.* He started to salivate.

Lizbeta nodded. Her blue-black eyes, like the obsidian spangle on her dress, were fixed on Redmond's. "Yes, I have concealed and twisted. I will tell you what you need. But know this, Dr. Redmond Fall—everything I have done, both now and backward through the millennia, has been to preserve the realms: the See, the Unsee, and the Mist. I hold the worlds of humans and of sidhe separate. On this point my sister May disagrees. That is what this is about. What it's always been about."

Redmond softened his tone. "This is known, my lady. May thirsts for greater and greater power." A pit deepened in his gut. "She steals what she cannot have. She dines on the blood of her subjects. She is a despot and a bully, though even those terms don't approach her depravity and cruelty."

"Sadly, yes. Even as a child that was true," Lizbeta said. "She'd find clusters of pixies and devour them. Our father, hallowed be his name, thought it cute. He called her his little carnivore. But Katye and I knew otherwise. There was a darkness in May from the start. We knew that as she grew, enough would never be enough."

"I would know of those early days," Redmond said. "For everything in this world… or any world, is caused. To understand the present, one must peer through the past." And that's when it hit him. He held out his hand and felt his own special magic course down his arms and through his fingertips.

Like a dancer, Lizbeta lifted her hand to meet his. "I know what you are doing, Redmond. You have a reputation."

"Yes." He let the emotions of the queen pass through her flesh and into his.

"It is a good reputation. It is why I came."

"That and the hope that I can contain your sister in my city of marble and magic." He smiled as her thoughts and emotions flooded into him. There was a first wonderful sensation of her magic, her special. In ways it was a bit like fairy dust, though it carried none of the haze or forgetfulness.

"Yes. This… you… are my last hope."

"Come with me." With her hand in his, he gently pried at her thoughts and memories. He glimpsed a horrific white beast shackled in the Mist. Its maw was smeared with blood as it rampaged on powerful legs over the shattered bones of dozens, if not hundreds, of magical creatures. He released her hand and nodded. Without turning he spoke to his two students. "The danger is real. Find Gark and tell him to close the gates. No one is to enter or leave without further notice and without my approval. I will be down shortly to reinforce the wards." He pretended to a confidence he did not possess. "We will get through this. Now do as instructed."

Luluba, in obvious awe of the rarely glimpsed Lizbeta, struggled to find her voice. "This is Queen May's doing."

"Correct."

"But they say it's a fire-breathing salamander."

"They do." And slipping into his professorial mode, he again took Lizbeta's hand and grilled his favorite pupils. "Tell me of salamanders."

Seamus, not to be overshadowed by Luluba, on whom he had a painfully obvious crush, spoke. "They start their lives in water with gills, fins, and tails. As they mature, they get legs and crawl to dry land. They hide beneath rocks and can change color."

"Continue," Redmond said, "but soften and open your mind. Like there's air between your ears."

Seamus nodded. "They are found beneath logs and timbers of houses burned to the ground."

Redmond looked to Luluba. "Take it further. Shift between the solid and the magic."

She swallowed. "There is a legend that says they are born in fire, like the phoenix."

"So a creature who is at home in different elements—water, earth, fire." He felt a rush of emotions flow from Lizbeta into him as he spoke. *She hides much.* Through the physical contact—her fingers entwined with his—images came. Like splitting his mind in two, he carried on the conversation while passively watching moving pictures of the great beast tethered by magic and surrounded by bones. "And all of this has to do with our bloodthirsty queen. It's time for me to learn what I must. You two do as instructed, and then join me for evening rounds in the hospital."

With nervous glances between them, the two sprites nodded, and with a breeze that wafted through the windows, they took flight on the currents and vanished out and down.

"They are dear to you, those two," Lizbeta commented.

"Yes." *And I have brought them into horrible danger. But I see no choices here. Yes, we could all take to the winds and fly far, far away. But no matter how far the currents would carry us, she would follow.*

"I can see why. They are young. He is obviously smitten with lovely Luluba, though she's not yet set on him."

"You observe well."

"Said the master to the neophyte." She took in Redmond's comfortable quarters, from the quarried dark amethyst floor to chairs and sofas in deep green and burgundy fabrics. Even the ornaments, polished globes and graceful mobiles, invited the viewer to pause and look inward. "I hear this is done on a couch," she commented.

"If you'd like, though for many, especially those who've known pain and who've suffered, a couch in a stranger's home may feel too dangerous." Still holding her hand, he led her to a pair of deep-burgundy chairs set apart at a forty-five-degree angle. He inhaled. *What the hell am I doing? This is madness.*

She sank into a chair. Her hand fell away from his. "Tell me what I am to do."

With a practiced efficiency born from thousands of such sessions, he sat across from her. *This is wrong. I cannot, must not trust her.* But what left his mouth was his very own *Once upon a time.* "Start at the beginning. Tell me about your childhood."

Two

FDNY Fire Marshal Finn Hulain sat at his desk on the fourth floor of the Bureau of Fire Investigation citywide north headquarters in Brooklyn and hit Send. He was sick of these bullshit reports from the deadly night of a thousand fires that had blazed through Manhattan and the other boroughs a month earlier. The stack that remained was massive, though more senior marshals told him 9/11 was a close second. But at least there, the cause was clear—Al Qaeda and Osama bin Laden. With this, the city was left with fear, uncertainty, and death. He muttered and hit the keys, "Bullshit, Send, Next."

He grabbed the file on top, a party store on Eighth Street. He'd been at that one… and more. Even now, just touching the memories, the smells of burned flesh, the dead, and cookies…. *Focus. Just focus.* The work helped… some, as he tried to quiet the darkness and depression that threatened to bury him. Some days, like today, it got so bad he thought about taking his service revolver, putting it under his chin, and…. He wouldn't be the first since that awful night, and he would not be the last.

A clerk interrupted. "Finn, there's a firefighter and some other guy wanting to see you." She chuckled. "If the blond guy is unattached, do me a favor and get me his number."

He swiveled in his chair and felt the dangerous tingle of hope. "The blond guy's eyes, what color are they?"

"Yeah, I was getting to that. They have to be colored contacts. They're purple. Send 'em up?"

"Yeah." And for a millisecond, his funk lifted. But with hope came a decade-old pain. The hope that Rory Fitzgerald was still alive, but that ship had sailed. He braced and waited. *It might not be him. Don't get your hopes up. And if it is him… I'm going to kill him!*

A knock at the partially opened door and Finn bolted from his chair. "Charlie!" He threw his arm around Rory's younger brother, who hugged him back. And then he took in Liam, Charlie's too beautiful boyfriend, who wasn't exactly human, with his surfer-blond hair and freakish violet eyes. He didn't know what to do first, keep hugging… or hit him. "Where the fuck have you been?" And without waiting for a reply, he threw his other arm around Liam. "Where the fuck have you been?"

Tears squeezed from his eyes as memories tore at his brain. The last he'd seen of Charlie and Liam had been following a crazy chase up the length of Manhattan from the burned-out store on Eighth Street to Fort Tryon Park, the whole thing too insane to be real. Charlie gunning his red Ford pickup as they were hunted by a fire-spitting salamander that looked like an escapee from *Jurassic Park*. He coughed and choked.

Charlie pulled back. "What's so funny?"

Finn wiped his nose with the back of his sleeve and, not letting go of either one of them, looked from Charlie, with his dark hair and clear blue eyes—*so like Rory*—to Liam. His head spun with the weird mix of emotions: relief, love, fear. "She tried to eat you."

"Yeah." Liam nodded. "I have that effect on people."

"It gets old," Charlie replied, his gaze fixed on Finn.

The seriousness in his expression, like a pin in a balloon, wiped all humor from the moment. Finn shook his head. "What the fuck, guys. Where have you been? It's been a month. No word, no…." Without letting Charlie speak, he laid into him. "How could you, Charlie? You of anyone should know. This is killing your family. It's killing me. Where the fuck have you been? Well?"

Finn pushed back from him in anger. It was hard to look at Charlie, like an echo of Rory, who would have been about his age when he died in the towers. Rory Fitzgerald, Finn's best friend since he could remember and the only man he had ever loved, though it had been unspoken and unrequited.

"Sit down, Finn." Charlie's expression was unreadable.

Finn nodded. *Let him talk.* He knew Charlie. He wouldn't have put his family through this hell if there wasn't a damn good reason. "So what is it? And please, just the truth, no matter how rabbit hole it gets."

Liam flinched.

Right, Finn thought as crazy memories returned. *There are rules around asking questions.*

And, *Liam's not human*. And, *A month ago I almost got eaten by a lizard. No, wait a minute; salamanders aren't lizards, are they? No, they're amphibians, and who the fuck cares?*

Liam shut the door.

Charlie pulled up a chair and faced Finn. Always more serious than his years, the young firefighter looked like someone had tromped on his grave. Liam sat at his side.

Finn tried to lighten things. "So, what's today's adventure? Vampires, werewolves, that Jewish clay monster that avenges the downtrodden?" It felt forced.

"Finn, we've got some shit to tell you, and then we're heading out of town.… Out of this world, actually, and the punch line is, you need to come with us."

Finn braced. "I'm thinking not for a weekend on Fire Island."

The pair sat stone-faced.

"Okay," Finn said. "This is no joke, but there's no way we're going anywhere without you letting your family know you're alive."

Charlie nodded. "We had no choice… or don't you remember?"

"I do. She… it was chasing Liam. And then the three of you vanished into that tree and… a month later you're back and telling me I'm going… to…. Some help would be appreciated."

Charlie kept his voice low and gripped Liam's hand. "We're going to the Unsee. It's where we've been, or rather someplace in between here and there called the Mist."

Finn nodded. As an FDNY Fire Marshal for over a decade, he'd heard crazy shit. Mostly when people lied to him. But Charlie was family, like a little brother. And unlike Rory, who had more than a bit of the devil in him, Charlie Fitzgerald did not embellish. If he said the sky had turned green, you'd best believe it. "I'm not blinking."

"It's not over, Finn. May did something, and she's not dead, and she's not finished trying to be the batshit-crazy queen of three worlds."

Finn launched into detective mode, his earlier depression replaced with a jangled excitement. "Spill it, Charlie. I've been down the rabbit hole. I'll just take it in and ask questions later."

"Good. So here it is." And with Liam filling in missing bits, they spelled it out. "So there are three queens who are unbelievably old. You met one the night of all that cookie-dough craziness."

"Yeah, and I'm still trying to get through all the reports."

"Silver lining," Charlie quipped. "I don't think you're going to get to those."

"This is really happening, isn't it?"

"Finn," Liam interjected. "Go easy on the questions. Where we're going every question asked is answered, but at a cost. It's a fundamental difference between the See and the Unsee. Here people ask questions all the time. It's remarkable how free people are with their answers."

"Yes," Finn said. "But they don't always tell the truth. And isn't that another one of the differences? You guys are obliged to stick to the truth."

"Yes, though many of us are skilled at finding the twisty bits where truth and falsehood are difficult to separate."

"Smoke and mirrors," Finn said.

"Yes." Liam fixed his startling violet gaze on him. "Let me tell you more of what we've learned and how you fit in…. Finn…. Hulain."

Something in how Liam drew out his name gave Finn pause. "So go on. I met the lizard queen, and I think we were all in the apartment of queen number two—Katye Summer. Though she had booked out of town." He started to laugh. "With a frog."

"Yes," Liam said without humor. "It's Lance, her lover."

"Of course," Finn replied. "You didn't even need to tell me that. And there seems to be an amphibian theme starting to develop. Cherchez the tadpole."

"Finn," Charlie said. "You got to take this stuff seriously."

"Sure… frog lover, cookie-dough fire. Shit! Just keep going. I won't say another word."

Liam smiled, and Finn got sucked into the blond's charisma… his glamour. Enthralled, he had no choice but to listen.

"Yes, Katye fled with Lance. We do not know where, though I'm certain she is safe… for now. It is the third sister, Lizbeta, who seeks our help. When you last saw us, May meant to kill me. To eat me. It is how she grows strong. She dines on her subjects and steals their magic. I believe she did the same with humans, though on this side, it's not their magic but their very lives on which she dines."

"Like a vampire," Charlie added. "I wonder if that's where the legends come from."

"It's possible," Liam said. "Therefore it is truth." Liam broke his gaze with Finn, looked at Charlie, and kissed him.

Finn was torn between looking away and fascination, and if he were honest, jealousy.

The obvious love, the total connection between Liam and Charlie was beautiful. *They fit.* And he stared and waited and wondered what it might be like to experience that. *You loved Rory. Yeah, and he didn't love you back... at least not that way.* Moments passed, and Finn drank in the expressions of the two men. As they parted, he saw the bond between them, a scintillating shimmer of molecules. A shiver ran down his back and the illusion shattered.

Liam turned to him and, like nothing had happened, continued. "Lizbeta is the queen who rules the Mist. She saved me as we tumbled through the weeping tree and into her realm. She managed to tether her sister."

"Good. Sister May tethered and all's right with three worlds."

"No, it's not," Charlie said. "There's more."

"Of course there is."

Liam went on. "According to Lizbeta, May split in two. We had one here, and the other is in the Unsee."

Finn coughed. "Come again? She split in two?"

"Go with it," Charlie said. "According to Lizbeta, May in her salamander form split into two identical copies and broke free."

"So let them handle it." Finn's anger surged, and he thought of the chaos and sorrow that had swallowed the city. "We did our part. We got the one that came over here and sent her…."

Charlie shifted in his chair. "I don't think they can. And we promised Lizbeta we'd help."

Finn tugged at his close-cropped flame-red hair, gone gray on the sides. His rational mind wanted to shut this out. And much as he loved Charlie, his return made everything too real… again. The city, the media, and everyone with half a brain had put together their theory of the night of a thousand fires. Then there had been the groups, some credible, some 100 percent crackpot, who'd tried to claim responsibility. *And here's the problem—you can't unsee what you've seen.* He gave a humorless laugh.

"What's so not funny?" Charlie asked.

"All of this. I don't want to know any of this shit. But you can't unsee what you've seen."

"Yes, that is truth," Liam said. "Once made, once seen, something which was nothing now exists."

"That's a bit heavy," Charlie said.

"It's a central tenet of magic," Liam explained. "It's how something comes from nothing. When we're taught magic, until we grasp the spell or incantation, it's not real. I believe that it's true here as well."

"You lost me," Finn said. "And I was doing so well with frogs and multilayered worlds."

Liam cocked his head and stared through a barred and grime-caked window. "The human world, the See, has science where the Unsee has magic. In science a thing does not exist until you can measure it or see it in a microscope or…. Charlie's Gran was telling me about great machines where you split apart bits of the world to see what power lies inside… nuclear accelerators. But until you do that and see the bits of creation, you don't know if they exist. But once seen, they are now real. Someone puts a name on the new thing, which is probably ancient, and maybe wins a prize. Magic is the same. It's pulling something from the invisible realms and making it visible."

"I'm getting a headache. This applies to our situation how?" Finn asked.

Liam nodded. His smile was radiant. "That remains to be seen. So yes, Finn, you've seen fairies and creatures who fled from the Unsee to the See. You've seen a mad queen transformed into a salamander. You've seen horrible destruction and death of both human and fey. None of this can be denied."

"Message received. And you want me to come with you down the rabbit hole. Which in principle, sure, willing to do. But here's the rub-a-dub-dub, and correct me if I'm wrong. Doesn't traveling between the worlds cost something? Like something big, like an arm or a leg… or your sanity?"

Liam and Charlie nodded. "Yeah, and that's the tricky part."

Finn waited. "And…."

"We don't have it all figured out," Charlie admitted. "Liam and I are good because—"

"Yeah, because you're bonkers in love, and that's protective. Not helping me here. I don't have that," Finn said with more bitterness than intended.

"It's true," Liam said. "This was not my idea, Finn Hulain." His pronunciation of Finn's name was again slow and deliberate.

Finn looked Liam dead-on. *Jesus, he's hot.* "We've been through enough. You can just call me Finn."

"Yes, Finn Hulain." Liam held his gaze. His violet eyes were both beautiful and disturbing.

He's trying that glamour thing. He wanted to look away. His head had the thought, but his neck wasn't following the plan.

Liam persisted. "Not my idea, Finn Hulain. But Charlie's Gran's. She saw what I should have but did not…. Finn Hulain."

"Enough!" Finn said, having a Pee-Wee Herman moment—*That's my name, don't wear it out.* "What's with the Finn Hulain crap? I know my name."

"Not its significance," Charlie said. "Gran saw it, and Lizbeta, when we told her about you, said it is no coincidence. You are a part of this. Possibly the most important part."

"In Fey—the Unsee," Liam explained, "we have no coincidence. What you call coincidence or fate is magic's smoke."

Finn braced, though gazing on beautiful Liam eased his nerves. *Charlie is one lucky man.*

Liam smiled as though reading the wander of his thoughts. "In the human world, magic is stuffed into children's stories, and even when it exists for real, you block it out or call it something else." He waved a hand toward the stack of reports on Finn's desk. "Even now you try to spin gold back into straw." He sighed. "You're not alone, Finn. Millions saw magic, terrifying magic that night, and the walls between the realms were the thinnest they've been since the Mist was formed. May nearly succeeded. She's not done, and you… Finn Hulain, are not a coincidence. You are part of this, child of Hulain."

Finn again felt the shudder down his back. He fought the urge to scream. He wanted done with all this madness, and in truth, just moments before Charlie and Liam had arrived, he'd again thought of ending it. And like a mantra, *I wouldn't be the first, and I wouldn't be the last.* "So we went through that craziness four weeks ago. Tens of thousands lost their homes, and hundreds died. You vanish into… the Mist. How long have you been planning this?"

"The same night," Liam stated. "Though once in the Mist, time works different. It's true for all three realms."

Finn wondered, *If I throw them out, maybe none of this is real.* He forced himself to look away from Liam to Charlie. His chest ached. This was family, and…. He looked at the mountain of case files still to be processed. *Not going anywhere.* And yes, they needed to be done so people could battle with their insurance companies, who were raising a holy stink about not paying for damage when the cause was undetermined. "I'm not saying yes or no. I need to talk to Gran, 'cause if she's the one who's saying I should come with, I need to know what the fuck I'm getting into. And you still haven't answered my question. Ever since I started hearing all this… whatever the hell this is, like rule one is you can't travel between the worlds without something awful happening. You've got your magic love thing, and I guess if you're half human and half something else, like Alex Nevus, you get a free pass. None of this applies to me." He gritted his teeth. "I have no love. And I'm pretty sure if I was part Tinker Bell, I'd know by now."

Liam inhaled. "There is a third way."

Finn waited as Charlie and Liam exchanged glances. "Well?"

Charlie hesitated.

"Spit it out."

"You won't like it."

"Say it."

Charlie looked at the floor and then at Finn. "Sacrifice."

"What?"

Liam clarified. "A sacrifice, Finn, a willing and knowing sacrifice. Someone takes the hit so someone else makes it through."

Three

REDMOND'S HEAD reeled as Lizbeta Summer, queen of the Mist, bared her soul.

"My sister is not one but has split herself in two. She means to retake the Unsee and attempted to do the same with the See. She failed there but will not stop. I have tried. She is beyond reason, perhaps she always was. I need your help, Redmond. I need you to hold her here, or at least the half that was returned to me. I need you to treat the madness that consumes her. She is broken and beyond reason."

Redmond seethed. "She should be put down."

"No, she is my sister, and no… just no. You are a doctor. You treat those with afflictions of the mind. I have heard of your work with the most incorrigible of villains."

She is impossible. This is impossible. Worse still, the smell that wafted through his tower's open windows—*fairy fire. She is close.* He tried to block out the intoxicating scent and focus on this once-in-a-lifetime opportunity— hearing the tale of the three sisters from one of them. "She was one and now is two…." He struggled to recall incantations and spells from his decades of training. But the one that came to mind was not an esoteric magic of higher learning but something taught on his mother's knee—a nursery rhyme of magic: "With a mickle and a care I will go into a hare."

Lizbeta was frantic. "Not a hare, a salamander. A giant and vicious creature."

Redmond pondered her response and her tone. "Not a salamander, my lady, not truly. Those do not devour our kind and grind our bones and steal our magic. The shape is salamander, but what your sister attempts goes beyond that." He stood and drew sigils in the air. *This madness must end.* It helped… some, but the smell of fairy fire and his years of addiction weakened his knees. His fingers shook as they traced symbols of magic and power.

Lizbeta watched, her lovely face etched with tears and fear.

He traced signs for the three realms, one next to the next: the See, the Unsee, and the Mist. He looked at Lizbeta. "You said May has split in two. You are wrong." He wondered if this would be a revelation. He wondered how much she hid, whether out of habit or deeper purpose. "There is a third piece of her. Tell me of that."

Lizbeta nodded.

So not a surprise, Redmond thought. "Without it she cannot be whole. Without it she cannot rule the three realms."

"I swear it was just the two pieces. I saw her split apart. I tried to stop her, but two only, and one is back, chained in the Mist. Damaged. Dangerous. I need your help. I cannot contain her much longer."

His gaze narrowed. *She does not know. How is that possible?* "There is a third piece. It is necessary for this to make sense. It is why she has failed. One who is not whole cannot rule the three realms. The trick is to find the piece that could bring her true power and destroy it. Unless, of course...."

"I cannot kill my sister. But...."

Redmond looked at her. "Give voice to the 'but.'"

"But… your words hold truth. Something forgotten."

"Speak."

"Love. There was a time my sister May loved, though anyone else would struggle to find that emotion in her strange relationship."

"The tale of the Hound."

"Of course, and not a tale… though at times he had one." She chuckled. "He was glorious to behold."

Redmond nodded. "More than a cautionary tale."

"Very much so, and how and when all of this began."

"Finally." He abandoned his sigils, which glowed and then vanished. He sank back into his chair. "You must tell all if I am to be of use. Do not decide what is or is not important. Speak without care." His voice soothed and lulled her. "Let go of caution and inhibition. Tell me all. Speak of the Hound."

She nodded. Her expression softened. "May blames me, and Katye as well. In truth she is not wrong, though she never understood our purpose. It was never to hurt or to harm her, for she is our sister, and we love her."

Redmond resisted the impulse to say *She is a monster who should have been put down centuries ago.* "Tell me what you and Katye did."

"We tricked her. And as is fair, she returned the favor. Although the perfect symmetry of it all, my banishment into the Mist and Katye's into the See to be with her sometimes human, sometimes frog lover, Lance, 'tis a twisted fate."

"Yes. I see that," Redmond added. "Three sisters, three realms, one to each. Because in truth, as three you are one, but as I now understand, at least two of you are no longer whole."

She pondered. "Yes, May split in two… and you would have me believe there is a third part, but I was there when she birthed a second salamander self."

"It's not what I meant." *She twists my words. What are you hiding?* "It's more fundamental, but your story brings us to that point. Tell me of the trick. Tell me of the Hound."

Lizbeta, lulled by the tenor of Redmond's voice and his curious brand of persuasion, not exactly a glamour but a sense of safety, that all is well and all secrets are best shared. "The stuff of legend and truth. My beautiful, albeit deadly, sister May…. Maeve, Mab, we have all worn different names. Just as the Hound sheds his mortal form and is reborn."

"Like a salamander in the fire."

"Interesting association, and yes. Coohulain was his name that time, and from birth he was a warrior without parallel. If I retold his adventures, you'd call me a liar. But before he had whiskers on his chin, he bested more than a thousand in a single battle. Once he and May got started, it became a contest of love, thievery, and betrayal."

"These are ancient tales," Redmond said. "The things told me by my mother or sung in ballads. You speak of a time before the three realms."

"Yes, and it's the story that birthed them. May and the Hound and the war between human and fey that lasted a thousand years. She stood at the head of one army and he at the other. Queer as it sounds, they would fight as bitter enemies by day, and by night come together in the dark with a passion second to none. They were obsessed with each other, both in love and in hate."

"And here we find the trick," Redmond observed as he studied Lizbeta for any of the physiologic giveaways of deception. *Does she really not see this?*

"If so, then you would be the first."

"Your sister Katye, the sister who carries the magic of love. This bears her mark."

Lizbeta met his gaze. "You are not wrong, but not just hers. I carry responsibility as well, as I tempered her magic with my own and draped it with a veil of forgetfulness and peace. The spell itself is a thousand times stronger than the addictive thrall of fairy fire."

"Please continue, as I would know the why of this if I am to be of use."

"You bring me hope," Lizbeta said.

"A dangerous commodity. Please continue. You cast a bond of love upon your sister. You bound her to the Hound… to a human, albeit a remarkable one. In the stories his name was not an accident. The man was both beast and human."

"We bound them both. One unto the other. Enemies and lovers."

"Tell me your purpose."

"May was set upon ruling all. Not necessarily a bad thing, but bad for her and for everyone under her. Worse still, as the war dragged on, century after century, it became clear that there would and could never be a lasting peace between humans and fey. We are too different, and it is in both of our natures to conquer. Barring a total genocide, there could never be a winner."

Redmond startled. This he had not foreseen. "It was you who separated the realms." The enormity of her power took him aback. This lovely creature with her sparkling gown and inkblack eyes possessed the strength of a god… as did her sisters.

"We saw no other way. Humans on one side, fey on the other, and something to keep them separated."

"The Mist."

"Yes, and not a bad plan. Of course, it was all in the execution. And key to that was that May could never know."

Redmond's jaw went slack, and he bit back dangerous questions, like *How did you do that?* But other thoughts came as well. "You didn't just conceal it from May."

"True, none could know."

"You lied to her."

"Of course not. We hid things. It eventually caught up with us, and when May learned of what we'd done, or at least some of it… well, she was cannier than I'd have thought. It happened fast. But that's putting the cart before the horse." Lizbeta leaned forward and sniffed. "Fairy fire. The part of her that terrorizes this realm grows close. I need your decision. We've not much time, and if you deny me… I fear all is lost."

"The war," Redmond said, "tell me how it truly ended. For the Mist not only separates the realms, it clouds the past. I would know the truth, and I suspect it's different from what is written in books."

"I was not wrong in coming to you. You see things others don't."

"Please, now is no time for flattery. Tell me how the war ended."

"In a contract and a truce between my sister and the Hound. There was an exchange, half for the fey and half for the humans. But the night before the documents were to be signed, the Hound played his own cruel trick on my sister."

"He declared his love," Redmond stated.

Lizbeta gasped. "It is impossible for you to know that."

"It's the only thing that makes sense. It's the only thing that's kept her from rolling across the three realms to retake all that she thinks has been stolen from her."

"Now it is you who conceals," Lizbeta said.

He pondered this unexpected information, though the growing reek of fairy fire distracted him. The great white salamander that was Queen May—or some part of her—approached. He needed to leave his most fascinating guest and do what was necessary to ensure the Center's safety. "It's obvious. He declared his love, and as we know, humans have no difficulty telling lies. In return for his love, I believe your sister gave the Hound a piece of herself. That is the key to all of this. It's not just that she's split herself into two or that she's damaged from travel between the realms. This is more fundamental. And at this point, my queen, if you will forfeit the cost, I would ask a question."

"Yes, do, and there will be no cost."

"If the Hound was human, or even one kept young through magic, he would now be long dead. So the piece of your sister that he took is either buried in some mortal tomb or…." He got out of his chair and stared out the seaward window. "No." He looked back at her. "You conceal still."

"I don't. I swear."

He chewed on her words and her visage, which emanated peace and sincerity. *There are traps and snares in her every sentence, and there is also truth.* "Where is the Hound?"

"I do not know."

I do not believe her. "So let's recap. You came to seek my help with your sister, while a second part of her wreaks havoc in the Unsee and heads straight toward the Center."

"Yes."

"You'd like me to contain the part that you say is broken, hold her here, and heal her mind if I can."

"Correct."

"Tell me your endgame. If I am able to do what you seek and return your sister to some semblance of wholeness…."

Lizbeta looked up, a sly smile spread across her lips. "You are clever. As you have so correctly identified, without the third piece, the heart she gave away millennia ago, she can never rule the three realms."

"You mean to reinstall her in the Unsee."

"She keeps the peace."

"She eats her subjects."

"No one is perfect."

Redmond's head swam. It's like Lizbeta came close to her true intent and then threw up a wall of her mist and scurried away. *So I hold May. I heal her. Life goes on as it had with her occasional attempts to rampage across worlds…. What am I missing? What is she not saying? It has to do with the Hound… who is dead and buried.* He pulled his hair back. One didn't turn down the request of one of the sisters. If this were May, a refusal would equal death. With Lizbeta, he was less certain. "If I do as you bid, tell me what must be done to ensure the safety of the Center and all who study, heal, and seek shelter within its walls."

"Thank you, Redmond."

"I haven't agreed."

She smiled and stood. From around her neck, she loosened a black leather strap, which held a marble-sized carved ruby in the shape of a dog's head.

Her glamour washed over him, and unable to resist, he stood frozen as she draped the amulet around his neck and pulled back his thick auburn hair to settle it. With dainty fingers she held the leather-bound jewel between them and then tucked it inside the open neck of his linen shirt. "This will keep you, and those you protect, safe."

Redmond's chest tingled where the amulet lay. "It's warm."

"It's powerful, and it's ancient."

"Tell me its name."

She backed away, and through the open window Redmond saw a cresting wave of mist. It spilled over the sill and settled around Lizbeta's feet. She whispered, "It is the houndstone. As long as you possess it, nothing here, not even my sister, can bring harm to you or the Center. Keep it safe, and keep it hidden."

Mist engulfed her and carried her up and away. As she retreated, a second dense wave rolled toward him.

And so the deal is struck.

He raised his voice to a pitch that was heard throughout the grounds of the Center. He sounded the alarm. "This is not a drill. Dr. Quick, my chambers, now! This is not a drill. Dr. Quick, my chambers, now." He heard the booted feet of his ogre and troll guards as they raced up the stairs and sensed others riding the wind and entering through the turret's other three windows.

Luluba landed on his right, and Seamus alit to his left.

"Tell us," Luluba whispered as the Mist neared and his chambers filled with guards brandishing chains, manacles, and torches dipped in a magic that stunned and paralyzed its targets.

"We are taking on a royal patient." He looked to a green-faced ogre whose bulk barely made it through the door. "Gark, she is to go in the forensic ward's lowest cell. I want two-to-one, line of sight, around-the-clock guards. More if you think it necessary."

"Yes, Doctor."

It filled the room, and from within its murky depths, a form emerged.

Redmond grabbed a stun torch from one of the guards and savagely poked it three times into the wispy swirls. Purple sparks flew, and the air crackled like moths hitting a flame.

Whatever was inside, which appeared part humanoid and part slick-white amphibian, gasped and crumpled to the floor. He swallowed and stared down as the Mist was sucked back through the windows and vanished over the Western Sea.

Luluba gasped as they beheld the unstable creature that shimmered and shifted on the stone floor. "It's Queen May… or…."

Redmond cleared his throat. *Show no fear.* "Gark, before she wakes, lock her up. I will cast the wards. Take no chances, and instruct your guards to do the same."

"Understood, Doctor." He motioned to four guards, who with a practiced efficiency lifted the spasming creature and chained her limbs and midsection to a floating stretcher.

Redmond watched. His heart raced. It was hard to catch a breath. In that moment, he would have given anything to undo the deal with Lizbeta. *This will not end well. This cannot end well.* As they carted the broken queen away, he thought *I will either succeed, or she will kill me, kill us all.* Not wanting to look at the shocked and frightened expressions of those who filled his chambers, he took to the air and, without the need of wings, flew out and down to meet the guards and his newest patient.

Four

THE HALF of May not imprisoned in the bowels of the Center gamboled in the shape of a giant white salamander through a riotous spring meadow of dew-dripped daffodils, crocuses, and bleeding hearts. She felt a crushing failure that tore her guts, though she did not have the right words to give voice to the ache. *Bad, nasty. Hatey little hafflings.* It was a shortcoming of her current physical state. Yes, she could spit fireballs, but sentences were a challenge.

The ache ripped inside her chest, though the feeling came from outside her body and, more pertinently, outside this realm. She knew that the other part of her, the pretty swirly dress part, had failed. She howled as she rampaged toward a gnome village's telltale clearing. *Down but not out.*

She hacked up a ball of fairy fire, and with her hard tongue, she pierced and shattered the projectile as it passed from gut to maw. Like a firework chrysanthemum, the pieces arced high and landed on the thatched and sod roofs of the quaint village.

Day was breaking as frantic gnomes scurried for safety. Dressed only in boxers, night slips, or wrapped naked in blankets, they quickly discovered that fire wasn't the worst danger. She was.

And while still stung by failure in another world, May unhinged her jaw, chased them down one by one, and gorged. It eased the hole inside. *More.* Her head swiveled from side to side. She breathed in and savored the different scents: fairy fire, gnome, and fear. *More, need more.* She sensed the thump-thump of a still-beating pulse and smashed her tail into the timbers of a smoldering hut. The walls shattered like matchsticks to reveal a broomstick-wielding mother attempting to protect her three young.

With an efficiency of movement, May's jaws widened farther. And with a single chomp, she swallowed them whole. *Yummy, yummy in my tummy.*

Bones crunched, and blood burst like grapes freed from their skins. *Yummy, yummy.* She felt the creatures' subtle magic course through her veins. But if she was honest, her hunger was never slaked.

Now, grinding bones and swelling large with stolen blood magic, if this wasn't happiness she felt, at least it tasted good. She rolled on the ground, crossing from one side of the village to the other like a wrecking ball, her skin impervious to fire and the tickles of demolished structures.

The new magic sharpened her thoughts. She had returned to this world with a purpose, and while eating gnomes held her appetite at bay for a bit, there was more important prey she needed to consume. *Hafflings. There are three. They are tricky tricky tricky.*

She flipped onto her feet and reared up on her tail and hind legs. Summoning her power, she drank in the currents. *Come out, come out, wherever you are.*

The scent was faint but undeniable. *I need but one. They are tricky. They cheat. Twice I have failed. Third time is a charm.* It would take cunning and skill. Her eyes turned from black to red as she visualized the trail of the littlest haffling. There could be no failure, as he was the last.

Third time is a charm.

She caught a noise from the woods that circled the smoldering village. She turned and sensed the presence of her swelling band of followers. She drank in their heady mix of fear, hunger, and anticipation. A tune played inside her head: *Fairy fire, fairy fire, come and watch my fairy fire. Fairy dust, fairy dust, try a taste, you know you must.*

She was about to turn away when her gaze fell on one with the head of a woman and the body of a praying mantis. *I know her.* She wore glasses, and her shiny dark hair was pulled into a taut bun. A name came. *Dorothea.* She paused and scanned the army of dusthead addicts.

Perhaps one or two could have been known to her. *Dorothea.*

As she stared, Dorothea separated herself from the horde and with head downcast moved, at first slow and then with the speed and grace of her insect limbs, to come within feet of her transformed queen. She knelt and spoke. "My lady, I know it is you. As always, I am your servant to command. My life is truly yours."

May tried to speak, but words were not possible in this form.

Dorothea nodded. "My lady, if you allow, we can share thoughts." And she extended one of her upper limbs.

May hesitated. But the words that rang in her mind as she gazed on Dorothea were *faithful, never betrayed me, good spy, sneaky.* She stretched her neck and allowed Dorothea to touch her temple.

As Dorothea's hand alit, May caught the haffling's scent.

"I see him," Dorothea whispered.

I smell him. I need him.

"Of course, my queen. You have wondrous things to accomplish. You need the haffling to conquer worlds. He hides from you. He is small, with flame-red hair." Dorothea shuddered. "He is with that woman, Marilyn Nevus, and her traitor husband, Cedric Summer. His name is Adam."

Yes. They hide far from me.

"But you are fast, your nose is true, and if you allow me, I will run by your side. I am now and always your true servant."

You are, and because it would be impolite, she masked the impulse to bite off Dorothea's head. Instead she nodded and broke the connection. *Good to have a friend. Don't eat her.* The other thought that added weight to Dorothea's devotion, *She's not dusted. She is true.*

May turned her head back to the haffling's scent trail. The added information from Dorothea painted a picture. *I need him. Third time's a charm.* She fixed the image of the boy and his hateful parents in her mind's eye, and like casting a line for a greedy trout, she spun a thread of magic and floated it over the haffling's scent. *I come for you. I will be whole. And I will rule all.*

With Dorothea at her side, an army of fairy-dust addicts at her back, and a clarity of purpose, she trotted off in search of the thing she needed, the thing that could make her whole, that could set her on the path of rejoining the three realms with her as their undisputed queen.

Five

BEHIND THE wheel of his Bureau of Fire Investigation SUV, Finn drove with lights and siren from Brooklyn to Flora Fitzgerald's, aka Gran's, apartment in Gramercy Park. Focused on the midday traffic and cursing those who didn't pull over fast enough, his attention got snagged by missing buildings, like teeth from a child's mouth.

On the night of a thousand fires, Finn, like many New Yorkers, had felt reality waver. He remembered 9/11. It was similar but different. After that they'd been barraged by shrinks and well-intended social workers, all trying to weave some magic of post-trauma inoculation. The main flaw in their approach was that most of them had trouble holding their own shit together. The one session he'd gone to, at the insistence of his then station captain, had made things worse. The therapist assigned to him had lost her brother in the towers and, overcome by grief, had to excuse herself halfway through. He'd told her he understood and would come back, though as he left her office, he knew he wouldn't. That he, like so many others, would shut up and soldier on, his every waking moment hounded with memories of that day and the ones that came after. Rory intruded into his thoughts, his dead station mates, the endless funerals…. For the first time in his life, he felt the fingers of true insanity. Thoughts he did not want to have hammered him. This morning's suicidal musings were far from his first. In this he knew he was not alone, as one of 9/11's dirty secrets grew and festered. Because it didn't end with the funerals from the towers. Those were the first wave, and it seemed that every week and every month saw another cop, medic, or firefighter end their pain with a bullet to the brain or a noose draped over a backyard tree or basement beam.

Over ten years later and the nightmares still came. He'd wake shaking and sweating, convinced that someone he loved was trapped in a house on fire, or that he was. Only for the last month, his night terrors had the added feature of white monsters, the smell of cookies, and beautiful New Yorkers who weren't exactly human.

He wanted to turn around. To not show up for this crazy-assed convocation with Liam, Charlie, and of course Gran. But no, that ship, the ship of pretending none of this was real, had sailed. Batshit crazy was the new reality. This wasn't over.

He pulled up to the front of Gran's brick building and parked behind Charlie's brand-new candy-apple-red Ford F-150. He counted the burned-out holes around this picturesque square, which had been used as the set in countless period-drama movies. Four historic buildings had vanished. On either side, the remaining nineteenth-century structures were smeared with soot.

It fed the sick feel in his gut as he gazed into the iron-fenced park, where residents rolled baby carriages and walked dogs. These buildings would never be replaced. Instead, developers were chomping at the bit and playing on the fears of displaced owners and tenants. Money would change hands and well-disguised seven- and eight-digit bribes would take place. Where glorious townhouses once stood, needle-thin luxury condo complexes, twenty and thirty stories high, would appear.

At least Gran's building had passed unscathed, as had Gran. The uniformed doorman, who had to be in his seventies, waved Finn through.

He headed toward the elevators. The doorman's familiar face tripped memories: he and Rory running in the halls or using Gran's spare bedroom as a safe spot for weekend adventures in Manhattan.

As the doors slid open, he caught the smells of cooking from different apartments, and the cabbage-rose carpet wrapped him deeper in a time warp. It didn't take much to imagine Rory behind him. *But he's dead.* He knocked on the door.

"Coming." Charlie's voice from inside, and then his blue-eyed smile, appeared as he cracked the door open. "Come in quick or we'll be chasing cats up and down the halls."

Used to Gran and Charlie taking in strays, Finn squeezed through, effectively blocking the escape of two boisterous tabbies. A Siamese whined from down the bookshelf-filled hall as Gran appeared from the kitchen. She greeted Finn with a hug and a kiss. She put her hands on either side of his face and shook her head. "You've lost weight. You can't afford to do that. Come in."

"I'm okay."

"And I'm the queen of Sheba."

"Who knew?" *God, she is still so sharp.* It was always impossible to put anything over on Flora. As teenagers, he and Rory would sneak into bars for some underage mayhem. Flora always knew and could tell how much each of them had to drink, down to the number of shots or beers. Though only once did she rat them out.

He took a seat in the familiar kitchen with its black-and-white tiled floor and glass-fronted cabinets filled with a hodgepodge of colorful dishes. Bacon crackled in a pan as pancakes browned and got flipped.

"Gran, tell Finn what you told us," Charlie said.

She stacked Finn's plate with butter-topped blueberry pancakes and a mountain of crisp bacon. She poured him black coffee and herself tea before she sat. "I don't see how any of you could have missed this. Though to be fair, I didn't see it at first. But Finn, you have a history with Queen May."

Finn blew coffee up his nose. "Yeah, she tried to eat me, Liam… and Charlie's truck."

"That's not what I meant. Now eat—all that's on your plate—and let an old woman talk. Finn Hulain… you do know where your name comes from?"

"Not so much."

"That's a pity. Your name—and I suspect if you climb up your family tree, you'll discover you're not the first to own it—is an amalgam of two of Irish history and legends' heroes: Finn McCool and Coohulain. As someone who's spent a lifetime poring through books, I can tell you that when you lay the stories one on top of the other, they're more alike than different."

Liam added, "In Fey what is coincidence is fact. So to follow what Gran says, they may be two, but they can also be one."

"Yes." Gran cast Liam a look. "Thank you for clarifying. Which brings us to you, Finn Hulain. Your history… your ancestors' history with May is significant. In fact, I think it's at the heart—" She chuckled. "—of this nightmare." She started to hum "I Left My Heart in San Francisco."

Finn looked from Gran to Charlie. "Has she lost it?"

"I haven't," Gran said. "But she has. You, or rather someone in your family's past, was May's lover."

Finn had a weird sensation, like he was falling. He thought back to the night of the fires.

He, Gran, Charlie, Liam, and Alex Nevus, the kid who'd been on that singing show, had frantically looked through ancient manuscripts in a luxury high-rise owned by May's sister, Katye Summer. The latter he'd not met, and according to her doorman, she'd left with a large frog in a carrying case the day before hell broke loose. "In those books, she was tricked by him… her lover. And there was some kind of pact between the fey and the humans, and in the end she got the fuzzy end of the lollipop."

"Correct." Gran stared at him. "Finn Hulain, you carry the blood of the man who tricked her, not just of her land, but worse. You broke her heart."

Charlie tried to lighten the mood. "Bastard."

"No laughing matter, Charles Michael Fitzgerald. For humans a broken heart is a pain that can drive women and men to madness, to suicide even, though most of us move on." She stared at Finn.

He nodded. *She knows. She's always known that I loved Rory. Maybe this is my karma.*

Gran nodded.

Liam spoke. "It's worse for us. We do not love readily, Finn. Our affections are hard-won. But once given, fey love is not taken lightly. It's magic." He glanced at Charlie. "When I fell in love with Charlie, I gave him a piece of me."

Charlie laughed. "Yes, and when I fell in love with you, you were naked and holding a Chihuahua."

Liam smiled. "You were glamoured. I was not, and this is truth." He placed a hand on Charlie's broad chest. "Inside, you carry a piece of me. It's what allowed you to travel between the worlds without breaking. It's a magic that humans still possess, albeit water-thin. If what Gran says is truth, and I can't see otherwise, you, Finn Hulain, possess something May needs."

"Wait a minute." Finn's thoughts swam. "I thought we were talking about a contract or something. There was a picture in one of those books, and May and this Hulain guy signed something. And we were thinking there's two copies, and to undo the bad deal, she's going to go on a paper hunt… or parchment hunt, or—"

Gran interrupted. "There was a contract, Finn. But the more I look at this and turn it in my head, it was not written on vellum but in flesh and blood. May gave your ancestor her heart, and if I'm reading things right… she wants it back."

Six

REDMOND FELT sick as he descended into the bowels of the Center's high-security hospital for the criminally insane. *I should not have agreed. I have put everyone in horrible jeopardy.*

As he passed specialized cells designed for their inhabitants, he ticked off the crimes that had landed them here. Each of these mental monsters, he had sat with and evaluated. Through the decades, and now centuries, he had become a connoisseur of the fey psyche. And no species or obscure disorder had escaped his laser-sharp dissection.

One called through the bars as he passed. "Doc."

"Yes, Farlark." He recognized the ferry-boat troll who had topped the news when he'd intentionally drowned a trip's passengers. At the time, he'd said a voice in his head told him to do it. As Redmond later learned in sitting with the murderous troll, his motivations had been far more twisted.

"Tell me who they got down below."

"You know I can't."

"Patient privacy."

"Yes, just as you wouldn't want me sharing your business."

"It's someone famous."

"Fishing gets you nowhere." Though he regretted his water metaphor. He looked in Farlark's cell. It was meticulously clean, the bed pulled so taut a pixie could use it as a trampoline. While it was said cleanliness was next to godliness, for this patient it was the kissing cousin and true motivation for his crimes, as he had divulged in one particularly painful session. Farlark had revealed his mother's obsession with tidiness, her cruelty to him as a child for even the smallest smear of dirt or speck of dust. It was the motivation for killing a boatload full of day-trippers. *They were dirty. I wanted to make them clean.* And yes, he had been hearing a voice, that of his mother, who he'd chopped to bits earlier that day. Redmond's trained eye took it all in. *It's too clean. The therapy is not working.* And then he spotted it. On the sink there was a definite, albeit faint, patch of soap scum. "Well done, Farlark."

Without looking, the troll knew what Redmond had seen. "It makes me crazy."

I think we passed that a while back. "Tell me your level of anxiety."

"Ten out of ten, but it was only a five before you brought it to my attention."

"Good work. And when it goes below a four, see if you can mess up something else."

"It makes her mad."

"She's dead, Farlark. Remember that."

"I know. I killed her, and she still won't let me go."

Redmond nodded. The normalcy of this interaction had calmed his fears. "It's often how it works with murder. You killed your mother's body, but she'd worked her way into your head long before."

"I want her out."

"It's a process."

"Yeah… a long one. That's what you said. But I'm making progress." His voice was like a little boy seeking a parent's approval.

Redmond did not withhold. "You're doing great."

And he headed down farther, each footfall on the stone stairs like the tolling of a funeral bell. *I don't want to do this. I don't want to see her.* He thought of Farlark and his dirt phobia.

The treatment was simple exposure: face the thing you fear, and in time, and with practice, it loosens its grip. *Yes, but that's when it's an unreasonable fear. The soap scum on his sink won't kill him. May could. And not just him… me, all of us.*

The air chilled, and his anxiety spiked as he passed cell after cell on his way down.

When he could go no farther, he had arrived. Outside, at attention, stood two ogres. "Karnick, Glebe, tell me of our prisoner."

Glebe, with his ridiculous bright orange Mohawk in the front and ponytail in the back, spoke. "She's all wobbly."

Redmond peered through the water window. "Good choice of words." For Queen May, if in fact she still was whole enough to even call her that, had no solid form. What lay half on the bed and half on the carpet was of no recognizable species. "I will go in."

"Of course, Doctor. We will follow."

"No. Stay here, but keep a close watch. If I need you, come fast, call for others, and use all means necessary to restrain her."

"As you wish." Glebe inserted the key. But it wasn't until Redmond drew a complex series of wispy sigils that it turned.

He held still and listened to the grinding of gears, both mechanical and magical. The water never stopped flowing through the iron-laced window as he was afforded a too-close and too-in-person glimpse of the once-powerful monarch in her lavishly appointed cell. His breath quickened and his pulse raced. *She killed my mother and father.* Distant memories flittered like pixies in his mind. Happy times with his professor parents and their friends. Glittering parties where he'd watch and listen from the bedroom stairs. *She killed them all.* And those she didn't murder—all the teachers, the doctors, the theologians—had been sent to camps. And their children, like himself, were enrolled in a prisonlike school where all that was taught was the world according to Queen May. It was on the grounds of that school the Center now stood.

He stared and thought, not for the first time, that the easiest and smartest course would be to take a sword and separate her head from her body. Even as he had that thought, the healer in him took inventory. *She is broken. And it's from traveling unprotected between the realms.* The queen's obsession with obtaining hafflings to protect herself as she sought to reunite the realms—all under her rule, of course—was no secret. *She failed in her last attempt.*

He observed the bedridden creature, with the worst case of travel sickness he'd ever witnessed. *Not just broken, but somehow an amalgam of creatures.* Fascinated, he watched as a humanoid hand appeared and grasped a pillow, while a slipper-clad foot turned into the claw of a salamander. Her face had the jaw and flattened nostrils of a beast, but her eyes, which followed him, were gold like a cat's, and her long blonde hair cascaded prettily over the embroidered bedspread. It seemed to have a life of its own as tendrils twisted on invisible breezes. A trio of tresses decided to form a braid as a length on the other side twirled in and out of a bun.

He replayed his discussion with her sister Lizbeta, who had all but admitted that the separation of the three realms had been her doing. In following that logic, Queen May's current state was due to her sister. At least her diagnosis, the kind a first-year medical student could make, was clear.

The creature on the massive bed with its profusion of dainty pillows kept him fixed in her gaze. The eyes occasionally flickered from amber to red. Her white maw gaped open, and an expression of frustration twisted her cheeks as she tried to speak. What emerged were grunts.

She strained as a broad tail emerged and swished from side to side. Had the furniture not been fixed to the floor, it would have upended tables and chairs arranged to give the cell a look of luxury and normalcy.

"Hello, my queen. I'm Redmond Fall. I will be your doctor."

No response.

"You are at the Center for Fey Development. I will come and chat with you each day. Perhaps I can help."

The creature coughed.

He smelled fairy fire. Like gas on a hot stove, his brain sparked. *If the other inmates catch a whiff of this... of her.... Not good.* He made a mental note to further seal her cell. But more importantly, he'd need to guard himself. For what he'd shared with no one was that he'd spent the better part of three centuries under the thrall of fairy fire's by-product... fairy dust. He'd been a dusthead and a slave to the drug. The false feelings of love and comfort it gave... for a while. Always leaving the user wanting and needing more. *She reeks of it.* Cautiously he leaned in. It was on her breath and in the snaking locks of her hair. As her form wavered, the smell was strongest when she was more amphibious. *Which makes sense.*

"My queen, tell me your pleasure."

Her head twisted, first with the flat head and broad maw of the beast, and then, with obvious effort, she pulled her humanoid face together. She gasped and blew air through her lips as though testing them. "My pleasure...." She halted. Her mouth twisted. "My pleasure is to be free of this place. Do that for me. For your queen." Her gaze, eyes first red and then amber, bore into his.

"That is not possible." *She tries to glamour me.*

She inhaled. "Hmmm. I smell something tricky tricky. I've no use for an inquisitive jailor. Off with you, for no amount of tricky in your pockets or around your neck will keep you safe." She attempted to rise, but her body couldn't decide on a form that would let her do that. She sank back. "I am weak, and you take advantage of this. Bad doctor. Very bad. Clearly you've forgotten your... hypocrite's oath."

"That's Hippocratic, my lady. And I am here to help." He felt the ruby well hidden in the folds of his shirt. *How could she know? What else does she know?* Her discovery of his talisman deepened his dread. *Even broken she is too powerful to contain.*

"Yes, well, we'll see. Do something about this," she said, as a human arm that ended in a salamander's talon swept up and down her unstable form.

Redmond nodded. *This is good. She has stated a goal that we can agree upon.* "I will try. The cause we both know."

"Yes." Her mouth broadened and went flat at the corners.

He waited, as it appeared that speech was impossible with a salamander maw.

Her lips reformed. "Travel between worlds. I was unlucky. The vessel I'd chosen was ripped from me."

"A haffling."

"Yes, they do not break, as they have one foot in the See and the other in the Unsee."

"They are rare," Redmond replied, his curiosity now stronger than his fear.

"I am aware. Now leave me, you annoying little bug. I do not want you tip-tapping at my thoughts."

"As you will…." He paused. "To help you maintain a stable form, you must focus. I can help you with that."

"Yes, and so starts the tit for tat. I know this game, Doctor. Neither a borrower or a lender be; what you give, no doubt you'll come and take from me."

"As you wish."

Not turning his back, he moved toward the door.

She spoke as he edged away. "Be careful, little bug, for when I return to myself, you will be the first down my throat, and no pretty bauble around your neck will stop me."

He had nothing to say. Her words were truth. He watched her form grow more solid with each moment. And for someone who had spent his career helping the most incorrigible of unbalanced criminals, creatures who had committed acts of outrageous brutality, he'd never once had the kinds of thoughts she triggered. *Fly to your chamber, grab your sword, and be done with it. One strike to separate her head from her body. Do it now.*

Seven

SALAMANDER MAY, with Dorothea at her side, scoured the Unsee with a singular purpose.

Find the third haffling, Adam.

Come out, come out. You can run. You can hide, but I will find you. In her wake she laid blood, destruction, and the mouthwatering smell of cookies. It was insidious and deliberate. Craters filled with fairy dust, like an all-you-can-eat buffet for addicts. So while the populace fled from her advances, more and more hung back and fell upon her leavings with rabid abandon. Their ranks swelled, and those who wanted to "just try a taste" were enslaved by the drug's false promises.

"A brilliant strategy, my queen," Dorothea gushed as ogre and pixie, highborn and serf, all turned to dust… heads. "They will follow you anywhere."

Yes, May agreed. Grateful to be able to communicate to Dorothea. Grateful to have a friend. And ever mindful not to eat her. *You follow without the dust.* Her limited reasoning wondered at Dorothea's motivations. *Tit for tat, what's in it for you?*

"You have raised an army. They are tied to you by the dust."

May lowered her head and nodded toward Dorothea. It had become their signal.

Without hesitation Dorothea's pincer-like hand touched down gently on May's left temple. The connection was strong and instant.

An army of dustheads. "They will not betray you." *You do not take dust.*

Dorothea sensed the queen's question and felt her presence inside her head, searching for motives. She held still. "My queen, I am yours."

May sniffed and searched. There was much to be found in Dorothea's head. Memories of happier times when she was not covered in this thick white hide. When she'd worn pretty dresses and had diamonds woven in her hair. She caught darker scenes of Dorothea with her enemies, of which there were always many. Dorothea laying down her traps. *She is faithful.* And then a thought so disturbing it caused her to recoil. *She loves me.*

"Yes," Dorothea whispered. An acid-yellow tear dribbled down her cheek. "I need no dust to follow."

May turned back and surveyed her army. *So many. I have so many. It's good.*

"And more each day." Dorothea swatted at her tear.

They'll do. May sniffed hard through her slit-like nostrils. *They will follow me anywhere for the dust.* Even the danger she represented, having just devoured the occupants of a village, would not hold them back.

"And if you grow hungry," Dorothea added, at times not even needing the physical connection to catch the wonder of her queen's thoughts, "they'll walk willingly into your jaws. And it is essential for your great work that you feed. Their magic fuels the fairy fire."

Yes, but you I will not eat. Her gaze alit on an ogre that towered over the others. *Tasty.*

He caught her gaze and then looked down. He dropped on bended knee, an obvious sign of submission. *No, he is mine.* He held motionless, the hundred yards between them no protection. *You may live… for now.*

"You can always eat him later," Dorothea suggested. "But as he is, big, dumb, and strong, he will be of use."

May turned to the west. She sniffed again. *Come out, come out. You cannot hide from me.* Her frustration welled and doubt clouded her thoughts. The other two hafflings were in the See. *Have they taken him away?*

"No, Your Highness. He is hidden, but he is here and near."

May roared. The sound of her anguish was echoed by her followers.

"He is here," Dorothea tried to reassure her.

But May's inner pain and longing were not slaked. *Where are you?* Tears fell and burned the ground. She wept in frustration and from a deep loss whose source she could not find. *I hurt.*

Dorothea reached out her forelimb.

May turned away. She stopped. Something had changed. Her focus shifted from the last of the haffling children. She turned inward. *Something has changed. I am close to myself.* Just hours before she had felt with certainty that something bad had befallen her other half, but the connection, the invisible links that held her parts together, had been stretched… between realms. Like the strings on a violin, her failure in the See had resonated, but now…. *I am close. I am here.* As she allowed her mind to wander and play at the connection with her other part, her rage boiled. *What have they done to me?* She butted her head against Dorothea and nearly knocked her over.

Dorothea braced and put her hand to May's temple.

Show me what they've done to me. To the other part of me.

Dorothea's clever brain reached into May's memories. She saw the queen trapped in her salamander form in the Mist. She watched as the queen split open her skin, and where she was one, she became two. One half vanished into the human realm, and the other was here. This was not the information the queen wanted. But the sequence of events allowed Dorothea to follow the trail. "Your sister Lizbeta brought your other half here… to the Center."

How dare she.

Dorothea, no stranger to May's rages, swallowed and continued. "They hold her prisoner deep within the earth."

How dare…. But then, as if a light switch had been thrown, the faintest whiff of something different pulled her back. *Haffling!* She sniffed again. There was no mistaking the youngest one. *He's here.*

"Yes, my queen. Here and near."

Hope swelled. May fixed on the direction where the smell wafted the strongest. It blew in on gusts that crossed the Western Sea's eastern shore.

She searched the verdant landscape, with orchards in bloom, rolling hills dotted with thatched-roof villages amid crumbling ruins of once-lavish villas. In the distance she sensed, rather than saw, the sea and, rising like a theater curtain, Lizbeta's wretched mist.

Using her lungs like bellows, she tasted the haffling's molecules. *He is close.* Her tail dug into the soft ground and disturbed a family of frosted mini-gnomes, which she scooped and gobbled.

As bones crunched amid muffled screams, she purred and sniffed. *Come out, come out, wherever you are.*

Dorothea pointed to a space between two crumbling structures not more than a mile away. "There. Something is concealed. I see the shimmer break between real and unreal."

Yes. She hacked up a small wad of fire and spewed it into the air. She watched as it arced high and then returned to the earth with a whistle and shriek. The missile struck something solid. She squinted as the air shimmered. She spat a second, a third, a fourth, and a fifth fireball. Like playing a game, she outlined the dimensions of a concealment spell.

"They will try to run," Dorothea advised. "They will have a bolt-hole."

May was on the move. She raced toward the hidden building, her thoughts riveted on a single goal—*haffling*.

Behind her, Dorothea struggled to keep up as May's legions of dusted fey swarmed forward on wing and foot. Five fairy fire projectiles would produce a prodigious crop of dust, which they would fall upon like jackals.

But May had no thoughts for any of them as she hurled herself into the concealment spell, breached it, and with a crash of glass, timber, and stone, she vanished from sight.

Eight

Finn observed the crowd swell in Gran's apartment. It wasn't just putting names to faces, but more complex as his reality of what it meant to be human and a part of this planet was assaulted. Dark-haired Alex Nevus and his boyfriend, Jerod Haynes, had arrived first. Which was fine, except a small black fairy with gold tattoos and pointy ears hovered on Alex's shoulder. Her name was Nimby, and he also knew that a month prior he wouldn't have been able to see her.

The others... creatures, beings, he didn't know what the PC term was for the model-beautiful crew. Many had artfully concealed surgical scars from pointy ears bobbed and other bits of unhuman anatomy that could be imagined, and occasionally glimpsed, from under their clothes. Here a tail, there a tightly folded wing with veins like a leaf. Some he recognized from the night of a thousand fires. Each had been targeted by May, their homes set ablaze as she followed behind and dined. As horrific as that night had been for New Yorkers, it held a special terror for those who knew its true cause and what May had attempted—an overthrow of worlds.

"The problem," Alex began, "is the passage between the See and the Unsee."

Finn looked at Alex, young and confident and, like Charlie with Liam, in love with his boyfriend, Jerod.

Someone for everyone... except me. He looked around Gran's crowded kitchen.

A murmur bubbled through the assembled, all aware of this central truth of the dimensions. Travel came at a cost. For some it would be their magic; for others, they'd sprout a deformity. But the most common was insanity. It had happened to Alex's mother, Marilyn, and it most certainly had happened to Queen May.

It added gravitas to what was being proposed. The two dozen or so creatures who had fled their world for this one had done so at tremendous risk. They were refugees who left with their lives and nothing else. It spoke to May's brutal regime. What was more admirable was they all appeared willing, eager almost, to bring the fight to her.

Charlie spoke, his gaze fixed on Liam. "The exception to the rule is love, requited and reciprocated."

Lianna, a sylphlike blonde woman, rolled her eyes. "That's great for the two of you. Me, not so lucky in that department. And that one"—her focus on Finn—"you're saying he has a part in this, possibly a big part. No predicting what will happen to him… to any of us. So we get over there, and suddenly you have a bunch of silly sprites and pixilated pixies. I can't see that being any use."

Alex spoke. "You're right. And that's why you don't go." He turned and made eye contact with everyone. "None of you do. Our numbers are small. We don't know what we'll face here… or there. The only ones to cross are those with a chance of making it in one piece." He looked at Finn.

"So who made you boss?" Finn asked, having met Alex before. And fairy world traveler or no, the kid was pushy.

Alex smiled. "My mom did. Here's the deal, Finn. If Charlie's Gran is right, you're needed. But I can't think of anything that will get you from here to there in one piece."

"Yeah, memo received." Finn took inventory of his life, living on the same street he grew up in on Staten Island. His mom, who knew he was gay but continued to try to fix him up with eligible women. His occasional forays into dating, mostly with guys who wanted a hookup and nothing more. And he thought of Rory and of how, after more than a decade, the pain was still raw. It was as though there were something hollow inside him, a hole that never closed. Sure, he loved his job, though not the mass of busywork waiting for him…. As they talked about the trip leaving people broken, he knew that wouldn't matter, because he already was. "I'm in," he said. *If I've got something May wants, she can have it. She can have it all. I'm done, and this is how I go out.*

Nine

REDMOND FINGERED the ruby against his chest as he looked through the water window of May's cell. He instructed the guards, "Keep me in sight." *She grows solid.* Thoughts tortured him with the undeniable truth. *I cannot hold her. And I don't have the resolve to kill her.*

"Yes, Doctor." The ogre inserted the key as Redmond drew the magic that turned it.

He entered. The queen's postpassage instability, or travel sickness as it was euphemistically called, had eased to the point where the beautiful blonde with amber eyes stayed mostly fixed. She'd done her hair. Half was up, and half hung loose around her shoulders. So too her outfit, half dark green satin party dress and half camo, gave her a harlequin appearance. "My queen," he began.

"Yes, odious little man." She smiled, clearly pleased at how much smoother her speech came.

In her brief hospitalization, Redmond had learned several things. The queen was carnivorous; she reeked of fairy dust, which if he weren't careful would become a huge issue for him; and given half a chance, she'd eat him.

"Tell me if your needs are being met."

She paused. "Tell me if you watch my every move."

"Of course." And while the fey did not lie, Redmond could have obfuscated. But to no good purpose. He needed her trust. "You are at the Center's Hospital, the Center for Fey Development." He chose his words with care, as there was no way to sugarcoat what this place was. "This is where the most dangerous criminal elements… those who also have mental disturbances, are sent."

She threw back her head and laughed.

It was unexpected. "You find that amusing."

She twisted her lips, and for an instant her mouth shifted back to the slit-lip maw of the beast. "I find it pathetic, little squeak. I am your queen. I will not be judged. Not by you, not by my sisters. So Lizbeta sent me here. Too amusing. I can't imagine how we shall pass the time, though I suspect you have plans with your clever brain." She inhaled. "And that smell, and I'm not referring to the fear that leaches through your pores and causes dampness under your arms. Show me what you conceal around your neck."

He felt her attempt to control his limbs. Not a glamour but a more brute form of control spell. *She's testing the waters, wants to see what of her magic still works.* It left him with a decision: *Do as she says and let her think I'm easily controlled or ignore. You need her trust. Earn it.* He resisted her thrall and stayed put. He met her gaze and pulled out the ruby.

A long forked tongue poked through her lips, the camouflage blobs of her outfit changed colors, and the half of her hair in a bun came undone as the other side twisted into a french knot. "Give me that."

"I don't think that's in my best interest, Your Highness."

She hissed. "You don't know what it is. It is not yours. It is mine."

"I do." He gauged her reaction. Her form was now unstable, though judging by the strain on her face, she was trying to control it.

"Then tell me." She lay back and tried to solidify her shifting appendages and errant ensemble.

He gazed into the gem. It glowed. "It's a houndstone."

"Not *a* houndstone, you moron. *The* houndstone. It does not belong to you."

"It was given to me by your sister. I'd say a gift from a queen makes it mine."

And then she did something unexpected. She wept. "It was not hers to give. It is mine. It was mine."

He gentled his voice and subtly applied his own unique glamour, which unlike the more standard forms, came not with the promise of sex or wealth or power, but with warmth, caring, and compassion. It was Redmond's special gift and what made the most hardened criminals pour out their hearts to him.

Whether weakened by the jewel or his glamour, May spoke. "It is mine." Her eyes misted with a milky haze. "It was a gift of betrothal… a gift of betrayal." She gasped. "And I had forgotten it."

He trod lightly and let the warmth of his healing magic fill the cell. "It is safe in here, my queen. Tell me your sorrow."

Like a switch was thrown, the haze left May's eyes. "You are tricky." She spat up an orange-seed-sized ball of fairy fire. It landed at his feet, and the ground hissed. "Damn!" Her eyes narrowed. "That was meant to be a direct hit." She appeared perplexed. "Of course, it protects you." She sounded tortured. "Like the sugary coating on a chocolate treat. It is mine. It was not Lizbeta's to give. And I do not remember. Tell me how she came by it. Tell me how I lost it."

As it burned through the carpet and created a tiny crater in the impenetrable rock, he smelled the fairy fire. *I have to get out of here.*

Hanging on to the bed with talons, she eyed him. "I see you're no stranger to dust. If you'd like to roll a couple of bunnies, I won't tell."

The hunger was strong—one hundred years sober and now this. "I'll return in the morning."

She chuckled. "Yes, Doctor. And you'd best hang on to your stolen bauble, though I suspect at day's end, I won't be the cause of your undoing. You will. And I will take back the thing that is mine...." Her voice drifted as her brow flattened. "I cannot remember how I lost it."

Backing out of her cell on shaky legs, all he could think of was how good a hit of dust would be. Like oil on troubled seas. It would give him peace. *It will ruin you.*

As if reading his mind, she croaked an ancient tune.

"Fairy fire, fairy fire, come and see my fairy fire. Fairy dust, fairy dust, come and taste my fairy dust."

Ten

MILES FROM the Center, salamander May panicked as she broke through the concealment spell. *No!* Her eyes blazed as the spell's force struck her, while a sword attempted to pierce her flesh. It tickled her shoulder. She pivoted, gripped it in her jaw, and shattered the blade. The spell was another matter. It tangled like a spider's web. The more she struggled, the tighter it clung.

She snarled and twisted as it grabbed and restrained her. Her stout limbs scrambled for solid ground as timbers and plaster fell all around. She panicked and thought of Lizbeta's tethers. *No!*

"Your Highness," Dorothea shouted from behind her. "Do not struggle. It feeds the magic. Calm yourself."

Had it been anyone else, May would have ignored the suggestion. But Dorothea had proved herself true. Through labored breaths, she slowed her struggles. And there, amid shattered walls, she spotted her target. The redheaded haffling boy, held tight in his mother's embrace, and behind them both, Cedric Summer.

"Traitors!" Dorothea shouted. "How dare you assault the queen!"

"She betrayed her people," Marilyn Nevus spat back. "She comes to steal my child, as she has done before. She cannot have him."

Salamander May grew calm in body while her emotions fumed. The spell loosened its hold. She broke free and, shaking like a wet dog, scattered the sticky shards that tangled in her talons and clogged her nostrils. *Nasty.* She sneezed, and trails of fairy fire burned what remained of Cedric's concealment ward.

With Dorothea at her right, she stomped into the once-hidden space. *Goody. And there are my three little pigs. And third time's a charm.* She stared at Adam Nevus, the last of the three haffling children, and stopped. In human years, he couldn't have been more than seven.

"My lady, tell me." Dorothea touched her side, and May's thoughts flowed to her.

He's too young. Too young!

"You can fix that."

Yes. I will age him. He will do. He must do.

The boy stared at her, his expression more curious than afraid.

I have come for you, child. Her gaze raked over his tiny hands, one clutched in his mother's, the other hanging tight to his father's pumpkin-colored cape. This should have been a moment of triumph, but something weighed upon her thoughts. His coloring, the red hair, the milky skin. He was blood of something both forgotten and familiar… *hound. Blood of the Hound. I should have seen this.*

"The Hound is but a legend," Dorothea blurted. "An ancient tale."

Forgotten memories intruded. Battles rich with blood. A dual-natured human who came to her by night… or she to him. *My Hound.*

She hesitated. And in that pause, no more than the space of a breath, Cedric gathered his family inside his russet cloak, and with an inrush of air, like a vacuum sucking the place clean, they vanished.

Dorothea shouted, "They get away. You must be quick!"

May tasted and inhaled the afterburn of their getaway, an acrid mix of ozone and char. She should have been frustrated or disappointed. But the emotions that bubbled through her like a well-seasoned stew were too complex to pull apart: anger, disappointment, and the bittersweet memory of something wonderful she'd once had. It resonated deep. *I was loved.*

"I love you, Your Majesty."

May looked at Dorothea. Her words were truth. *Different love. Blood of the Hound. I can smell it. Smell him. I will find you. But then…. How could this hurt so much? How could I have forgotten?*

Dorothea kept her gaze fixed on May and gingerly touched her shoulder. "My lady, among my species we have little use for the male. Or rather, two specific ones. They give us babies, and then we bite off their heads and our babies feed on their bodies."

Not a bad system. But the Hound….

"Tell me," Dorothea urged. "There's something you seek to remember."

Yes, something hidden. Something important. Something I have forgotten.

"It involves the Hound."

Yes. She cocked her broad white head. *His smell…* and then it came to her. *He took something from me…. No, that's not it. I gave him something.*

"Tell me."

How have I forgotten this? She growled as the answer came. *No.* She shrugged away from Dorothea's touch. *This is not to be shared. Tricked.* She growled.

Dorothea filled in the pieces, though she did so with caution. "To not remember something and someone so important reeks of magic."

May smashed her head into a wall. The building shook as enchanted blinders fell away.

She pictured her two sisters. Lizbeta with the magic of the Mist, which carried peace and forgetfulness, and Katye, who emanated love and all its deceptions. And his image came to her. Tall with locks of flame red, a body stronger than any mortal man, and eyes that could hold her in thrall. *Hound, I remember you.* Tears of blood and acid streamed.

Lost in reverie, she did not feel Dorothea's gentle touch on her flank. *I will find you. I will take back the stolen part. I will take back my heart.*

"Finally," Dorothea stated. "You now have the missing piece… you know what must be done to become whole and to march in glory across the worlds as the one and only queen. Though it pains me to see your hurt, this is marvelous news."

Take back my heart. I will be whole. It's why I failed. This is how I shall succeed. Take back my heart. A cancerous doubt grew. *So long ago….*

"Yes," Dorothea said. "Humans do not live that long. Not even here. Though your heart, as the rest of you, approaches immortality. It must still beat. And if I may be so bold as to comment on the males of the human species. You must take back your heart, and if by some chance he still possesses it, then bite off his head. In my experience, it's the only satisfying way to end a relationship."

Eleven

ON THE receiving end of salamander May's assault, Marilyn Nevus, a seventh daughter of a seventh daughter, watched the air waver as the edges of her husband Cedric's protection wards unraveled. "It will not hold." She clutched her haffling son, Adam. Cedric's arm enfolded them both.

"It will hold," he said without assurance.

It will not, she thought, as spiderweb cracks spread across the plaster walls and debris rained down from above.

For his part, Adam, only two years old in human time but so precocious he'd skipped several years through fey influence and appeared around seven, did not shed a tear. He held silent as fairy fire whistled down and the building trembled.

A missile landed on the porch's flat roof. It sizzled and burned through shingles.

Marilyn smelled the fire as it caught on the dry timber. She leaned back and whispered in Cedric's ear. "We must leave. If she does not break through the ward, she will burn us to death."

"It's her way." And he wrapped his wife and son within the folds of his cape.

Despite the warmth of his body, her teeth chattered. "Where?"

He shuddered. "No questions."

In a less fraught moment, she'd have spat back that she'd ask all the damn questions she wanted. But now…. *It's all up to him. I have no power here.* She felt like screaming, so sick of running, of this constant fear that at any moment May would come for one of her children. She tried not to think of brave Alex and soulful-eyed Alice. At least she'd recently received word from Cedric's nephew Liam that they were alive, and while battle-weary, they were well.

Though the memory of that conversation left her with fresh fears, especially the way Liam and his boyfriend, Charlie, hedged their words as they told her of Alice. *Something is wrong with her. I can feel it.*

Another shriek of fairy fire hurtled toward them. In the awful moments before it hit, she knew their time here was up. From the periphery she saw flames on the porch and from back in Adam's bedroom.

"It's time," Cedric acknowledged as he twirled circles in the air with his wrist and extended a forefinger.

Hiding Adam's face in Cedric's cloak, she braced as a creature unlike anything she could have imagined pierced through the ward and through the walls. It tangled in the spidery threads of Cedric's magic as a disembodied sword attempted to pierce its flesh, only to be shattered like a toothpick.

"Hurry." She was unable to rip her gaze from the slobbering white lizard with its spewing nostrils and razor-toothed maw. *What is that creature? I've seen it… her, before. It cannot be. That is what has become of Queen May.* Her gaze landed on Dorothea, a vile insect of a creature, ever eager to do May's bloody bidding.

"Traitors!" Dorothea shouted. "How dare you assault the queen!"

"She betrayed her people," Marilyn spat back. "She comes to steal my child, as she has done before. She cannot have him." And with an inrush of air that made her want to vomit, Cedric's arms tightened around her and Adam and they were up, up, and away.

Below them the creature howled. It reared back, aimed, and shot a ball of fire straight toward them. She fell into Cedric as he twisted and feinted to the right. She felt heat as the missile whistled past them.

"Fairy fire," Cedric hissed as they soared higher.

There was nothing to say, but Marilyn wondered at the weapon's source. If that thing was May, or some part of her, it would not have been meant as a killing shot. At least, not for all three of them. *She has come to take Adam.*

Despair threatened to overtake her. *First Alex, my brave boy, then Alice.* Her rage, never far from the surface, roared to her aid. It pushed past the sick clutches of hopelessness. *She failed before, and she will fail again. If that creature is her… she is not well.* In a clear voice, she asked, "Where to?"

Cedric recoiled at her use of forbidden interrogatives.

"Where to?" she repeated. I will not be cowed by her.

He whispered, "I have a thought, and you won't like it."

She turned into him and pressed her lips to his. She held her hands tight over Adam's ears. "Tell me." Though she knew what he'd say. It was the only thing that made sense.

"We must send Adam to his brother and sister in the See. Alex and Alice can protect him… we cannot."

She gasped. It felt like she'd been sucker punched. "Yes, it's the only solution. I will go with him."

"Dearest, you cannot, and you know that is truth. You are mad beyond repair in the See. Our oldest has reached majority and can be a legal guardian to Adam. It would be good for them to spend time together. And they have your changeling doppelgänger as well. Ripped from your own true flesh."

She hissed and continued to shield Adam's ears. "Are you mad? He's too young. I will not send a seven-year-old, who in fact is only two, alone on the back of a puka. I will go with him." This was not to be argued, and while Marilyn loved Cedric, brave he was not. Even robbed of her reason in the See, she'd do what needed to be done. "Will May follow us?"

Cedric gazed down at the creature, little more than a pinpoint on the ground. "She will break if she tries. I cannot say how. But the queen we knew grows ever more unrecognizable. With our three children safely tucked away in the See, she cannot follow. She will break. Adam will be safe there. They will all be safe."

Marilyn prayed that he was right. Still, the plan carried horrible risk. But in times of war, which this was, mothers faced unbearable choices. She gazed into Cedric's beautiful face. Much of this was his fault. She had forgiven him, though at times like this it was difficult to remember why. With her fingers twined in her son's silken red hair, she spoke. "Call the puka."

Cedric shifted in the wind, his course now clear. He tried to soothe her with his voice. "He will be safe there. This is what must happen."

Marilyn held her tongue and tried not to think of the horror that awaited her. An awful doubt took hold as she remembered how difficult— almost impossible—it had become for her to think clearly in the See. She had been broken by the trip. Sane in this realm and bereft of all reason in the world where she'd grown up. Her every waking second hounded by nonsensical voices and rambling thoughts, one disconnected from the next. But even more awful was the realization I have to send my last child *away*. She clutched Adam to where she could feel his heart beat against her chest.

I will fight for your return. And if I must, I will die to keep you safe.

Twelve

REDMOND STOOD in front of the packed Level Four Psychopathology class. His head felt like it might explode. *I can't believe I did that. This is bad. So bad.* Sunlight streamed through the windows in the round auditorium. Dust motes glittered in the rays. His eyes teared, and his thoughts were dragged to the sound, sizzle, but mostly the smell of the fairy fire and residue of dust in May's cell. And they traveled from there to…. *I did not do that.*

Yes, you did.

Centuries of being a functioning dusthead, with endless practice of pretending all was well, had not been wasted. As he moved around the room, casting sigils into the air illustrating today's topic—eating disorders that afflict the fey—he was at war with himself. What made matters worse, and the excuse he'd given himself last night to have *just a taste*, was May. *It was the stress. Yeah, right. It's always something. It always was… is.* Hidden from his eager-eyed students, he ran the litany of all the reasons to have a taste, and then a bit more: *stress, celebration, fuck it all, check out, get high, boredom….*

Moving on autopilot, something he did better than most, he rattled off criteria for each of the eating disorders that affected fairy, pixie, ogre, sprite, gnome, troll, and so forth. He heard the words stream through his lips. These were addictions too, only they involved food. He weighed the pros and cons of his own love of dust. On the plus side, the dust bunny he'd gobbled last night had sent him into a beautiful world that not even May could touch. He'd felt happy and free, and like nothing bad existed in this world or any other one.

Followed by waking up with a crushing dustover. No stranger to the rhythms of dust addiction, he knew how the day would go. A pounding headache, like wearing a hat three sizes too small, accompanied by absolute resolution to never touch the stuff again. But come midday, there'd be a shift. He felt it now, and it wasn't yet ten. His head would clear, and the hunger would start. By eventide it would be unbearable, and only one thing would slake it—dust.

A redheaded pixie in the front raised his hand, Colum something. His tiny wings twitched with nerves. "I don't understand how Brownie Eating Disorder… BED, works."

Redmond, as he'd done during the centuries of his rampant addiction, focused and coped. "It's complex, but once you understand the subtle psychosis involved, it makes sense. Let's start by having you tell us what you *do* know of that disorder."

Colum flitted onto his desk and, like a contestant in a spelling bee, restated the subject and then dove in. "Brownie eating disorder mostly affects ogres, but occasionally trolls and giants."

"Correct," Redmond stated. "Though there have been exceedingly rare reports of water worgs and even one of a cyclops, but continue."

"It's a binge-purge phenomenon. The ogre has a building need to eat brownies, while simultaneously resisting the urge to do so. Eventually the craving becomes too intense, and rather than eat one or two brownies, they'll pillage and devour an entire village and then turn around and vomit them all up." Colum looked to Redmond.

"Spot on so far."

"But it makes no sense."

From the back right of the room, a group of cliquish brownies mumbled and nodded their green-capped heads.

"It does if you understand both the history of the disorder and the psyche of larger creatures. It ultimately comes down to the grass is always greener. Very large creatures wonder what it might be like to be small and slender. A thousand years ago this disorder was unheard of. Quite possibly it did not exist." He looked over the classroom. All eyes were on him. This was a hot topic. "So tell me what is different between then and now."

From her usual seat in the front row just in front of his podium, Luluba shot up her hand. "The culture has changed."

"Say more."

She stood and without trepidation launched into a thoughtful analysis. "A thousand years ago, the fey concept of beauty was broad. Ogre, troll, and such were merely one's species and did not carry added connotations. You could be a lovely troll or a graceful ogre. That changed." She lowered her voice.

"Say it. These walls are safe."

Luluba's composure wavered as she launched into what could be considered treason. "Queen May began to define beauty and used herself, her sisters, and her species to define it. If you weren't from one of the four-season families, such as you, Dr. Fall, you were outside her standard."

"Well done, Luluba. Let's hear from others. Explain how the standard of beauty occurred, and for ten thousand gold stars, relate that to Brownie Eating Disorder."

Around the room hands and related appendages shot up. He called on a student with the limbs of a praying mantis, the pointy ears of a pixie, and a humanoid face. "Yes, Flikka."

She rose up on acutely angled limbs. "I think I have this."

"Let's hear it."

She paused and gathered her thoughts. "I'll work backward from the ogre puking up the brownies." She gave an apologetic nod to the green hats in the back. "Creatures with BED describe intense remorse, guilt, and shame after they purge. And yet they get pulled back over and over, sometimes destroying the same village multiple times a day. So it carries elements of both compulsive behavior and obsessive thought. They spend hours ruminating on either giving in to the urge or resisting it."

Redmond's breath caught. *This is close to the bone.* He nodded, dreading what she'd say next.

"So yes, it's an addiction. It has strong similarities with certain anxiety disorders, but the piece that's missing is, for lack of a better term, a kind of psychosis… a beauty psychosis. On some level, the afflicted ogre or troll believes that they can be other than they are. When you're doing therapy with them, a common theme is the belief that by resisting the urge they could magically transform into a four-season fairy. To my knowledge that spell does not exist."

"Correct," Redmond stated and then added, "There are certainly ways—not pleasant ones—where we shift, but starvation is not one of them. And then they give in to the urge and feel both physically sick and disgusted with themselves on numerous levels, but because the behavior gives them that giddy in-the-moment relief as they're engaging in it, they go back to it over and over again."

Flikka's eyes sparkled. "It is a type of psychosis. It's thinking something impossible might work, even though you know it won't. I think that's true of all addictions. That maybe this time the hit of dust might make you feel good forever, even though you know for a fact it won't."

Shit! Keep it together. Flikka's observations were too sharp. "You know, I think I've just taken you from ten thousand gold starts to twenty-five. Well done, Flikka." He glanced at the wag-on-the-wall clock. There were ten minutes left to go. Normally he loved to teach, but now… *It's just one slip. You don't have to follow this path. Today is a new day. You don't have to use.* But in his gut, like an ogre trapped in the cycle of BED, he knew. *Once a dusthead, always a dusthead.*

Flikka, emboldened by praise and imaginary gold stars, quipped in her impression of a human voice, "It's just so unfair."

The hundred-plus students burst into laughter at the ancient joke about one of the obvious differences between humans and fey.

Redmond smiled. Though he'd never met a human, it was widely known that they had a ludicrous belief that the world should operate with a sense of fairness. A concept which, when placed against the cruelty and beauty of nature, made zero sense.

After class, Luluba tagged at his heels as he headed toward the asylum and his dreaded session with May. She was troubled, but in his fogged state, Redmond didn't notice.

"It's her," Luluba said in a tremulous voice. "She's back. I don't see how that's possible." She lowered her voice. "She's locked up in the hospital. She can't be both locked up and free… as some sort of fire-breathing salamander."

Redmond listened with half his attention. The other part ruminated on how he'd make it through today's session with the coalescing and convalescing queen. "It's rare, what she has done."

"She's carnivorous," Luluba stated.

"Yes, they both are." They approached the first security gate outside the forensic hospital. Uniformed ogres inspected their palms to verify their identities. The outer wards came down, and he and Luluba entered. He emptied his pockets in bins as a flock of pixies scanned for contraband.

"So the salamander is her… and what you have locked up is her," Luluba whispered. "I don't understand how that's possible."

Despite his funk, Redmond chuckled.

Luluba caught his drift. "If it's possible, then it's probable, which means it's true."

"Exactly. Queen May split in two. The difficulty being, or rather her problem is, she is in a severe schizo-diddled state that is worsened by her frequent forays between the worlds. Her cleverness and machinations have cost her."

"You can fix her," Luluba said with admiration.

"I believe so. Our problem is that by fixing her I screw each and every one of us. We know what she's capable of. What I don't yet grasp is the method behind her madness."

"Queen of three worlds seems a good place to start. She's power mad. It's narcissism on steroids. It's always been and always will be about her her her," Luluba stated.

"Yes, but deeper. The creature you describe devouring all that come in her path is a symptom." He paused. *She suffers from her own addiction to power. It's a hunger without end.* "It's a part of May, and what we have locked deep in the earth is another part. But even with the two put back together, she will still not be whole, and that's been the mystery. Some crucial piece has been lost to her." He turned to Luluba as they approached the sweeping circular stairs. "No." He read eagerness to join him. "You see your patients, and I will see mine." He had few illusions about May's capacities. From the moment Lizbeta had first come with her proposal, he'd known the truth. *This will not end well. One slip and I'm dead.* His head, clearer than an hour ago, still rang with traces of a dustover. He paused. *And you've already made that slip.*

Thirteen

IT FELT familiar and strange as Finn took the Fort Tryon Park ramp off the Henry Hudson Parkway and followed Charlie's SUV up the steep, winding drive to the castle-like Cloisters.

He'd never gone inside, though he knew it housed the Metropolitan Museum's collection of medieval artifacts. He parked and got out. It was near dark, and the grounds would soon close.

It's Tuesday, he thought as he took in his surroundings. *It's May. The sun is setting, the trees are green, and I'm out of my fucking mind being here.* He watched as Charlie, Liam, Alex, and Jerod piled out of Charlie's pickup truck. *I'm just with a bunch of guys... and one of them has a bare-breasted fairy with swirly tattoos and butterfly wings on his shoulder. Nothing wrong with that.*

"This way," Charlie said as he took Liam's hand. "Come on."

Finn trailed behind as they left the asphalt drive for one paved walkway after another and then through a hedge and onto obscured deer trails that cut through the otherwise gracefully manicured acres of the park. The ground squished from recent rains and last fall's leaves. Here and there he glimpsed the glittering gray surface of the Hudson River hundreds of feet below.

What am I doing here? He looked up and caught Nimby staring at him from atop Alex's shoulder. Their gazes connected. She nodded but did not speak. Instead she threw her arms around Alex's neck and kissed him on the cheek.

Alex turned. "What is with you?"

"No questions," Nimby said and turned back to Finn. "Ask no questions. Remember that."

"Okay," Finn said, his gut telling him to get out of there. A twig snapped under someone's heel. He startled. A leaf brushed his face. *Why is*

Nimby staring at me? Every time he looked up, those red eyes were on him, studying him. "What? Why are you looking at me?"

Nimby shook her head. "No questions, Finn Hulain. Neither a borrower nor a lender be. If you give, it must be free."

"Awesome." The unmarked path they'd followed led to a meadow that had escaped the park's ground crew.

"Shit." It was too familiar as the night of a thousand fires thundered back. Because there, in the middle of an overgrown field of dandelion and wild pansy-faced viola, towered the weeping mulberry. It was into the bower of that tree that Charlie had followed Liam and the beast and they had vanished… for a month.

Charlie whispered, "Into the breach." And he and Liam went hand in hand through the tree's dense curtain of limbs and heart-shaped leaves. Jerod and Alex followed Nimby, whose gaze never left Finn, seemed terrified. Perhaps it was a trick of the dimming light, but to Finn, it appeared as if the leaves parted and swallowed her.

"Crap." He inhaled deep and, putting his hands in front of his face to avoid getting scratched, followed.

It was pitch-black inside. Finn pulled out his cell and clicked on the Maglite. Alex and Charlie did the same.

Nothing happened.

"It's not working," Alex said. He looked at Liam, born fey but stripped of much of his magic as the cost of his passage between realms. "Tell me what you feel."

"Nothing. The only magic in this place is love. Mine for Charlie, yours for Jerod. Even Nimby's for you."

"Awesome," Finn groaned as he shone the light on Nimby, who was trembling. She bit into her lip with a sharp fang-like tooth. She looked like she wanted to scream.

"There is magic here," Nimby said. Her eyes glowed red. She screamed, "It's coming! It's tricky, trappy! Alex. I love you. I'm sorry. Goodbye…."

Finn felt it too. A tingle in his belly, not like nerves but like bees. It buzzed. "Guys, something's happening."

He searched for them with his light but found only darkness and the red eyes of the terrified fairy. "Something's happening. Alex! Charlie! Guys, where are you?"

Nimby howled. *"No questions!"*

The buzzing belly bees spread. Stunned into silence, Finn felt the air rush out, like being sucked through a giant vacuum. "Holy shit." The earth canted, and his feet left the ground. His stomach lurched, and he had the sensation of floating and then of falling. Something landed on his shoulder. Tiny claws gripped his shirt and broke through his flesh. Jabs of pain and Nimby's frightened voice as she clung to him. "I've given away my Alex. My Alex. I have little time and must soon pay. Oh. No no no." The fairy looked at Finn with glowing eyes. She spoke fast, as though needing to confess before whatever was about to happen arrived.

As they fell, she clung to his shoulder as her words tumbled forth. All the rules for the fey. Like she was reciting lessons to a child. "Questions come with cost, so ask none. Neither a borrower or a lender be. At day's end, everything must balance. What is taken must be replaced. And the travel between worlds always comes at a cost. The fey will tell you the truth, but it's often laced with tricky and trappy."

Finn tried to speak.

"Shh. I speak. You listen. You have a part to play and a path to follow. I do not know what it is, but if you listen, and not with your ears, you will find it. Open yourself to the winds. It's how magic comes in. Not through the brain or the ears or the eyes or the nose. You've another sense, Finn Hulain, though humans have fallen out of practice."

The air shifted, and a salt breeze washed across his face. Bile rose in the back of his throat, and like an elevator coming to a stop, something cushioned their descent onto a moonlit meadow. His feet touched down, and he gazed up at a star-filled sky and a bloodred crescent moon.

He whispered, "Alex! Charlie! Liam! Jerod!" There was no reply.

Nimby's teeth chattered.

He looked at the little fairy as she did deep knee bends on his shoulder. Her hands flew to either side of her face, and she grinned, though it seemed more grimace than smile. Her lips parted, and at the top of her tiny lungs, she sang and did whip-fast pirouettes on his shoulder. "I'm a little teapot short and stout…." She did not stop.

Fourteen

ALONE IN his chambers, Redmond stared at two brownish dust bunnies he'd purchased after work. They looked like small dirty eggs. *I should have bought more. You bought too much. One is too much. You know that.* It's as though a part of his brain had separated from him. *Or maybe this is just who and what I am... a dusthead. Once a dusthead, always a....* He tried to hold on to the rational part of himself. The part that had achieved so much in his life, that had built the Center into the premier institute for the psychological study and betterment of all sentient beings in the Unsee. But it had become so much more. It was a haven... the haven. *What are you doing? Shut up already and eat it.* He was at war... with himself. He knew this battle was lost.

Yesterday he'd finished work and found his way to the alleys of the capital. *The horse knows the way...* to the streets where a hundred years earlier he had skulked in the shadows waiting for his dealer and his fix. His face concealed, hidden by a dingy scarf. Little had changed; only the prices of dust had come down. *It's too cheap. Someone... something has flooded the market.* He'd pulled out the coin and paid the blue-skinned sprite. It was easy.

"And here I am. Once a dusthead, always a dusthead." Saliva welled in his mouth. As he reached for the bunny, a high-pitched noise came through the windows. The song of a lone female pixie.

"I'm a little teapot short and stout. Here is my handle. Here is my spout. I'm a little teapot short and stout. Here is my handle. Here is my spout...."

He paused. *Is that real? Am I hearing this?* He wondered if the off-kilter singing was a symptom of one of the later stages of dust addiction, where hallucinations were common, though more typically visual than auditory. He went to the window and peered into the night, toward the meadows that ringed the Center. The cool air helped, and the little creature's song reeked of madness. *At least it's not my madness.*

Careful to not handle their sticky surface with his bare skin, he pushed the dust bunnies back into their clear package and dropped them into his stash box, hidden inside a drawer. He locked it with a chant.

"Duty call." He belted on a robe and flew on the currents into the night. He mentally cataloged the patients. There were only a few pixies in the current census. It took a lot for someone that small to do something so big that it could get them locked away at the Center. *Someone has gotten out. But who?* He thought to call security, but having a troop of uniformed ogres hunt down a lone pixie seemed overkill.

Riding the cool night air, he followed the song. It didn't vary, the same two lines over and over. As he neared its source, he hovered and reassessed the situation. Yes, one mad tattoo-covered pixie, dancing and singing, and something unexpected… a human man seated on the ground with hair the colors of fire and ice. The pixie's tune changed. She pointed up at him. "Twinkle, twinkle little star. How I wonder what you are."

Sounds like my cue, and more curious than cautious, he touched down. The man's gaze followed him. His jaw hung slack, and his incredulous expression told Redmond he was a new arrival. It also spoke to the cause of the pixie's obvious madness… travel sickness. *One broken little pixie. But why and….* "You're not from around here," Redmond said as he took in the odd duo, seemingly dropped in the middle of a heavily protected field.

The man stood and started to speak. "Wha…." And then stopped. "I'm trying to figure out how to do this without questions."

"Someone has prepared you. You are from the See." *Redmond took in the well-built man, with his flaming locks gone silver at the temples and dark, soulful eyes.* Neither young or old and… beautiful.

"She did," the man said, motioning to the little fairy who was oblivious to either one of them as she trilled from nursery rhyme to nursery rhyme with accompanying jigs, reels, and a bit of ballet.

"Row, row, row your boat, gently down the stream. Merrily, merrily, merrily." She giggled and made rowing gestures. As her wings beat out of tune, she spun in circles.

"She's broken," Redmond stated. Something tugged at his heart as he realized that human and fey alike had to pay for the travel. The pixie was pixiellated, but the human…. Redmond shifted to a more clinical appraisal of the situation. *The pixie is broken, but the man… a fine-looking man.* "Tell me your name."

"Finn. Tell me yours."

He paused. Normally it would be Dr. Fall, but that's not what came out of his mouth. "It's Redmond, and you're on the grounds of the Center."

Finn extended a hand.

While not a fey custom, Redmond knew what was expected. What was unexpected was the moon's glow in Finn's eyes and the strength in his grip. It mesmerized, and the contact was like a cleansing wind that washed away Redmond's earlier despair. "Tell me if you're hurt," he said.

Finn shook his head. "No pain. Confused, but nothing hurts." He looked down at their still joined hands and then back to Redmond. The two stood, seemingly frozen, each thinking the other would speak.

Nimby broke the spell. She sang at the top of her lungs. The pitch grew higher and higher, like a teakettle set to boil. "Ring around the rosy, a pocket full of posy, ashes, ashes, we all fall down." And then she screamed.

Fifteen

SALAMANDER MAY howled, though she did not know why. Something tore deep in her chest. She thrashed on the ground and spat random projectiles of fairy fire. Some immolated members of the drug-hungry throng that trailed her. Here and there a pixie, sprite, brownie, or ogre went up in flames. It smelled like cookies at a barbecue.

Dorothea stroked her shoulder. "Tell me your pain, my queen."

The ache in her chest was unexpected. *I know this.*

"Show me," Dorothea urged. "Let me help."

May saw flashes of the Hound, a red-haired shifter. A spell learned on her mother's knee flashed through her mind and out of Dorothea's lips.

"With a mickle and a care, I will go into a hare."

No. May pictured the tough rabbits and hares that populated the Unsee, as well as the occasional puka who held obeisance to the Goddess of a thousand names whose symbols were the owl, the moon, and the hare. *Not a hare… a hound.*

She sniffed. Something was different. *Something lost and something gained.* She pounded the ground with her tail, her thinking even more muddled.

"Your sisters' spells still cloud these memories. You must be stronger than their magic to take back what's been stolen."

Yes. Good friend. Good advice. Mustn't eat her. Instead she grabbed an ogre from the ranks and bit off his head. The magic in his blood and bones helped clear her thoughts. *The haffling, third time's a charm.*

She howled again as blood trickled from her maw and stained her hide.

"The child fled, Your Majesty. We were there. You must remember."

He's gone. I was there. I don't remember.

"Because of the spell," Dorothea stated. "It lingers. It's sticky and tricky. The instant you turn away from it, it grabs hold again. I am under no such enchantment. I will be your memory."

Rage, frustration, her sisters' magic blinded May. But something else, it filtered up her nostrils and sizzled in her brain. *Not a hare… a hound.*

"Exactly." Dorothea hesitated. "He was both enemy and lover. And from what I glimpse in your mind's eye, he was both human, though remarkable, and had a second nature. He shifted into a beast, a dog, though unlike any I've encountered."

May, with the ogre's booted legs still in her mouth, shook her head from side to side. She bounced once to clear room in her belly and sucked the last of him down. *It helps.* She let her thoughts drift to wondrous nights spent in bed with the Hound of Hulain. *I remember.* Though it was hard. She saw a massive curtain-draped bed with a beautiful man naked and twisted in the sheets… in her arms. Their nights of passion. But just as she tried to hold on to the feel of his flesh on hers, a wall of forgetfulness clouded the edges of her thoughts. *No.*

"I am here for you. I will hold all your memories. I will remind you that you gave him your heart and that we hunt for it now. But there is something more. It's gone beyond a memory."

His scent.

"Yes," Dorothea stated. "You smell him, and not just in your mind's eye. If he has smell, then he is real… he is here, though I can't say how such a thing is possible.

He's here. He's back. He's come back for me. She inhaled deep. *I know that smell.* It rolled around in her brain, and no amount of Lizbeta's and Katya's tricks could push the intoxicating blend of musk and man away. *He's come back for me.*

Dorothea nodded. "This troubles me. The Hound should have perished more than two millennia ago in human years. When a fey snatches a human babe, they last a good couple hundred years, maybe even three, of their time, but not this long."

May barely listened. The smell rekindled wondrous feelings. His flesh against hers. Darker feelings intruded. *He hurt me. I hurt.* She turned on her hind legs to where the scent came strongest. *I will find him.*

"Yes," Dorothea said. "You will, and I will help."

If salamanders could have smiled, May would have. *I will find him. There will be no tricky. There will be no trappy.* She turned to look at Dorothea, with her pincer gently rested on her flank. *Take back what's mine.*

"Take back your heart," Dorothea echoed.

And bite off his head.

"Yes, and bite off his head."

Sixteen

Finn's mind reeled. Moments ago he was in Fort Tryon Park, and now…. He stared at the guy, or whatever he was…. Redmond. *Ears a bit pointy, but everything else….* His eyes traced the outline of the man's body. Even with his long blue Harry Potter robe, he was graceful and practically floated. Their gazes locked. *Why is he looking at me like that? God, he's good-looking. I wonder how old he is? Thirties, twenties, forties?*

And I'm staring like a schoolgirl. Finn looked away. *What the hell is that?* He stopped and gazed up at a towering citadel that glowed a silvered orange by the light of the moon. *Okay, not Manhattan. Just go with it. And where's everyone else? Why does everything smell so strong? Why am I smelling him? He smells good. What the hell? Where is everyone?* He wondered if maybe the others had landed at random points. *But why is Nimby with me and not with Alex? And is it okay to think questions and not ask them? Fuck fuck fuckity fuck…. God, he smells good. And looks even better.*

Nimby lay on a rock and sang and rocked and occasionally screamed. "Poor thing," Redmond said, and he scooped her up.

Finn braced, wondering if he'd need to defend Alex's fairy. But Redmond's touch was gentle. *He's done this before.* The urge to ask questions was intense. But he'd been warned…. *How do you talk without questions?* "Tell me what's wrong with her."

"Travel sickness. In her case it's pixielation." He tapped his forefinger three times on the center of one of Nimby's tattoos. Like an off switch, the fairy closed her eyes and fell asleep. He tucked her into a pocket of his robe. "It's common." Redmond's gaze narrowed. He scrutinized Finn.

So that's it. "You're wondering how I broke," Finn said, knowing he was neither haffling or in the midst of some blissful love affair—that ship had never come for him. But TMI for this guy, at least TMI for now. He looked around. *Where's everyone else?* It was just the two of them. He thought to shout out for Alex, Charlie, and the rest. But with Nimby silenced and the warm night air filled with strange scents and this beautiful man, loud noise seemed wrong. "There were more of us," he said, hoping the sound of his voice would push away the weird. But it kept coming. Like the way colors here were different. The moon was orange, and the grass in the meadow was too green for the middle of night. And Redmond, from the blue of his robe, to his auburn hair tied back in a ponytail, to his eyes that seemed mostly green but held other colors….

"I don't see or sense anyone else," Redmond said, not taking his gaze from Finn's.

Finn felt his cheeks color. Gooseflesh prickled on his arms. *What the fuck?* He thought of Charlie's Liam. *Is he trying to glamour me? It wouldn't take much. And man, his hair looks soft, and his smile… not good-looking, beautiful. Teeth a bit pointy… probably not a vegetarian.*

"Come," Redmond said and broke the connection. "Let's see what can be done for your pixie. She's a Nevus fairy, and I've not seen one…." He turned back to Finn. "In a very long time."

How he said it made Finn reappraise his earlier age estimate. While Finn did not sleep around, there were times the urge for human contact, the touch of another man, was so strong he'd go to places. There were many in New York—where guys could find something brief and anonymous, though the ache it filled was fleeting. But one thing he'd learned: everyone looks better and younger in the dark. But in the moonlight, as they crossed the meadow toward the imposing all-white city, with oddly angled towers and smooth soaring walls, he was entranced by Redmond. Every time he turned, he wanted to drink in his features, his high cheekbones, the tiny wrinkles at the corners of his eyes. The way the slightest breeze caught in his silk-fine hair. "Tell me what this place is."

"It's a university, a fortress, a hospital…," Redmond said. "The Center for Fey Development. Though most call it the Center."

"You work here," he stated, careful to keep the inflection down at the end of the sentence.

"I do." Redmond swallowed. "I founded it. Though it was built on something even older. A temple to a goddess that's now largely forgotten. After that it was a school…. I was raised here."

Finn stared up and took in the scale of the beautiful white city, like something from ancient Greece or Rome. "I'm thinking you're older than you look."

"Time works different here, Finn. We don't age the way you do. Our lives are measured on a different scale, a larger scale."

Finn wanted to ask just how old, but that seemed unimportant… and rude, as they passed under an arch guarded by two hideous creatures in blue uniforms. He bit back the obvious *What the fuck are those?* and watched Redmond give the briefest of nods as they passed. It was hard not to spin his head back and just stare. *Some kind of guards… but Shrek, only not cute Shrek.*

"So Finn, and I imagine there's a surname as well, tell me your business here."

"I'm not certain." And Finn deliberately lobbed the thing Gran had said was important. "My last name is Hulain."

Two things happened as those two syllables left his mouth. Redmond spun back and clamped his hand firmly over Finn's lips, and a scream, like a mortally wounded animal, shook the foundations of the city. It came from within the earth and simultaneously from somewhere far in the distance, two separate screams, but somehow connected.

It reminded Finn of the wail of sirens, only more primal. And as they stood and listened with Redmond's warm hand on his face, a thought hit.

That's the sound of a heart breaking.

<h1>Seventeen</h1>

Redmond kept his hand clamped over Finn's mouth as the stereo screams filled the night. He could feel his questions. They practically burned his flesh. *What the hell was that? Who are you? Where am I?* But Redmond, who had answers to all those questions, had darker thoughts. *She knows you are here, and the wheel of fate has just been spun.*

Despite the ice-water terror that ran through him, Redmond felt something else. The human's lips, his hot breath against his palm.

Finn nodded and gripped Redmond's hand to pull it away. "I'm good. Tell me what the fuck that is."

"Not a what, exactly…, a who. It's our queen, Finn. Though lately she's not been herself. More like two selves, and truth be told, there's a third part she's just come to understand. And I now know why you've dropped from the sky and landed here. Damn."

"Tell me." Finn gripped Redmond's wrist. "I know some, or think I do, though it's all batshit crazy."

Redmond smiled as May's wails crested and finally stopped. "Madness is my business. I am a psychiatrist."

"So that's what this place is. It's a nuthouse."

"We use kinder words, but yes. It's an insane asylum and a place for others to work on improving themselves. It's also a university. And…." Redmond's words stuck in his throat.

"Tell me," Finn said.

"It's a shelter. It's the only place in the Unsee that Queen May has not breached. Though she has tried."

"But you said she's here now… or a part of her is. I'm guessing it's not for a round of getting over daddy issues."

"No, and this is my particular specialty. Those whose insanity leads them to harm others."

"So mad and bad," Finn commented, drawing on his own experience investigating arson.

Where oftentimes the motivation was the fire itself.

"Precisely. And while I don't mind," Redmond said, "at any point you could release my hand… unless you don't want to." He faced Finn and felt his breath and the beating of his heart in the inches between them. He hoped he wasn't wrong, because he saw desire in Finn's eyes.

Finn's voice was gruff. "Maybe this is my insanity. Maybe this is how I broke." And he closed the inches between them and pulled Redmond into a kiss.

Redmond did not resist. Their lips met. Finn let go of his wrist and gripped the sides of his head. Redmond felt transported to a realm of bliss as they locked together. Someone gasped, and Finn's warm mouth was on his neck.

It lasted a lifetime and not long enough. Breathless, they pulled back, and the night was again split by the ground-rocking roar of two beasts, one from within the Center and the other far in the distance.

Nimby awoke in Redmond's pocket and sang, "Peas porridge hot. Peas porridge cold. Peas porridge in the pot nine days old."

Finn whispered, his breath hot against Redmond's cheek, "That's her."

"Yes." Redmond couldn't focus. His fingers twined through Finn's. He knew enough to be afraid, but those feelings would not come. "This won't end well."

Finn nodded. "Yeah, I get that. I take it she's your patient."

"Yes."

"A well-locked-up patient."

"One hopes so." And from inside the neck of his robe, Redmond pulled out the ruby houndstone on its leather strap. In the moonlight, the gem glowed and pulsed with the rhythm of a heart.

Finn reached for it, and the color flared. He touched it, and…. "Holy shit!"

"Tell me," Redmond said. *There's magic here. Something is happening.*

Finn's eyes sparked red with the gem's pulsing aura. "It's like energy, raw power." Finn closed his fist around the stone. He looked at Redmond and, with a quick and decisive pull, severed the cord from Redmond's neck. "This is mine."

Redmond stared, transfixed. Finn's form wavered. Subtle at first, his hair, which had been close-cropped and military, lengthened. His red-and-silver locks sprouted and glistened in the moon as they lengthened and curled around his broadening shoulders. Where they had been of equal height, Finn gained five inches, the fabric on his shirt strained, and buttons popped to reveal a broad chest. And his eyes, which had been deep and warm and brown, glinted with the red of the stone. Finn's lips curled into a smile. He looked toward the distant city and then at Redmond. "Tell me what you see."

"I see a legend reborn."

"Speak plain, Redmond. I need to know."

His use of his name and something in his voice quieted Redmond. During that wonderful kiss, he'd let hope blossom that in the midst of horrible danger, something wonderful had fallen into his life. But now…. "I see you, Finn Hulain. I see the Hound."

Finn opened his fist, and where he'd held the talisman, all that remained was the leather strap. "Tell me what I am."

Redmond thought of the dust bunnies waiting for him. A dull pain blossomed within his chest. "You are the Hound, Finn Hulain. She, that creature howling in the night, she is yours, and you are hers." *And I had you for one unlikely and wonderful moment. But you are not mine. You are hers.*

Finn's eyes narrowed as he focused on Redmond. He placed a hand beneath Redmond's chin, not letting him look away. And as the little black fairy sang about love betrayed, Finn's words washed over Redmond. "And you, Redmond. With whom do you belong?"

That it was an unabashed question shocked Redmond, but more than that, the truth was a vice around his heart. He met Finn's gaze—*and now you are not just a handsome mortal, but a legend.* He knew that whatever connection he'd had with Finn was gone in this transformation. "I belong with no one." He pulled back from Finn, and trying to hang on to what little self-respect remained, he masked his emotions. "You came with a purpose, Finn, and that lies within those walls." He looked down at Nimby, cradled in his pocket. *I must clear my thoughts.* "Let me tuck this brave little thing into a healing cradle, and then I will return. Wait here. It's time you became reacquainted with your betrothed."

His chest ached as he rose on the air. It wasn't the elephant thump of angina or even a muscle pain. It cut deeper. He let the pores of his skin drink the night air. *I need to get away from here. Away from him.* A breeze off the Western Sea lifted him high and fast. *Don't look at him.*

Don't let him see. Don't let him know. It was just a kiss, a lie made flesh by the burn that lingered on his lips. The feel of Finn's stubble clung to his fingers, as the ghost of his breath and the flick of his tongue played on his neck. *He's not for you. He is hers. He is taken, and I have been a fool.*

Warm currents swept him skyward, and he gazed back on the transformed mortal. The beautiful man was taller and stronger than when he'd found him in the meadow with his barking-mad pixie. His hair now curled around his neck in a mixture of fire and ice. *Stop looking at me. Don't look at me. Why does he stare? I should have known.* He forced a laugh as he thought of the man's ridiculous name, Finn Hulain—*two heroes wrapped in one*. But what squeezed through his lips was a rasp of pain. He lost track of his purpose—to get little Nimby into a healing cradle. He drifted directionless on the currents, unable to rip his gaze from Finn, from the Hound. He blinked back tears and tried to meet Finn's stare. As the distance grew, he saw Finn's mouth open. *He's trying to say something.* But what came through his lips was not a word but a howl, like an animal, like a dog, *like the Hound.*

And so it begins, Redmond thought as he vanished into the clouds.

Eighteen

DEEP IN the earth, May woke screaming from a tortured dream. Her shrieks split the air as she struggled to remember where she was, who she was. For a panicked moment, she couldn't move. Then like a switch was thrown, she ran her hands down the length of her body. *What form am I?* Her fingers played over smooth limbs, breasts, hair. *I'm back to me.* She felt a thrill beneath her feet and knew its cause. "Fool me once," she muttered. The sound helped her focus and steady her shape. She heard footsteps. *He's coming. This is not possible, and so it is real. He must not see me like this.*

When she'd seen the doctor with the houndstone, she'd known that fate was about to loose a wicked arrow. She smelled his musk on that cursed jewel. But prepared she wasn't.

She heard voices and checked herself in the mirror. *Not like this. I must be beautiful for him. Hair up or down?* The air sparkled as gown after gown appeared, was altered and then replaced. *I am Queen May. I am….* The door swung open, and there he stood. Tall, handsome beyond compare, with shoulder-length flame-red hair streaked with silver, strong jaw, and penetrating eyes. *He is perfect, and I am broken… because of him and my conniving sisters.*

Ancient hurts skewered her afresh. The jealousy, the fear that not only had he betrayed their love, but that… *he was unfaithful. Dog! Lying filthy dog!* Any traces of her sisters' magic vanished in his presence. *I can see clearly.*

She couldn't breathe. *I will not let him see the effect he has on me.* "Hello, Hound."

"My queen." He bowed, and beside him she saw the doctor, his gaze fixed first on the Hound and then her.

She made several rapid conclusions. First, the Hound was not exactly as she'd remembered him. Yes, it had been more than two thousand years ago, but still. The face, the features, he was the Hound, her hound, and the standard of male strength and beauty. It was common back in that day when commenting on a newborn to say, "Let him have the strength and beauty of the Hound. Let her be as lovely as Queen May." He looked different. *There's something more.* It tore at her. *He is whole, and I am not. And he has my heart as well. How?*

How? What do I not see? And so it starts with lies and infidelity.

"Shall I enter?" he asked with the slap of a question and a curt nod of his head. Not even close to the courtly bow she was due. His eyes sought out hers.

"Questions cost," she replied, as her hair decided it was unhappy as a french braid and would rather be a ponytail.

He smiled.

Her knees weakened, and her dress shortened to midcalf and went from a deep blue brocade to quaint country gingham.

"I'm prepared to pay." He smiled and cocked his head as he studied her rapidly evolving costume.

"You lie." She struggled to remember all the reasons this creature was poison. And too distracted to keep even her outfit in line, she felt the salamander return. And wouldn't it be nice to bite off the Hound's smiling head. *Best to eat those we love. At worse they give us a bit of indigestion.*

"I am not fey," he stated. "It is my right to lie, as it is to ask questions, cost or no."

"You've made some effort to come here." A tail formed at the base of her spine. *He cannot see me like this.* She kept her voice level as the appendage grew and threatened to poke out beneath her shortening dress. "I'd thought you dead and buried."

"As I've been… many times." He squinted and appeared perplexed. "I do not share in your longevity. What you see is me, and it's not me. It's flesh of my flesh, blood of my blood. My name is Finn, or you can continue to call me Hound if you prefer. And madam," he said, stating the obvious, "I do not recall your having a tail… at least not of that type."

Damn him. Her white tail wagged from side to side. She tried to will it still. *It has a mind of its own.* "You could have lived forever." And there it was; her defenses fell, as did her tears. "You could have had everything."

Finn crossed to her and took her hand. His voice was deep and kind. "What have you done to yourself?"

She pulled back, though he would not let go of her hand. He looked back toward Redmond. "She is your patient?"

"Yes."

"She is broken. I mean seriously broken."

"True."

"How?"

May struggled to free herself from his grip as her tail thumped like a puppy's on the stone floor. "Let go. You have no claim here."

"They say the fey can't lie. I never believed that."

She looked at her hand in his. "It is no lie." She slipped from his warm grip. "If I am your patient…. Redmond… I do not give you permission to talk to this creature. This Finnish hound. Leave! Run away, dog. I have no bone for you here." As harsh words tumbled from her lips, her tears streamed, and memories, now free from magic, returned with a crushing force. "Get out!" She pointed to Redmond. "You, little man, stay. I have need of you." Her body trembled as she moved as far from Finn as possible. *Yes, I'm broken, and stupid me not to see the cause. Everything makes sense, or nearly so.* She glared at the Hound, with his stupid grin, flowing red locks, and lying brown eyes. But there was more. *He holds the key.*

She watched as he bowed and left. She studied his every gesture and how he glanced and smiled at the doctor. *They hide something from me.* She felt pain and looked down at her chest expecting to find a wound, but the hurt was all inside. *He made a promise.* Her throat tightened, and she choked back a sob, because the truth hurt as bad now as it had two thousand years ago. *He broke his promise, and he broke my heart. No, it's worse than that. What is still hidden? What did my sisters do to me?*

Redmond, aware that he no longer possessed the protective houndstone, kept a wary eye on May as Finn—or whoever or whatever he was—left the cell. His pulse raced. *Is this how and where I die? And how has a single kiss rattled me so?* He sorted through the race of emotions. *I should be more afraid.* He felt the tingle of Finn's lips and the strength of his—*the Hound's*—hand.

May voiced his present danger. "You've lost your little charm. Though it was never yours." She spat at him, and the air blossomed with the smell of fairy fire.

Redmond steeled his nerves. *I will appear calm. She must not see or smell the clamor of my thoughts.* "True." He recognized the opening gambit of tit for tat. "He said it was his."

"Once. He gave it to me… and then he stole it. I wonder how Lizbeta came by it. Tell me."

Redmond waited. This much of the story he knew, the tale of the three sisters, children of the prior reign, daughters of gods.

May paced, stopped, and stared at Redmond. "Of course. Hound! Dogs sniff after one and then another of the sisters. I should pity her. But then… you come by the stone. I would know her game. My misty sister. She hides from me, as does the other. Tell me of that one, of lovely Katye. I would know." May's voice turned singsong. She pranced and grimaced as her costume, tied to her moods, was torn… literally. Half became a twirly tulle-flounced bubblegum-pink party dress, and the other trailed the floor in midnight-black lace.

Redmond felt her power pulse. *The moment she can control it… I will be no more.*

She threw a glamour at him. Houndstone or no, her cell and the entire Center were well warded. But in the short time he'd spent with May, he knew her ego would lead her to believe she was above that. "I cannot speak to your sister Katye. As a child, I'd glimpse the three of you from the distance. I've never met her."

May ditched the glamour and spat again. Fire illuminated the space as it arced in the air and landed with a sizzle inches from his feet.

Redmond's heart skipped as a tiny blue-and-orange flame burned into the rich carpet and created a glowing crater in the stone floor. His knees weakened with the smell. *Help me, Goddess.*

May stared from the flame to Redmond. "Yes, it is delicious. Or so I'm told. I'm immune to the stuff. I see that you, dear doctor, are not. There's no harm in a little taste." She hummed and then belted in a throaty alto, "Fairy fire, fairy fire, come and see my fairy fire. Fairy dust, fairy dust, come and taste…." Her tune stopped. "But you know all this. Please, don't mind me. Get down on your hands and knees and roll yourself a bunny. It's what you want. It's what you crave… it's what you need."

Redmond shielded his thoughts, though this was less mind reading or control on her part than a serious lapse in judgment on his. *This is how I die.*

"Seriously, Doctor, I don't mind if you roll a bunny or two. I find that so cute. Dust bunnies." She hummed the familiar spell. "With a mickle and a care I shall go into a hare."

For a heartbeat he wondered if she wasn't about to shift into a rabbit, or more likely, back into the ravenous salamander. But no, she'd made a joke… and he'd made a connection.

"Yes," she offered. "It has many meanings. As do the words of the Hound. So he's here. It's no coincidence, and he comes at the bidding of my sister… most likely the two of them together. In fact, that you got the stone from Lizbeta"—May's eyes glowed—"she did not get it from him, but from Katye." Her hands flew to the sides of her head. "Yes, now we have a song that sings. But…." She paused and glared at him. "The truth still hides from me. Yes, the stone is back where it began, though he is not the Hound I knew." She sank into a chair and appeared confused. "He gave me the… I cannot remember. And I gave him something in return, something important. I was so young when we met. I had not tasted love, never known what Katye took for granted, its power. Its magic. It's her hand behind all of this. She's always been jealous, of me, of my special, of the greater work before me, to take the three realms and put them back as one. I will make Fey great again. She is the cause of my misfortune. I will make her pay. I will make them both pay."

Nineteen

FINN WATCHED the gears on May's cell door. *What moves them?* The air shimmered as the intricate mechanism whirred and clicked. *Don't freak.* Which, now standing outside the unstable queen's cell with her otherworldly guards, was difficult. Exactly what was one supposed to say to eight-foot green… *I'm thinking ogres, but what if that's not PC?* Erring on the side of less is more, he gave a polite nod to each, his focus on the queen… and more so, on Redmond. *I just kissed a guy who flies. Yeah, not the strangest thing here….* The feel of his lips, the taste of him, the strength of his body had been seared into his brain. *Just a kiss and then….*

He took stock. *Still me, but this body.* He imagined how he appeared to others with his shins poking from the hem of ruined cargo pants that a few hours earlier had covered his now-too-small New Balance walking shoes. He toed off one, then the other. *Much better.* He stared at his feet. *What the hell? Fur, it's almost like…. Jesus, where else?*

Panic surged. He tried to keep his expression calm. He glanced at one of the guards. *At least I'm not green.* His shirt was split at the seams, and a quick hand to the chest let him know that the thick hair wasn't just on his toes. It felt soft, and for an instant he wondered what it would be like for a lover. *Some guys like them hairy. Done is done. Okay, I'm a bear now.* Then as his hand traveled from chest to abdomen, he made another discovery. While always fit, first from football, then from the rigors of the FDNY, and more recently from long runs and the gym, *I'm cut.* His fingers, larger than he remembered them, splayed across hard muscle ridges on his abdomen, something no amount of push-ups or crunches had ever given him. Over the years he'd realized that great abs were created in the kitchen and not the gym, and unfortunately, while he'd run several marathons, he had zero interest in a life of protein shakes. He counted the valleys of his new eight-pack. *So I've got a hot hairy bod*, and if he'd been alone, he'd have explored further. *Is everything bigger?*

He turned at the sound of Redmond's voice from inside May's cell. He noted the thick door and the walls built of boulder and mortar. *I shouldn't be able to hear them… but I do.*

What's happening in there? It's not safe for him. He began to pace circles, his head down, his nose catching whiffs, *just like the night of a thousand fires. Fairy dust.* But other scents, ones he knew, though not in a conscious way. Only now… *fear, that's the smell of fear… and of Redmond.*

Like a connoisseur swirling wine, he caught hints of musk with a rancid overtone. *Fear.*

He stopped and sank cross-legged to the floor, his nose and ear to the door. He sniffed and let the conversation from inside waft through his enhanced hearing. Redmond was in trouble. *I should not have left him alone.* His pulse jumped, and he found that if he opened his mouth, his olfactory acuity grew more intense. His tongue poked between his lips, and he tasted the air.

What was difficult was the content of their conversation.

He heard the words and sensed the context, Redmond's voice like a balm that soothed everything. And when May spoke, it was as though she were an open wound. If he'd not known the murderous thing that she was, he could have felt pity.

But how can he? How can he be her doctor? From their brief interaction, he knew this entire world lived in terror of their queen. Between the lines, he'd gathered that Redmond had suffered at her hands and had not willingly allowed her into his center. *What is he saying?* Frustration at not being able to pull apart the meanings of the words and sentences welled. *Chill, Finn. Maybe you don't need that.* His nose, as though it had its own mind, sniffed across the door's unyielding surface. The air tingled around his face, and as he inhaled, the lock trembled.

I could break through. He smiled and listened to the soothing tenor of Redmond's voice. *So not only can Redmond fly, he's got some kind of soothing magic. He is so cool.* He pictured Charlie's Liam and how he literally stopped traffic, and people always gave him stuff. *This is different. I could listen to this voice forever. Just curl up at his feet…. What the fuck?* He hung on Redmond's shifting tones. His fear was unmistakable, but he held his ground against May. *I got your back, Redmond.* Finn looked at the guards, who stared back with red-rimmed eyes.

They're afraid. With his mouth open and tongue hanging out, he drew in deep. *They're afraid of her... but of me too. Why the hell would two eight-foot whatever-the-hells be afraid of me? So much to ponder,* as he compared the scent of ogre fear to that of Redmond, to his own curious musk and heat. *I smell good.* Images came with the scents. *I smell like a baby.* He pictured Danny Dog, Rory's Irish setter he'd gotten when they were both six. *Not like a baby... like a puppy. And everyone's been talking about this hound, and you're hairy, and one plus one equals....*

The conversation inside the cell shifted. There was fury and power in May's voice. Finn tensed, ready to break through that door or go down trying. The smell of fairy fire was stronger. But then Redmond did that warm thing with his voice, and it seemed to calm things.

I will not stray. I will stay. The sickly sweet stench burned his nose. He shook his head as fresh images were sparked by the smell. *Obviously magic... but more. Calm down and let it come.* He glanced up at the ogres, who were as far from him in the darkened antechamber as they could get. Embedded in the fairy fire's reek, he caught a whiff of something primal. His stomach turned as he made the connection. *There's blood and bone in fairy fire.* He had seen her in action when she'd attempted to eat Liam. *It's not just killing. She's feeding.* He pressed an ear to the door, turned, and licked it.

Bile rose in his throat. *Redmond, what have you done?* From the experience of watching Alex's sister, Alice, he knew too that fairy dust was a highly addictive narcotic. *Please no.* He licked the door a second time. *Shit!* There were traces of the stuff coming from Redmond. It was more than he could take. *I finally meet a guy and he's an addict... and probably not human.*

He threw back his head, and without thought, voiced the emotions that surged within. It shook the walls. *I can sing.* And he did. *I sound good.*

His voice woke patients in their cells. Some joined in; others howled. As his booming tune led the strange choir, he stood. While still attending to Redmond and Queen May, he took a fresh inventory. *I'm wicked strong. I can hear and smell everything. Having trouble understanding words... don't care much about that.*

As his song swelled, those who'd been singing switched to noises more animal than human. His own tune held no words, and as he stared down at the torch-lit floor, he was not surprised... well, maybe a bit. Where he'd had feet, albeit fuzzy ones, he now had massive paws, four of them. *Oh well.*

With his long pink tongue lolling from his mouth, he stopped his tune and loped three easy circles in the hall and settled outside May's cell. His attention was riveted on Redmond.

Healer, heal thyself. With his body coiled taut as a spring, Finn guarded the door and prepared for battle.

Twenty

MARILYN NEVUS shook, though she tried to hide it from Adam, as the towering black puka in the form of an enormous stallion emerged from the depths of the Western Sea. She glanced toward the direction they'd come and scanned past the beach, the dunes, and the meadow. *I do not see her. We may have time.* She focused on the one bright spot in a day filled with terror, a chance to see her other children.

She pictured dark-haired Alex, her eldest—*He's in college, in NYC, another world. He wants to be a doctor.* And Alice with her curtain of blonde hair and crystal blue eyes that spoke of too much pain for someone so young. *She's a teenager now.* She bit back the rage that came when she thought of them and of how much had been stolen. She calculated what grade Alice would be in. *Eighth? Ninth? A mother should know this. I should know this.*

With her eyes on the puka, a creature both ancient and deadly, she reassured herself that Adam, a haffling like his siblings, could travel unharmed. *And that's why May pursues them.* As for her, now protected by Cedric's true love, no further damage could happen. *Too little too late.*

She found Cedric's hand as her other held Adam's, whose gaze was riveted on the fierce stallion that stood on the stilled water. Its hide glistened with green-black algae.

She took comfort in Cedric's touch. All her sorrows had begun with his beautiful face in a mirror. For him she had sacrificed everything. She glanced back. "I don't hear her anymore."

Cedric nodded and sniffed. "There's no fairy fire." He followed her gaze from the deadly certainty of May's hunger back to the fire-eyed puka, who was known for dragging many a traveler to a watery grave. But in this he agreed with Marilyn; it was the surest way to travel between realms. Even now, as he stared at the beast who toed a hoof into the sea, he felt the beast's power. Even the Mist that marked the end of one realm and the start of another wavered with the puka's every movement.

Marilyn spoke. "This means something. She would not just give up the chase."

"Agreed."

"This is madness." She stared at the puka as her thoughts raced through any other possible means of escape.

"Tell me," Cedric urged.

"If she's not chasing us and she can't cross without breaking further… then something more important has diverted her attention."

"Perhaps she's been captured," Cedric offered. Marilyn cocked a brow.

"Just saying. Perhaps you need not take this insane journey."

"Stop!" She loved Cedric, but he had a bit of the craven that crept out in tense times. "Use your gifts, husband. If she's not chasing us, you must discover why. Because if it's more important than our child, that can carry her from world to world, it's also more dangerous."

Cedric nodded and opened his senses to the wind. It was unnecessary, for even with her human ears, Marilyn heard it.

"Dogs," she commented. "Why are dogs howling?"

"Please don't do that," he said, referring to her dangerous use of questions.

"Cedric, grow a pair." She focused on the swelling chorus of baying dogs and then on Cedric's concerned look. "Tell me."

"It can't be."

"Spit it out!"

"Her boyfriend is back."

The puka's hoof again tapped the water's surface. It grew impatient.

Marilyn nodded. "There is work for us both. You must learn her purpose, Cedric." She pulled her husband into a kiss, and before he could protest, she gathered Adam. *He is so young. What will this do to him? He will see my madness on the other side.* She paused. *And you have no choice.*

Not knowing what to expect, she held Adam's hand and walked with him into the water.

The puka, for whom every journey was purportedly different, hardened the sea's surface. Fear clutched at her throat as she approached. The puka grunted once and then knelt.

Barely able to breathe, she lifted Adam onto the beast's strong back. It was slick to the touch, and black-string algae clung to her fingers like spiderwebs.

Fearful the beast might take off without her, she hoisted herself behind Adam. She gripped him tight around the middle, while her free hand sought for any purchase on the puka's slick hide. There was none. She braced with her thighs. "Breathe in and out deep," she instructed. "And when I tell you, hold it." And she prepared for a journey that few survived.

Twenty-One

REDMOND'S THOUGHTS raced between May's rage and the reek of fairy dust from where she'd spat. "Tell me," he urged, and his voice warbled with the soothing grace of his special healer's magic. While he felt jangled, its effects on her were obvious.

May stared at the door where Finn… the Hound… had just left.

He watched the planes of her face shift from rage and the gaping sore of betrayal to… *calm.*

"Yes," he said. "Find this moment and only this moment. You may lie back on the couch, should you wish. It is soft. You are safe here." *Though I am not.*

"I am never safe," she replied but did as he suggested and sank back onto the pillow-strewn recamier.

"Tell me of that."

Her expression softened. "It hurts."

"I know. And to hold it in only makes it fester." Despite the danger, he chuckled at a memory.

"You laugh at my sorrows."

"Never, Your Majesty. Just a memory from my training."

She turned and looked at him, her eyes back to the beautiful amber. "Then tell me. I could use a touch of humor."

"You might not find it amusing. But as part of a doctor's training, we must taste all of the specialties, including surgery, which I enjoyed greatly. But for those who heal through steel, there is a truism, and I believe it applies to your pain. Pus under pressure must be lanced."

She winced. "More gross than funny, but there is truth there. So you would know my story. Tell me, Doctor, tell me your years."

"Near five hundred."

"So well after the war and my sister's mist. Though it's only now her treachery is laid bare. Even as I think of it, of her… for it's Lizbeta that brought me to you. It's Lizbeta that summoned the mist. It is her that clouds my thoughts even now."

"That's not the story we've been told."

"I know." She rested her head back and looked at the wood-coffered ceiling. "In truth these games of yours reveal things. You are of some use with all your scratching at my thoughts."

"Good to know."

"Do not mock me. I am your queen, and though I may be down, this story is far from over."

"Yes." He softened his tone further. He pressed his special. "Tell me what you've learned of the Mist and of your sister. What we're taught, what's in the record, is that the Mist came at the end of the war and separated the world of the humans from the Unsee. That before then, the races mixed freely."

"She tricked me. And what makes it the more painful, even humiliating, is that it is I who thought I had tricked her. Only now I see her fingers on all of this. She summoned the mist. It reeks of her special."

"Her special is peace," he stated.

"You say that as if it's a good thing."

Redmond held his tongue and nodded to encourage her story. Important things were being uncovered. As she spoke, he too wondered at Lizbeta's motives. Her special and the caress of the Mist addled one's thoughts. The words May now spoke were a radical departure from the history of the Unsee as recorded and retold.

"My sisters conspired against me. They wanted an end to the Thousand Year War." She squinted her eyes, as though trying to see something on the ceiling. "They united their specials against me—love and peace. How they could do this to their own flesh and blood, reeks. Katye, it was her that must have called the Hound. It was her who created the abominable enchantment that separated our warring days from our lusty nights. Wait a minute." Her breath quickened. "I can see it. I can almost see it."

Redmond held still, aware that May was on the verge of something important.

"Sweet Goddess, no." She looked at Redmond with an expression twisted with pain. "She caused me to give him my heart. She caused me to break off a piece of myself. And she knew. She knew…." The words choked in her throat.

"Tell me," Redmond said.

May's hands flew to the sides of her head. What came through her lips was more a cry as tears tracked down her porcelain cheeks. "She knew. She knew he was a dog. She made me fall in love with a dog." She trembled. "Everyone knows that dogs sniff every crotch and ass they can. He played me false and stole my heart." She turned on Redmond. "Tell me how you came to be so close to the Hound that he took my stone."

"He just took it," Redmond said without guile.

"You must have been standing close."

Her observation startled him. *She is in pain, and when vicious creatures are in pain, they attack. What have I done? She is beyond cure. Only death or life imprisonment will keep her from her dream to tear down the Mist, reunite the realms, and be queen over all. She knows. She suspects. It was a single kiss. He is her betrothed. It's what is recorded. It's what....* He ran his fingers through his hair. "Forgive me, Your Highness, but the story you tell is much different from our history books."

She shook her head, as though trying to clear it of his special. "I do not lie, though he did and does. What makes this worse is now I believe he was a party to the treachery." She convulsed and coughed. She spat a tiny missile of fairy fire onto the carpet.

Redmond edged back as a wave of the dust scent rolled across the room. *I cannot take much more. I need to get out of here.* He struggled for words and saw that she too was in distress. Having held her form mostly together for the session, her costume and hair now shifted, but worse, her hands now ended in razor-sharp talons. She growled, and the building shook.

I need to get out of here. But the tight quarters and the dust reek made it hard to think.

Get out. Get out now! Whatever calming grace his special had on her was gone. Yes, she appeared drained by all she'd laid bare in the last few hours, *but there's something in her eyes, its....*

"Doctor, doctor, doctor." Her words grew less intelligible as her face turned amphibious, with a sloping brow and mouth that grew ever larger as her lips disappeared.

Around them, the air filled with the sound of inmates who first sang different tunes in different keys, and then one by one the words and music turned to barks and howls.

What is happening? Redmond thought. *Is this the howl of my banshee?* His mouth was dry. He pulled at all the magic inside him to steady his voice and strengthen his special. "We should end for today. You did exceedingly well."

"Yes, Doctor." And in the blink of an eye, the reflective May was gone and the predatory one leapt from the couch and stood inches before him.

He met her gaze. His knees trembled as he watched her eyes shade from amber, to black, to red. The corners of her jaw unhinged. He tried to move, to reach for the door. *I'm paralyzed.* Too late he realized the tables had turned. *I am glamoured…. This is how I end.* He listened to the roar of the inmates as his heart pulsed in his ears.

May's tone growled and mocked. "You did exceedingly well too. You have such a way of getting at my secrets, all the hurty twisty places inside. Like shucking meat from an oyster, well done, exceedingly well done. 'Pus under pressure.' I will remember that, just as I will remember how tasty you were swimming down my gullet."

Paralyzed, he watched her mouth gape wide like a python preparing to devour its prey.

He'd had a talisman to protect him, and now….

Something crashed behind him. Unable to turn, he watched as she pivoted. She glared at an intruder Redmond could not see. He tried to read her expression, outrage and something else, something he'd glimpsed through the last few hours—pain. *Heartbreak.*

Her glamour broke, and he turned to flee. As he did, he came face-to-face with a legend. An Irish wolfhound taller than he even on all fours, with lustrous red-and-silver fur and a broad square head.

The dog arched its back, growled, and stalked May into the corner. It sniffed at the patch of fairy dust, lifted a hind leg, and peed on it. There was a flash of silver and a hiss like air being let out of a balloon.

Redmond stared at the spot. The drug's smell vanished, and Redmond's head cleared as though a switch had been turned from On to Off. He watched as the beast's lips pulled back. It snarled. Its intent was clear. He was going to attack.

She is still a patient here. Above all else, do no harm. He was torn. *She is too dangerous to ever leave this place. And can you contain her?* "Stop!" he shouted.

The beast did, its bared teeth inches from May's exposed throat.

He does not fear her. And she, she has swallowed ogres and trolls. Why is she so frightened? He glanced back to see the two guards staring transfixed in the doorway. *What am I to do?*

The beast stared back at him with large soulful eyes. May tried to speak.

It barked and sent her tumbling onto her ass. All traces of the salamander had vanished.

She appeared tired and gaunt.

The Hound growled and sat back on its haunches halfway between him and May.

Redmond wondered, *Why doesn't she attack? What is this effect he has on her?* He backed toward the ruined door where the two guards stood. He left May's cell, and as he did the Hound followed at his heels. Redmond stopped and reached out a hand. The Hound lowered his head, and he stroked the wonderful fur, soft and silken. He scratched between his ears and looked into the animal's eyes.

The dog nudged the side of Redmond's face. His broad tongue licked his cheek.

The touch calmed him, and then the Hound turned around three times and lay down in the smashed opening of May's door.

From inside her cell, May sobbed and cursed first Redmond and then the Hound. He summoned his head of security. "Gark, put her in the reflective cell."

"It will not hold her long."

"I will repair this one. Double the guard until then."

"As you wish. But if she eats my guards…."

"I know. They don't grow on trees."

"Would that they did."

"Yes." Redmond stayed as the guards cautiously restrained May. He noted how the Hound never strayed from his watch at her door. It was odd, seeing something in the flesh that he'd always considered legend and fairy tale. He thought of the broken sprite… *Nimby*, tucked away in a healing cradle. *Perhaps in her rambles she holds a clue.*

He stepped back as the nervous battalion of ogres transported May to a different cell.

Unbidden, the Hound followed. Redmond nodded as it passed and felt a sense of loss. *Of course the Hound follows his queen, his betrothed.* He listened as their footfalls faded into the bowels of the earth. He thought of Finn's question after their kiss. "And you, Redmond. With whom do you belong?"

Rather than think of the answer, he thought of dust and the peaceful oblivion it would bring.

Twenty-Two

IT WAS midnight in Manhattan as the puka rose from the depths of the Hudson River.

Marilyn, her mouth tight over Adam's, had given him all her air. Her sanity vanished as they left the river floor. A chill rooted in her flesh. Panic took hold as she sought to feel a pulse in her son's neck.

My child is dead. I have killed him. She gasped as they broke the surface. "Say something!" Adam lay cold and still in her arms. She blew breath into his mouth and felt the rise of his lungs. "Adam!" She'd never taken CPR and couldn't imagine his small body could take the violent chest compressions. Instead, she gave him breaths one after the other, her fingers tight in the crook of his neck by the carotid artery.

A beat flickered against her forefinger. He opened his eyes.

Water gurgled from his lungs as the puka surged toward the shore and the brightly lit riverside park, which even at this hour had joggers, dog walkers, and couples who strolled hand in hand.

Clutching Adam with one arm, Marilyn dismounted. The chill water of the Hudson did not support them as it had in the Unsee, and the weight of her clothes and of Adam's barely conscious body threatened to drown them both.

Her booted foot found purchase on the river bottom, but with the next step, there was nothing. She pumped her legs as they tangled in her long skirt and robe. *I will not die.* Here and there she caught glimpses of the surface and unintelligible sounds as she fought hard for each inch that brought them closer to the rough boulder breakwater. *Yes.* She bounced off something solid, keeping Adam's head above water. She sank back, *yes again.* Her foot landed on something hard, and with gratitude but no words for it, she came to the cold, slick rock that separated the river from the land. Winded, she rested her head against a cool flat stone. She kissed Adam's cheek and didn't move until she saw the flicker of his eyelids. He turned to her.

"Tell me this place," he whispered.

She opened her mouth but knew from painful experience that what would emerge would frighten him. His body trembled in her arms, and they were soaked to the skin as she stood knee-deep in the Hudson. The river's chill water lapped against its reinforced bank. "Shh," she tried to say, but what she'd meant to soothe came out like the scream of a teakettle set to boil. *Get him safe. Find your son, your other son. Find your daughter, who went down the rabbit hole. I am the mother of kings.*

She scrambled for purchase on the slick rocks.

Her efforts were observed by late-night strollers and joggers. "There's someone in the water."

"Someone's fallen in!"

"Call 911."

People ran to her aid.

No! Stay away. And that's when she knew she'd traded one peril for another. Her words would not come… at least not any that made sense.

"What are you doing in the water, lady?" a man asked as another went down on his belly and grabbed her hand.

A crowd formed as she shinnied up the rocks with the assistance of the strong stranger.

Adam clung to her and helped as best he could.

"Was she trying to drown her kid?"

She wanted to say *I'm Marilyn Nevus, this is my son Adam, and we need to find my eldest, Alex.* What came out as she and Adam stood in a circle of curious and not-so-friendly onlookers was, "I am the mother of kings, and of the girl who went down the hole. Stand back, lest my fire burn you to ash." It did not help.

"She's out of her nut."

"Call 911."

"Screw 911. I saw a couple cops not far back." And the man raced away to find the authorities.

"Somebody should get that kid. She tried to kill him."

Her teeth chattered, and before the opening in the mob closed behind the guy who'd just left, she picked up Adam and, jostling through the crowd, she fled.

Some followed her.

"Hey, lady, you need help."

"Where you think you're taking that boy?"

"I bet she kidnapped him."

She screamed as they pursued. "Keep your pitchforks and your fire. You have no power here. I am the mother of kings and of the girl who went down the hole." She cried into the night and cursed the clang and clatter of her thoughts. But she did not slow. She ran with her precious Adam in drenched clothes that tangled between her legs.

"Mommy, put me down. I can run."

"Yes." She managed and grabbed his hand. *Where am I?* Without direction she fled the park and crossed one street after the next, going in whichever direction the stoplights allowed. She'd once loved this city, had come here as a young woman to be an artist, and she had known success. Gleaming SoHo galleries displayed her work. Museums had begun to include her in their collection. And then she'd glimpsed Cedric in a mirror. "I am the mother of kings and of the girl who went down the hole." *I am broken.*

Holding Adam's hand tight and keeping to the shadows, she lost the last of their pursuers.

She covered him in her wet robe and avoided the gazes of strangers. On some level, she knew how she looked. The rub of her damp boots raised blisters on her heels and the balls of her feet. Her calves ached as she walked and walked. Free from the angry crowd, her thoughts cleared enough for her to remember that the street numbers could guide her. If they were going down as she walked, then east was on her left and west and the river from which they'd come was on her right. It was all she needed.

Adam struggled to keep pace. Wordlessly, she hefted him onto her back and felt the comfort of his arms around her neck. *Find Alex. Find Alice. I am the mother of kings and of the girl who went down the rabbit hole.*

She arrived at the corner of Avenue B and Third Street. *I know this place.* She turned and scanned for the brick apartment building she'd once called home. Her gaze tracked down the block. *Where is it?* Not wanting to at look at the wreckage of a burned-out building halfway down.

"Tell me what's wrong, Mommy."

She gazed back and forth. *No.*

She stopped in front of the boarded-up husk of a structure. Plywood walls had been constructed around its first floor, concealing the entry from the street. Posters slapped on the plywood read No Trespassers. There was a number to call if someone suspected any public hazards.

"Mommy."

No. What little plan she'd constructed was gone. In a city of many million souls… *how?* Before despair could overtake her, she caught the whiff of something bad, something familiar. She put a hand to the rough wood barrier wall and pressed her nose to it. *Fairy fire.*

"Mommy."

No. Tears fell as she let her and Adam's combined weight slump against the wall. *All for naught.* She whimpered. "I am the mother of kings and of the girl who went down the hole." But then, through a knot in the wood, she caught a flash of movement from the basement of the boarded-up building. The place that had once been her home. *Someone's there.*

"Mommy." Adam struggled down from her back. His feet found the ground. "Mommy, tell me this place."

Her back screamed, and her feet burned with angry blisters. She'd hoped this was the end of her trials. *Get Adam to safety.* She tried to speak, testing each word for insanity as it passed her lips. "Alex, your brother's name is Alex. Your sister is Alice."

"I know," Adam said. He stared into his mother's face.

"This is the See." She grabbed for his hand, and he pulled it away.

"Tell me what's wrong, Mommy."

She read terror in his eyes and knew she was its cause. She steadied her breath and on a stream of air floated a simple sentence. "We have to find Alex and Alice." *That was good. That was normal.* "For I am the mother of kings and of the girl who went down the hole." *Crap!*

"Okay." He stared out at Third Street between Avenues B and C. "Those lights. They're not fairy lights." And his gaze bounced from window to window and then to the occasional car that passed in front of them at that late hour. "That's a taxi."

"Yes." She nodded. "Come." Barely able to manage even simple words and fearful of what might pass through her lips, she gripped his hand. "Come."

Shattered glass twinkled in the moonlight as she found a crude door in the plywood wall.

It had been padlocked, but its shank had been cut. The smell of fairy fire washed over them as they entered the burned-out husk of her former apartment building. Fear trickled down her spine, and gooseflesh popped on her arms. She paused. *Keep Adam away. Danger. Is May here?* The cloying sweet smell of fairy fire and burn came strong from below. With Adam's hand gripped tight, they headed down the basement stairs.

"Mommy...." She clamped her other hand over his mouth and shook her head.

She stopped dead at the sound of hushed voices from below. *I should not bring him... and what? You'd leave a seven-year-old, who's really two, on the streets of Manhattan. Not the first time.* Before the guilt of her life with Alex and Alice could return, she pressed on. *I am the mother of kings. I will not fear.*

What they came upon, slumped on ruined mattresses stained with char and body fluids, was unexpected and sad. A group of three, a seven-inch-high silver-haired pixie and two fairies, a fair male like Cedric and a female with hair that caught the light with reds and golds. The two sidhe had had their ears and teeth surgically altered to make them appear human.

Dusted to the gills, they barely noticed her approach.

"I am the mother of kings...." She grabbed for the edges of sanity and managed to pull out a cogent statement. "I am Marilyn Nevus. Help me." She swallowed and planned her next words. She bit her lip and drew blood. The pain helped clear her thoughts. "Please help me... I need to find my children."

Twenty-Three

REDMOND'S THOUGHTS were dark as he flew up and into his chamber window. *I have been a fool.* His focus was riveted on the dust bunnies. Exhausted, frightened, and confused, he resisted their pull. *It would be nice to... check out. No May, no Hound. Maybe just a little....*

Are you insane? You think you can do a little? You never could. What's changed between today and the several thousand other times you said you'd do just a little? A war raged inside him between his rational mind and the promise of the drug's quick, albeit evertooshort, bliss.

Why did he kiss you?

He spoke aloud. "It's what she said. He is a hound and sniffs at everything and everyone. It meant nothing. Stop acting like a child. It was a kiss and nothing more. If it meant so much to you...."

No, do not say the thing that plays around your lips. If you want love, go out and find it.

He shook his head, and his gaze came to rest on the cabinet where the bunnies awaited. "No," he said with force. "No." His feet edged closer to his stash.

Waves of exhaustion clouded his eyes. He stopped and ran all the reasons why he shouldn't get dusted. He ticked them off:

It will slow my thoughts.

It will make me less able to battle a threat that could kill us all.

It will leave me with a dustover like a vise around my head.

Once I start, I will not stop.

It hurts my body.

It kills my soul.

But like a gremlin buried deep inside of him, a single reason to gobble dust gurgled forth. *It will make you forget. Forget him, forget the kiss that still burns on your lips, and most of all, forget the danger you have brought into this house, a house you built to defend and to protect.*

As if it were someone else's body, Redmond watched his hands rip open the drawer, pull out the carved chest that lay within, open it up, and…. *Two of them. I'll just do one.*

The gremlin inside nodded and chuckled. *Yes, one now and one for later….*

His fingers landed on the soft, sticky ovoid lozenge. The first touch of flesh to drug blew away any resistance as the potent narcotic seeped through the pores of his skin even before it found its way to his lips.

When he'd first experimented with dust, it had been a mystical experience with candles and an obsidian orb. There was a cult of dust that venerated its properties and not just its high. Back then, he'd savored the scent and the heightened senses and abilities that came with the waves of its rush, as though his every molecule was open and connected to the Unsee. Now, as he popped it without ceremony into his mouth and under his tongue, there was none of that. *Just this one*, he thought, hating the lies he told himself. *The fey don't lie.*

"But addicts do," he said aloud. "And that is what I am."

But true to its dusty promise, the pit of self-loathing fell away with the drug's first kiss.

If I could but sleep.

As the elevator rush of dust hit, he stared longingly at the chest where a bunny remained.

You said just the one.

How many times have you said that? Just the one, and then… I'll be done. Maybe if you finish the last one, that will be it.

Even high, the war for Redmond waged. *You said just the one. But that's not enough.*

His disgust returned. Not even the dust was giving him what it promised: release, forgetfulness. *A hundred years clean and it's like it never happened.*

He turned from the chest, aware that he would eventually give in and not only gobble the last bunny but pursue more. *A hundred years clean… gone.*

He turned toward his curtained-off sleeping chamber, and letting his clothes fall as he went, he lay down. *What have I done?* He stared at the star-painted ceiling and tried to remember why he had fought so hard to get sober. He remembered the first two weeks of detox, like being gutted and turned inside out. All the while hiding it from his friends, his colleagues, and his students. *The fey don't lie. And we sure as hell don't tell the truth.*

Dust sweat oozed through his pores as sleep overtook him. His last thoughts before going under were of Finn's lips on his and the hint of a minor victory… *I just had one. I just had one.*

He fell into dust-fueled dreams. White stallions stampeded through the ruins of the capitol, trampling all under hoof. He realized that only he could control the berserk beasts. Though it wasn't exactly control, as they would not do as he commanded, but they did stop their destruction. He ran after the most magnificent of the horses, and the dream's tone shifted as he turned in bed. He groaned aloud as the stallion, no longer exactly an animal, with silken fur and deeply corded muscles, begged to be stroked and kneaded.

The dream shifted, and he was in bed with the beast. As a lucid dreamer, Redmond's analytic mind watched from a hazy vantage point and marveled at the symbolism. *What does the beast represent? My addiction? The patients at the Center? But it… he… I am aroused. This is hot. He is hard. I am hard.*

In the twilight between wake and slumber, sensations intruded, as though the dream had leapt the rails of one realm and… his fingers tangled in soft fur, and there was something against his cheek, like the pelt of an animal not yet full-grown.

His eyes blinked open to sun streaming through the window. And to a large redheaded man, naked and hard in all senses, in his bed.

This is still a dream. He rolled into the strong man with his tousled mane of red and silver. *Horse… mane,* he mused, noting the weird ways dreams pulled and played with words and puns. *A beautiful dream.*

But so much heat… must be the dust. So warm, so… firm… so…. He put a hand on… *Finn.* He traced his fingers over a firm abdomen and held his breath. *This is one solid dream, and Finn is in my bed. What does this mean?*

Finn growled. It reverberated up Redmond's arm.

No dream. He held his breath and watched Finn… *is he even still Finn Hulain, or is he the Hound and Finn is no more?* A sad thought, as while it was just a kiss, it was the best of his life. He stared at Finn's face as his lips curled into a smile.

Redmond whispered, fearful that perhaps it was a dream or possibly a dust hallucination, though he was not prone to those… at least not in the past. "I thought you were betrothed to her. That she was yours and you hers."

Finn did the unexpected. "Morning, cupcake." His strong arms pulled Redmond close. "Now is no time for talk, Redmond Fall. I am Finn Hulain." His tongue flicked over Redmond's forehead.

He shivered at the touch as Finn's words cut through his fears.

"And I am the Hound that lived thousands of years ago. You do not know my side of the story." He placed a finger under Redmond's chin, lifted it up, and kissed him.

If this is a dream, Redmond thought, his mind and body on fire with desire, *may I never wake*. He did have one strange and not fully formed thought before giving in to what would be the best sex of his life. *I should be dusted over. I'm not. Odd....*

Twenty-Four

MAY FUMED in her new cell. She reeled from the revelations, both those made explicit by the Hound and by what she'd reasoned out with her handsome, albeit nosey, doctor. *He is of some use… and I will kill the Hound.* The pain of his betrayal both then and now had shifted to things more familiar and comfortable… rage and bloodlust. *What will his magic taste like?*

Though even that brought memories. The feel of his flesh against hers, the stroke of his fingers, the certainty of their lovemaking. The oblivion and rapture of being in his arms. *Lies! It was all lies. Unfaithful dog. They played me. And even still their magics cloud my thoughts. Damn them.*

At least now she had the truth and the cause of her prior failures. *How could I not have seen this?* A central tenet of the Unsee is that to rule you must be whole, and she was not. And not in the manner she'd earlier thought. *It was them all along.* Like ripping through dense layers of webbing, the truth emerged. She tilted her head and spotted tiny filaments of shattered blue-and-pink magic. Her mouth twisted in disgust. "My sisters. My sisters." She spat fire to the floor and immolated a footstool. "They conspired against me." *I can believe nothing and no one. I am alone. His love was false. The Mist…. Goddess protect me, how could I have believed her? It was all a fairy tale. The Mist that just appeared, that took our parents. It was her. It was her all along. It is she who wants to rule.* Moves and countermoves from the distant past returned, and she realized that all the times when she'd thought she'd been the one in control, her sisters had been steps ahead of her, dropping crumbs that she had followed.

"Enough," she said aloud, hating the maudlin cling of self-pity. "I may not be whole, but I know what needs doing. I am Queen May. I will make them pay. They shall taste my fire. They will burn. They will all burn.

But first…." She looked around her cell and then to the heavily bolted and warded door. "Help me," she cried out loud enough to be heard by the guards on the other side. "Something's wrong!"

"Tell the problem," an ogre grunted back.

"I must see the doctor. Please, bring me Dr. Fall."

"Tell me the problem," the ogre demanded.

Morons. She tossed a glamour over the two of them, uncertain if it would penetrate through the cell door. "I can't tell you, but I can show you."

"We're not supposed to enter."

"I'm in pain." She pressed her magic. *They are warded.* She doubled her efforts. "I am helpless against ones as strong as you." She twisted the glamour and played with their testosterone-riddled egos.

She heard them argue on the other side, and like a fisherman playing out the line, she let the shimmer and want of her glamour reel them in. The lock turned.

And as she readied her escape, she thought to stop and thank the doctor. But first, *a quick snack.* In a well-practiced move, she turned, and with razor-sharp talons sliced each of her guards open from the notch of their necks to their navels. They were dead before their brains could even register the need to scream. The air hissed and filled with blood scent as she unhinged her jaw and in six decisive bites—head, torso, legs, head, torso, legs—devoured two full-grown ogres.

She belched. *Much better.* With a closed fist, she tapped below her sternum several times and belched again. *Much, much better.* She pulled her face back together, and free from the cell's wards, her feet lifted off the ground, and following the curve of the stairs, she wafted up and out.

Twenty-Five

MARILYN TRIED to follow the rapid prattle of the three dusted expats as she held tight to Adam's hand. It took all her will not to grab him and bolt out of the cellar that reeked of dust and desperation.

"She can't be trusted."

"She's the hafflings' mother."

"She's off her rocker."

"Poor kid."

"She won't know about her daughter."

"We shouldn't, but we can't leave them here."

"If she's here with the boy, the queen won't be far."

"Good point, I'm out of here."

And where there were three, now stood a lone female with auburn hair and a tiny silverhaired pixie with the wings of a monarch butterfly. "I'm Sabina, by the way, and this is Peony."

She listened to the clamor of her companion as he hustled up the stairs and out of the building. She shrugged her shoulders. "Males, pretty but craven."

"I heard you call Daddy that," Adam said. "Tell me what it means."

Marilyn nodded and tried to smile. It came out as a grimace as she fought to conceal the addled porridge of her thoughts. Not letting Adam's hand go, she followed Sabina and Peony out of the burned-out basement and back onto Third Street. *Are they helping? I am the mother of…. This could be a trap.*

"Murray Hill," Sabina said. "That's where you'll find your children and the changeling copy of you who raises them."

"No. Not anymore," Peony chattered as she flitted around Sabina's shoulders. "Murray Hill burned, burned, burned."

"Right. Peony is correct." She looked at Marilyn. "I know," she said with compassion. "You are broken, and you try to hide it. There is no need. For we too are not right."

"Dust," Marilyn managed, careful to not say more as phrases and rhymes swarmed her thoughts like angry bees.

"'Tis true. Your son Alex will not be glad to see us."

Marilyn's breath caught. "You do know of him." Not certain if they'd been leading her on and had some ulterior motive. After all, what might May pay for the last of the haffling children and his mother?

"Of course. Alex is hope."

Marilyn stared into the beautiful sidhe's dust-enhanced eyes. They were hazel with flecks of gold, red, and blue. Years in the Unsee had taught Marilyn much, including this fey's lineage. "You are a Fall."

"Yes, my family is Fall, and my story is not for today. Today we find your children. They are not in Murray Hill." Her tone was kind, almost like that used when talking with a child… a very slow child. "I was mistaken."

"It's okay," Marilyn said, sensing a depth to Sabina's admission she could not fathom.

"It's Gramercy," Sabina said. She stopped in front of a subway entrance and scanned the numbers and letters of the available trains. "We can get there from here."

Peony looked wistfully at the cars and cabs whizzing up and down Avenue A. "There's always Uber," she suggested.

"Show me your credit card," Sabina said with an edge.

"Dusted," she admitted. And then to Marilyn, "I did have one. It was my Visa."

"Yes… dusted." Sabina shrugged as tears squeezed from the corners of her eyes.

"Tell me," Marilyn said.

"Mommy, no."

She looked down at Adam. "What's wrong?"

"Don't ask, Mommy. It makes them feel bad."

Peony flitted to Adam and hovered in front of his nose. She glanced from him back to Sabina. She alit on his shoulder. "Special boy," she chattered. "Haffling for sure but something extra."

Marilyn shuddered both at Adam's pronouncement and the pixie's words. *Did he break?*

He can't break. He's a haffling. They don't break. Not like eggshells. I must walk on them.

Sabina nodded, wiped back her tears, and produced a poker hand of well-worn MetroCards from the sleeve of her stained blouse. "Come." And as a train shook the ground, they headed down.

Voices whispered in Marilyn's head. *We go around and around, we find the little girl, and we bring her hey nonny down.* She focused on other passengers. A couple made eye contact and then quickly looked away. *What must I look like? Mad Marilyn, mother of kings. Shut up. Eggshells. Walk on eggshells. Try not to break them. Shut up.* She blocked her ears with her hands. It did not help. *Shut up.*

A club girl dressed in black with glittery makeup and purple streaks in her hair looked at Marilyn, was about to say something, and then… "What the hell is that?" She pointed at Peony perched on Adam's shoulder. She jabbed her companion, a thin dark-haired man with kohl-lined eyes. "Do you see that?"

He narrowed his gaze. "What am I supposed to see?"

Marilyn gripped Adam's hand and tried to tease apart the conversation. *Something's different. Something's not right as rain.*

"It's since the fires," Sabina explained. She smiled at the girl and her companion and pressed a faint concealment charm across the aisle.

"They see… saw, Marjory Daw," Marilyn hissed. "Yes… some do. Most still don't. And some do."

"Things are breaking."

"It appears so."

"I'm a bit broken," Peony added.

"Just a bit," Sabina said.

"But I'm still pretty." She smiled at the darkly dressed duo who could no longer see her.

Sabina rolled her eyes. "Yes, you're a beauty."

"Thank you."

They got out at Twenty-Third Street and headed northeast to Gramercy Park.

Marilyn held tight to Adam's hand as he stared wide-eyed at a new world with needle-thin high-rises and streams of cars that stopped and started with the rhythm of green, red, and yellow lights. For her part, it overwhelmed her. Jangled rhymes skittered in her head as she tried to make sense of burned-out and demolished buildings. "What happened? So many. It wasn't like this when I left it."

"May happened," Peony said. "Mad, bad May, and now some can see us. The walls cracked."

"Eggshells," Marilyn said. "We walk on them."

"Not a problem," Peony said. She played with a lock of Adam's hair. "I can walk on eggshells all day. But the rest of you… it won't go well."

"It rarely does."

"Yes," Peony replied. "You're broken."

Marilyn said nothing as they headed into the quiet streetlamp-lit block of Gramercy Park. Even here beautiful turn-of-the-century buildings had been destroyed. "Was there rhyme and reason?"

"Us," Sabina said, and she stopped in front of a redbrick apartment building. "She came for us."

Marilyn nodded. She pictured Cedric. *She will come for him.* The enormity of what she intended hit hard. *I am the mother of kings. I may never see my children again.* She crouched down by Adam and smoothed back his hair.

"Mommy?"

"Shh." *Please words. Please come.* "The worlds are collapsing. Safer here. Understand?"

He nodded.

"You are the first, and you are my last. Though I was seventh of seven."

"Born with a caul," Sabina added.

"They say so."

Like a schoolchild, Peony sang: "Through the seventh daughter of the seventh daughter, the haffling child comes. They dance and play around the Mist. They travel where they may. 'Play with me. Play with me,' they sing into the night. But play with them, play with them, and you break as they take flight."

Sabina nodded. "This is where your children are… now. I'll go up with you, but I cannot stay. Your son Alex does not want our type near his sister… your Alice." She looked away. "I do not blame him. I was not always a dusthead."

"There's places for that," Marilyn said, almost lucid. "Places for help."

"Not here, and not for us," she replied. "And I cannot go back. It's certain death, breakage aside."

"True, but worlds collapse, and I am the mother of kings and of the girl who went down the hole."

"Thank you," Sabina said, able to discern what lay beneath Marilyn's words. "You too give hope."

"It's springy," Marilyn replied as they entered the building.

The doorman looked up. He smiled. "Marilyn, I'm losing it. I could swear you just went up." He peered at Adam and then at Sabina.

"Not up at all—through, under, around."

Sabina tugged her hand before the man's polite questions could start. "Come, Marilyn." And they got away from the doorman before his bemused smile and curiosity changed to other things.

Marilyn watched as Sabina pressed the number twelve. The button lit, and they headed up. "Why are you nervous?" she asked, pleased at how her words sounded. But then babbled, "Nervous, pervous, no need for service. We deserve this."

Adam wiggled his fingers from her firm grip. "It's moving. This is a magic box. It's moving us."

Sabina smiled. "It's an elevator, Adam." Then to Marilyn, "I would go back if I could. In all senses. But I am well and truly dusted, and I do not have the constitution for living life more broken than I am."

"Trust me, bust me, but do not dust me. I certainly, pertinently understand." She wanted to bang her head against the mirrored walls. "Broken, token, I was bespoken." A scream welled in the back of her throat as they came to a stop and the doors opened.

"Not your fault," Sabina whispered as they came out into a hall with faded cabbage-rose carpet and doors in either direction. "Come. Here. It's number 1211." She knocked on the door and waited for footsteps. "Good, someone's home." She backed away.

"Don't. Please stay," Marilyn said as the handle turned.

Sabina shook her head but did not move.

The door cracked open, and an old woman looked out. On the floor a furry paw batted manically into the space.

The woman gasped. "Marilyn?"

Marilyn looked from Sabina to the woman she'd never met.

"I am the mother of kings and of the girl who went down the hole."

"Of course you are. I'm Flora Fitzgerald. And that must be Adam. Come in." Flora saw Sabina and Peony lurking in the hall. She shook her head.

"They helped me," Marilyn said. "Help they need."

"I am aware." To Sabina, "You should leave before they see you." She paused and made a cooing sound as she caught sight of Peony. "A pixie. And such a beauty. Come back in the morning, if help you truly want. I believe there is a way. I've had some success."

Sabina, with Peony peeking out from behind her right ear, backed away. "Thank you."

Flora sighed, and with a practiced move, bent on arthritic knees and swept up two tabbies by the scruff of their necks. "Come in quick, and close the door behind you or we'll be chasing the terrible twos all over the building."

"Two's company," Marilyn said as she let loose Adam, who was fascinated with the cats.

She shouted back, "Goodbye, Sabina. Goodbye, Peony. I will not forget."

"You are welcome, mother of kings." And without another word, they left through the elevator.

"What is five?" Flora asked as she pulled Marilyn into her book-crammed hallway and shut the door.

"A party."

"Then welcome to the party house. Come. I'll make tea and fetch those you came to see."

Marilyn panicked. "Wait! What? Here, they brought me here."

"Right place," Flora said, having no difficulty following Marilyn's train of thought. "Wrong apartment. Sit. I'll tell you a story while we wait for them."

"You are the wise old woman. Can you help Sabina and Peony?"

"Two out of three. And possibly."

"I pick wise and woman," Marilyn replied. "And they are broken and broken again with dust." Sick of crying, she could not stop. "She used to fly, that one. And now…."

Flora gazed at Adam, who was on the floor playing with the tabbies, Aldo and Andre. Three older cats, including a demonic Siamese, watched from the darkened living room. "And you are the mother of kings and of the girl who went down the hole. I'll make us tea."

Twenty-Six

FLUSHED WITH passion's afterglow, Redmond drank in the man… beast… hound in his bed. "You are beautiful."

Finn smiled and placed Redmond's hand to his furry chest. "Back at you." He pulled him into a kiss.

Sparks exploded. *I have never felt this.* Something screamed, though it was neither fey nor any known animal. He pulled back. *No.* Recognition dawned. *Someone has escaped.*

Finn immediately put a name to it. "Like sirens. Didn't know you had them here." He turned to the source of the noise. His heightened senses tried to tease apart the wails.

A harsh rap came at the chamber door.

"Not good." Redmond rose from the tousled bed, picked a robe from off a chair, and belted it on.

As the siren peaked and dipped, they heard other sounds. Cries of the patients from their locked cells.

Naked, Finn followed at Redmond's side.

The size of him and the heat that emanated from his body were a comfort to Redmond. "Whatever is on the other side of that door…."

"Yeah, got it. Not good news."

The rapping grew louder. A gruff voice boomed out, "Dr. Fall. Dr. Fall."

Redmond drew a sigil in the air with his forefinger and thumb, and the lock twisted and turned. "Enter."

An ogre in blue, his chest and shoulders bedazzled with epaulets and badges, appeared.

He was winded and seemed unfazed by the naked man.

"Gark, tell me," Redmond said, though in his gut, he already knew.

"Dr. Fall, the queen has escaped, and she's eaten two of my guards. We're understaffed as it is. I'll need replacements. Third shift is always the hardest."

Gark's words washed over him. A problem with ogres was that they weighed all issues the same. May's escape was catastrophic. "Tell me what happened."

Gark did, or as much as he knew. He pointed outside the window to the direction of the siren and the howl of the inmates. "That woke me. I investigated. I found blood. I'll need replacements."

"The queen," Redmond interjected. "Tell me of her. Tell me where she went."

"Gone," Gark stated. "Had she still been there, I imagine you'd be down a third. Two is bad enough. As we discussed, ogres do not grow on trees. She sure can eat." The last was said with admiration. "She could be anywhere."

Finn sniffed the air around Gark. "She clings to you. There could be clues in her cell."

Redmond nodded and vanished into his closet. He returned with a soft robe. "You are lovely to look upon, but I do not want to share."

Finn shrugged and covered himself. He breathed in. "And there's the rub a dub dub. You know what she wants."

"Yes, so while she's escaped, she will return." His eyes met Finn's. "There is much I still do not understand. You were hers."

"True, or true enough, though what I heard during your last session makes me question how true my former self had been."

"You heard that. I can't imagine how. That door is impenetrable to the senses."

"Not mine. I have a new set, and they shift as I do. At my most houndish, my nose and ears are outrageous. So not words, not exactly, but impressions, emotions… I'm still figuring it out. Before she tried to eat you, she talked of things that had gutted her, and over her pain, I caught images of a former hound." His focus shifted from the queen's scent to Redmond. "We know that she is shattered. By her own hand and by…." He grabbed Redmond's hand and placed it over his chest. "And by this. She would rip my heart from my chest. She believes it belongs to her. She is wrong. Or at least in part."

Redmond held his breath as his fingers played in Finn's soft chest hair and felt the pulse of his heart. "Yes, she is wrong, and that will not stop her. She will return."

"But here's the deal, Redmond. Maybe a thousand years ago, whoever was the Hound gave her his heart, and then again, maybe he tricked her. I think that's what happened. You know all's fair…. But he's not me. Whatever she thinks I've got, it's not for her… it's for you."

Redmond's heart skipped. *It's too fast. This can't be love.* His mouth was dry, and more than any drug, he needed to look upon Finn's face. He gazed up. *This is love. How is that possible?* "She needs the stone. Because maybe you didn't give her your heart… you most certainly took hers. That's what the stone is. How I did not see that…."

"She can try."

"She will kill us all." *And there lies the twisty snarky fey way. Yes, I get love… for three heartbeats, and then we die.*

"And eat us," Gark added.

But three heartbeats of love are better than none.

"She can try," Finn repeated. He grabbed Redmond around the waist and kissed him.

Gark snarled. "It's all hearts and flowers, but I still have shifts to fill and disgruntled employees who are talking unions."

Redmond pulled back. *Three heartbeats are good, and I have responsibilities.* "Do what needs doing," he told Gark. "I'll approve bonuses for all based on loyalty and hazardous duty."

"Thank you, Doctor. You just can't imagine the stress of having to staff the wards 24-7. Someone's always calling out sick or eating someone sick… or getting eaten." And without stopping in his litany of woes, Gark left.

Twenty-Seven

MARILYN'S TEARS would not stop, though her thoughts clanged without reason. She gazed around Flora's tidy kitchen. *All three at once. Alex, Alice, Adam.* It was an all-you-can-eat buffet of joy and anguish.

Unable to stay seated, she went first to Alex, her dark-haired champion. "So old, a man."

"Not that old," he said.

Marilyn observed how he gazed on Jerod with love and then on blonde-haired Alice with something more… concern.

"What is wrong?" she asked. She turned. *He's too quiet.* Bad memories haunted her. *I was not a good mother to them.* "I made you lie and cheat."

"We did what we had to," he replied.

Something's wrong with Alice… and he doesn't want me to see it. Tricky Alex, some things never change. "You will not lock me up."

"I hadn't intended to, and now there's no need for that."

"They have me." Marilyn's changeling double, dressed in a spring floral with her hair tied up and back, smiled at Marilyn.

Marilyn felt a dull ache in her side, where years earlier Queen May tore flesh to make the changeling. The pain was different now…. *She sits in my place. She rears my children….* She looked over the pass-through into the darkened living room where Adam played with the tabbies. She grabbed the sides of her face.

Changeling Marilyn spoke. "You are doing the right thing, Marilyn. If you had a choice, of course you'd keep your children with you. Though Alex is truly grown and wants to spend little time with me." She smiled. "I embarrass him."

"Tell me," Marilyn said as she turned in place, making note of what was right and what was not. "Your fairy. Where is your fairy? Where is Nimby?"

Alex nodded. "Gone. We have much to tell you."

"She cannot go. That was part of the deal."

Alex looked from her to Jerod. "What are you talking about? What deal?"

"Balance, Alex." Marilyn's words choked in her throat. "Tip the balance and something tumbles back." A strangled cry came from her throat. "Up and down the scales go. You can't have one without the other."

"Shh," Changeling Marilyn cooed. "I think I understand. Let me try. I am after all flesh of your flesh, though not exactly your child."

Marilyn nodded as Flora pressed a mug of hot tea into her trembling hands.

"Your Nimby," she said to Alex. "You were gifted with at birth." She looked to Marilyn, who nodded. "Good, and I suspect the gift was from your father."

"Yes, Cedric. You met your father," Marilyn gushed. "He's a fairy."

"And he sent me Nimby?"

"Yes, to protect. To guide. To dance on your shoulder and on the head of a pin. For I am the mother…. Crap!"

"I've got this," Changeling Marilyn said. "Just as I was created to maintain balance between the worlds, your Nevus fairy was like a weight in the balance. Cedric tricked your mother in love; a scale is tipped. He then gets her heavy with a child at May's bidding. It tips further, but then he falls in love, and something swings a different way. At your birth, Alex, you did not enter the world alone. You came with a gift from your father."

"Nimby."

"Yes, not birthed by your mother but by your father."

Marilyn nodded. "True, and boy was I surprised." Her eyes were wide. "She flew out of his mouth."

Changeling Marilyn continued. "And all around you and your brother, sister, your mother and father, the warriors you gather on the way, like Liam and Charlie, and now Finn, wheels turn, and weights shift."

"For I am the mother of kings and of the girl who went down the hole." Marilyn stared at Alice. *Why is she silent?* She walked over to the teen, who would not meet her gaze. "Alice."

Alice pressed back against the cabinets, her face hidden in the curtain of her straight blonde hair.

"Daughter," Marilyn pressed. *Something is wrong.* "Look up. Look at me." Alice shook her head but did as asked.

"No." Marilyn gently pulled back her daughter's hair. She was shocked at the dark circles under Alice's eyes. "So thin. You must eat." She remembered how young girls in the See developed horrible problems with food. *Is that this?* Marilyn felt her daughter's shoulders. "Anorexia."

"No." Alice shook her head and pulled back from her mother's touch.

"No," Alex affirmed. He glanced at Jerod.

"Tell her," Jerod said. "Maybe she'll know what to do."

"Tell me," Marilyn said as she looked from Alice to Alex. "Tell me."

"It's dust, Mommy," Alice said. "I didn't know, and now…."

"I am the mother of kings and of the girl who went down the hole. This is May's doing. I could kill her. Perhaps I will…. How much dust?"

From her veil of bangs, Alice met her mother's gaze. "None now. And I suffer."

"It was worse before, wasn't it?" Alex asked.

"Brother, I love you and Jerod both. But you do not know. You in your happy shell of love and premed—'Gee, I got another A'—cannot know. I won't bore you, but I suffer, every day, every second."

"As much as before?" Jerod asked.

"Different." She slumped cross-legged onto the floor and wrapped her bony arms around her knees. "Then it was physical, now it's worse. I was happy when I was dusted. I was free of everything bad that's ever happened to us… to me."

"I'm so sorry," Marilyn managed, uncertain how to help.

"Not your fault… but then again, it was all your fault. It doesn't matter. Shit happened, Mom. Really bad shit… because of you and the crazy. Kids shouldn't know how much evil there is in the world, and we learned young… because of you and the crazy. So yeah, babble about being the mother of kings and of your holy daughter. I ain't buying it."

"It's not her fault," Alex said.

"It sort of is," Alice replied. "None of this would ever have happened."

"There's truth in what she says," Flora added. "But done is done. You can't unmake an egg."

"Yes," Marilyn said. "And for my sins, for falling in love with your father, I got scrambled."

Alice snorted. "That's us. A whole lot of scrambled eggs. So I was dusted, Mom. And now I'm just sad all the time. Not a little sad. Not fourteen-year-old emo sad, and maybe sad is not a good enough word. I live in gray and black. There are no colors." She looked to her brother. "You don't get it. And why should you? I don't want you to know, and I can't believe I'm rambling like this. It's mine. I'll own it. But the dust… I know it wasn't real, but for whole hours, even days, I was happy. And now… is this all there is? Am I ever going to feel normal? Am I ever going to stop thinking about the shit that happened to me in that house?"

Marilyn stared at Alice, too thin and curled on the floor. "What have I done?"

Alice stuffed a fist into her mouth.

Alex sat next to her and went to put an arm around her.

"Don't." Alice shrugged it off. "You can't fix this. And I'm sorry for being such a shit. I'm happy for you and Jerod. But I'm fucking jealous. You get the happy ever after, and I'm the girl who got raped by a pervert."

Marilyn froze. *I knew this. I let this happen to my little girl.*

"You can't fix me, Alex. And I do appreciate everything you've done." She swept her hair back and looked him square on. "And I do mean everything. Sometimes child-molesting creeps fall down stairs and break their heads." She whispered, but everyone in the kitchen heard, "And sometimes they need a push. I'll get through this. What's one more bad thing? Do you remember *Sadly*?"

"Of course. Today on *Sadly*."

She smiled. "Yup, today on *Sadly* we find Alice addicted to fairy dust. Though I've been without it for so long, maybe this is just a protracted withdrawal."

Changeling Marilyn looked to Marilyn. "Do you know how long it lasts?"

Marilyn did, and did not want to say. *Years, decades... some say once dusted never undusted.*

Alice looked up at her mother. "You don't have to say it. I think I know. Today on *Sadly* Alice realizes that she is well and truly fucked... forever."

"Don't say that," Alex said.

"It's the truth, unless someone has a magic happy trick they can pull. It's like every good feeling I ever had left when I stopped using dust. There's nothing left in here, but... the bad stuff. And can we please talk about something other than me. Tell Mom about Finn... and Nimby."

"Sure." Shoulder to shoulder with his sister, he looked up at the assembled. "It's weird having the two of you here," he said, looking at the carbon copies of Marilyn. He focused on the one with the disheveled hair and raggedy Renaissance-fair robes. "But first, how did you get here? 'Cause we tried to go through the mulberry in Fort Tryon Park. It didn't work, or rather it took Finn and Nimby."

"Puka," Marilyn said.

Jerod, who'd been playing with Adam and the cats in the other room, joined them. "One nearly killed me." He went to Alex and Alice and slid down beside them. "I nearly drowned." He jabbed Alex in the side. "Though I did get some nice mouth-to-mouth."

"Please stop," Alice said. "I could vomit."

"I think I did," Jerod said. "I can still taste all the seaweed and crap. So where did you come out?"

"The Hudson," Marilyn said.

"Makes sense," Alex said. "It's like this world and that one are pieces of bread in a sandwich."

"And the Mist is the filling," Flora offered. "Three realms, three sisters, and all of the fey balance holding them apart."

"I must return," Marilyn said. She stared into her teacup. *Please give me words.*

"Dancing daisies and a dog howls in the night."

"It's the Hound," Flora said. She settled across from the two Marilyns. "Would it help if I spoke and you nodded if I have it right or not?"

"Yes… thank you."

"There is war and chaos in Fey," Flora said. Marilyn nodded.

"You have brought your son Adam here to keep him safe."

Marilyn nodded again and looked to Alex. "Please. Please."

"I know what to do," he said without hesitation. "And with Changeling Mom it's not like before. Everyone thinks she's you, so no need to go through all that social services bullshit… and she's pretty cool."

Flora continued, almost like she could read Marilyn's mind. "The Fey need a ruler. Without it they fall into war and chaos. It's probably why they've tolerated May as long as they have, for even a despot who snacks on her subjects is preferable to anarchy."

Marilyn nodded. Her fingers trembled, and she had to put the cup down. *I'm about to lose my last child. I have been a horrible mother.* She looked at Alex and Alice. *I made them suffer.*

Flora reached across the table and grabbed Marilyn's hand. "This is not your fault," she said. "Your children are strong. Adam will be safe here. And when the time is right, you will come back for him. You are doing what you must."

"Good words," Marilyn said, *but are they true? My last child. I am losing Adam. Though wasn't he the first?*

"The rub," Flora added. "And please stay with us, Marilyn, as I think you can help. The rub and possibly an explanation for why May is barking

mad, despite having traveled inside your haffling children, is that there is
another reason she is not whole. It's obvious at this point, but what I now
see is that she's not been whole for millennia. Probably close to the time of
the Mist and the separation of the three realms."

Marilyn strained to make sense of Flora's words. There was truth
here, truth she'd need to hang on to and bring back. "Not whole, how?"

"Her heart," Flora said. "She was betrothed to a man, a human man, but
something more. He was the Hound. It's not clear if the love was reciprocated,
but the two had tremendous fun for quite a long time. If one believes in
legends, and Irish history is ripe with them, the love between Queen May and
the Hound lasted from before the Roman Empire fell to well into the dark ages.
It was with him the deal was struck, and the worlds were separated to end the
thousand-year war. Knowing enough of the history… or what the Irish call
history, I suspect there was a trick on the Hound's part, and that's where he
took back the piece that kept her whole. He took back his heart, though perhaps
he never gave it. More importantly, he kept hers."

"Everyone howled," Marilyn said. She threw back her head and bayed.

The room quieted. All eyes were on her.

"The two who passed through," Flora said. "One was Alex's little
fairy, poor creature. She wasn't all there to begin with, and I shudder to
think what's become of her. But the other, the man called Finn Hulain, I
believe I know why he was let pass. Like all in this room, we are not brought
together by chance but by fate. Finn Hulain, a man I've known since he was
a little boy, is the Hound, or some incarnation of him. It is he who possesses
what May most covets. It is he who must battle her."

Twenty-Eight

"I NEED clothes." Finn rummaged naked through Redmond's closet. "This is not anything I'm used to." He chuckled and pawed through robes of green, blue, purple, and rust, many of them festooned with intricate embroidery and jewels. "Where's gray, black, khaki, olive green?"

"Questions, Finn," Redmond cautioned.

"I know, but really. On you it looks good…. I don't like to stand out."

Redmond laughed as he took in Finn, with his flowing mane, imposing height, and body that, well…. "I will find clothes that suit. For now, let me see." He pulled out a deep green tunic and loose white shirt that would just cover Finn's ripped chest. "It's the britches."

"I'll wear a kilt."

"We're not Scots."

"Right, I need to keep my crazy fairy worlds separated."

"The snark does not suit."

"No." Finn grabbed Redmond from behind and held him close. "It helps. I may not have broken coming through. But finding that I can turn into a dog and can hear and smell things in a way that is so not human…." He nuzzled Redmond's neck.

"Tell me." Redmond turned into him and gazed up as his hand splayed over the expanse of Finn's chest.

"My senses are different, like, altogether. Smells and sounds are thoughts, though putting them to words is not as easy as with sight. It's like"—he ran the back of a hand down Redmond's cheek—"they bypass words and go to emotions. No, that's not quite right. Emotional knowing. I feel something and, without rational thought, know whether it's truth or a lie."

"Give me a for instance."

"Sure." His cheek brushed Redmond's. "There… and that. A thing you hide from me. It seeps through your pores."

Redmond froze.

He sniffed again. "And now the thing you hide turns to fear. But nuanced. It's not the fear of May coming to eat us… that's different. This is deeper. It's old." He inhaled hard and shook his head as if swirling a Bordeaux. "There are traces of things… disgust, loathing… desire… but mostly… hunger." His eyes narrowed. "You are afraid to tell me something important. Something you hide. And now I am good and truly curious."

"I…."

"You wish you could lie, and you cannot, Redmond. Nor would I want you to. Even now I've tripped your fear higher. Your pulse quickens, and not just from touch. You fear that once I learn—"

"You will not want me."

"Do you murder kittens?"

"Please, no questions."

"Why?"

"Because they cost."

Redmond gave a half smile.

"To whom will I be in debt?"

"Please stop."

"Answer the question, Redmond."

"To the person of whom the question has been asked."

"So to you. I will be in debt to you?"

"Yes."

"Good. So tell me this secret, Redmond, and because I have asked so many questions, it's clear that regardless of the awful truth, I will not leave your side until you weary of me and send me away… like the hound I have apparently become."

"Tell me of that." Redmond attempted to dodge the interrogation. "Tell me of the Hound. He is inside of you."

Finn growled. "No. And remember I am a dog with a bone. It is not so easy. I feel the heat of your fear. You need not worry. I will know this thing that brings you sorrow. But first, to your diversion." He played a hand through Redmond's hair. "The Hound is spirit, and I am flesh. He is, I suspect, immortal, and I am not. He does not exist without a vessel, and as far as I can tell, he is an apt companion. For it is I, Finn Hulain, that steer this body. Although when we get all fuzzy and four-legged it's more him than me, though I'm still inside of here. I smell, I hear everything. The eyes… not as good. The sense of direction and of purpose, it's unreal. And I like it… a lot."

"So you are not the one who gave May the houndstone."

"Correct. It was the Hound and another… whatever I am to it. And considering the stone found its way to your possession via May's sister Lizbeta, he… whoever he was, gave it and took it back. From what I've seen of May, she did not give it up willingly. He either stole it or took it by force." He breathed in deep. His back widened, and his belly swelled like a Laughing Buddha. "So that's it."

Redmond stiffened.

Finn scowled. He sniffed Redmond's neck, and then he licked it from the notch of his sternum to his ear. "Fear not." And buck naked, he left the closet.

Redmond's gaze followed. He found it hard to draw breath as he stared at Finn and dreaded what was to come.

Locked onto the scent, Finn nosed out the delicate inlaid table with its single drawer. He opened it to reveal Redmond's stash—a single dust bunny. Without pause, he pissed on it. "How much are you using?" he asked as his stream hit the bunny. The sticky ovoid hissed, and with a brilliant silver flash, like an old-time camera, it vanished.

"Too much," Redmond admitted. He paused. "And none since yesterday."

"Are you hurting?" Finn asked.

"Strangely, no." He looked at his stash, or rather where it had been. There was an acrid tang of ozone… but no more bunny and no pee. He ran a finger inside the drawer. No trace of either remained. He brought it to his nose. "Nothing."

Finn nodded. "Redmond, we've just met, and I have little—no, wait, let me rephrase that—I have no experience of love. Other than I loved someone deeply who could only love me like a friend or a brother. And he died way too young. But in one day, I have walked between worlds, and I have found the most amazing and smart and funny man… with a killer ass. I kissed you before I took back the stone, so I don't think what I feel is magic."

Redmond shook his head. He shut the drawer and walked to Finn. "It is magic. When the worlds were separated, all the magic stayed here with two exceptions—love and art. Those exist in all realms."

Finn lowered his head and touched his forehead to Redmond's. "You feel something for me."

"Bastard, you just want me to say it first."

"We'll say it together."

And they did. "I love you."

An explosion rocked the room.

It was followed by the whistle and scream of fairy fire missiles. "Shit," Finn cursed. "Do I ever catch a break?"

They gripped each other's hands and raced to the eastern-facing window.

"Son of a bitch," Finn muttered as he smelled and heard the formidable mixed-race army that approached the Center.

Redmond drew a sigil to enhance his vision. He fleshed out the picture. "They are at the outer lake," he explained. "It's why I chose this location. The waters are deep and wide and provide a natural moat for the Center. She has brought an army."

"Tell me what you see, all of it."

"I see her. She rides a massive white salamander, which is a part of her. She looks solid. Her armor is a deep purple, and it glitters. A swarm of pixies is braiding her hair with colored diamonds."

"Okay, that I don't need to know. I smell them, and everything reeks of dust."

Redmond nodded. "That's how she's doing it. Goddess preserve us." His vision bounced from ogre, to pixie, to sprite. "They're all dusted. She leads an army of addicts."

"She's come for me," Finn said.

"No." He gripped Finn's hand.

"It's true. We both know it." He hugged him tight. "But listen to me, Dr. Redmond Fall." He smiled. "And me ending up with a doctor."

"It's no time for jokes, Finn. She means to eat you, to take your heart. To make herself whole. To—"

Finn placed a finger to Redmond's lips. "Yes. To fill the hole. And the more I think of it, it's not my heart she wants, but hers. That's what that houndstone thingy is. Like a cage for her heart, and right now it's inside of me."

Their eyes locked, and Finn continued. "Having finally found you, I'm not going. Not without a fight." He kissed him with every fiber of his being. He wanted… no, needed Redmond to feel no doubt of his love. But more, he knew with the senses of the Hound and his years investigating fires that things could quickly go south.

They pulled apart, the air thick between them.

"I know something, Redmond. And I don't know how I know it."

"Tell me."

"There is little doubt that fate brought me here. Brought me to you…
and to her."

"Agreed, to argue chance at this point is ludicrous."

"But here's the thing. And don't ask me how I know this. I just do. At
this moment, fate has been suspended. It's like a fork in time that could go
to the right or to the left. What happens now has not been written."

With their lips inches apart, Redmond whispered, "I see the possibility
of such a thing, and so it must be truth." He closed the distance, and like the
halves of a circuit being thrown, they kissed.

Finn's pulse sped. He loved Redmond, without doubt or hesitation.
But for the first time in his life, he knew that he was loved, without condition,
without "I love you as a friend." In that kiss, a lifetime of want and despair
vanished, like a dust bunny pissed on by a hound.

Twenty-Nine

REELING FROM the kiss, Redmond shifted into crisis mode. *He loves me. I am damned if I'll be eaten… at least by her.*

He summoned Gark and the guards. His hands shook as he sent out an emergency sigil to all who resided within the Center. He placed words onto the magic. "This is not a test. This is not a test." He'd always known this day would come. Queen May had tolerated the Center for centuries. He'd given her a reason to not raze it to the ground, but now she couldn't care less about housing the Unsee's most unsavory and unstable criminals—*The guests.* He'd always wondered why she didn't just eat them all. Now was not the time to ponder. "This is not a test," he stated one more time. "The Center… our Center is under siege. The queen's army is upon us. United we will not fall. I need all to meet in the grand auditorium in five minutes. The guests are exempt."

He turned to Finn. "Come. Throw on something and stand by my side."

"You don't like me as I am?"

"Another question in my debt. And as I said, I do not share."

"Good to know. I don't share either, and I intend to dig myself deep into debt. What do you think of that?"

"We mustn't tarry. And we must retrieve your broken Nevus fairy."

"My what?" He smirked.

"Your Nimby. We must prepare for all eventualities."

"I ain't leaving."

Redmond grabbed a fistful of Finn's chest hair.

"Oww!"

"All eventualities, Finn. While fate may have taken a break, we can't diminish our options. She came with you for a reason. We need her now."

"Fine, I'll follow, and you lead." Finn picked up the shirt and green tunic Redmond had picked out. The former ended at midabdomen, and the latter split from calf to armpit with his first step. "Screw this." He ripped them off, grabbed one of Redmond's blue robes, and belted it around his waist. It fell to just above his knees and gaped over his hairy chest. "It's this or nothing," he said. "The naughty bits are covered."

"It'll do," Redmond said. He averted his gaze and damped down his arousal. *We're under attack. Stop thinking about....*

Minutes later Redmond stood in front of the packed auditorium. Behind him to the left stood Gark and his uniformed lieutenants, and to his right was Finn with Nimby, swirling like an asteroid around his head.

Those who could not find seats, stood—or flew—five and six deep around the periphery.

Still more flooded the broad square out front.

"The Center will not fall," Redmond said. "She will lay siege. Our walls are thick, our foundations run deep, and the magic that protects us will not be breached. Not by her, not by anyone."

"Tell us what to do," a troll mother surrounded by her children shouted from the balcony.

"Stay calm. Stay within these walls. We are prepared for this day and for months to follow if need be. We have food and water. We are secure. No one leaves these walls. No one is to enter without being vetted by myself. And this is perhaps the most important thing." He took a deep breath. *I am such a hypocrite.* "No one is to touch or taste fairy dust."

A missile whistled overhead. The room fell silent as it screamed toward the ground… toward them. It exploded at the Center's outer wards.

Redmond held still. He glanced back at Finn.

"She is here for me," Finn whispered.

Nimby sang, "The worms crawl in and the worms crawl out. The worms crawl in and they wiggle all about."

"Don't even think about it," Redmond whispered. He turned back to his anxious audience. "She will attempt to pull us apart and to create dissension within these walls. We must hold firm. For should we fail, have no doubt that our queen will not forgive, and every single one of us will be marked for death… or worse."

"We shall fight!" a tiny pixie dressed in a battle helmet and purple tutu screamed from the chandelier. Her cry was taken up by dozens of others in an odd array of warrior dancewear.

"We shall," Redmond said. "But now we batten down and wait for our moment. Our walls are strong." He scanned the crowd from one end to the other, from the ceiling down to the insectopods with their mishmash of bug and humanoid limbs and heads, clustered deep in front of the podium. "Our walls are strong."

A family of frosted mini-gnomes piled onto a single seat repeated his words. "Our walls are strong."

Without prompting, others joined in. *"Our walls are strong."*

Finn, with Nimby buzzing around his head, came to Redmond's side. "What's happening?"

"Watch. Listen."

"It's magic."

Nimby clapped her hands and changed her tune. "With a mickle and a care I shall go into a hare."

"Yes. Collective magic. They all came here for a purpose. Mostly it was to find a life free from May's insanity. This is their home." The chant swelled, and the room filled with a golden glow that pulsed and grew. Redmond raised his arms over the crowd. He made a motion for silence. And like a conductor, he brought the sound down. "Our walls are strong. Stay within them. Keep your children safe. And above all else, stay far away from fairy dust."

With missiles flying overhead, he watched the Center's residents disperse to the streets and their homes. He wondered how many would survive.

"I can stop this," Finn said.

It was all Nimby needed to pick up with a Supremes' song she'd learned in the See. It came with well-crafted choreography that started with one hand on her hip and the other in the universal sign for Stop.

Redmond looked past Nimby's antics. "You can, Finn. But you were not born into our magic. In that she has the advantage. Magic does not travel in straight lines, but it is twisty and carries options. As you said, on this day fate takes a holiday. There is choice here, and there is strategy. She batters our walls and incites us to panic." He gazed on Finn and realized with crushing certainty that any moment might be their last. "Once she has what she wants—" He rested his hand on Finn's chest. "—she will resume her prior objective. Many will die."

Finn nodded.

Nimby shifted her tune. "We're all worm food in the end. We're all worm food in the end."

Redmond caught something in Finn's expression. "Tell me what runs through your head."

"*Veritas ex Cineribus.* Truth from the ashes. It's the logo of the Bureau of Fire Investigation." Finn stared out over the departing crowd, many of whom still chanted "Our walls are strong." But it wasn't his eyes that fed him information but his nose. "It's them."

"Tell me."

Finn paced across the stage. Nimby circled his head.

"May is a creature of fire and magic. She eats her subjects," Finn stated.

"Yes," Redmond said, "and that is the source of both fairy fire and fairy dust."

"She is a cannibal." Finn stopped and met Redmond's gaze. "And the ingestion of dust…."

"Yes, I get it," Redmond said. "Trust me. I'm not proud of the fact. She has enslaved her army."

Finn pointed a finger at him. "No." And without explanation, he left the auditorium.

"Finn!" Redmond shouted, but either Finn didn't hear, or Nimby's constant songfest distracted him. "Finn!" Redmond ran after him, accompanied by several of the ogre guards and a handful of students.

Finn headed to the outer walls. He climbed the zigzagging flights of stairs and looked out over the fields and past the broad outer lake toward May's massed troops.

Redmond flew to his side as May, from her perch upon her salamander self, made eye contact first with him and then with Finn.

She shouted and fueled her words with magic so they could breach the distance. "Hound, you can end this."

Finn nodded. He whispered to Redmond, "We know that she has created an army of addicts. They follow her out of need. They have lost any semblance of free will. Tell me, can they be healed?"

Redmond grew quiet. The first time he'd beaten his addiction had come at a terrible cost. He'd had one of his students lock him in a cell deep below the earth. For more than a year he had wished for death. The mechanics of dust were simple and cruel. It fused with every molecule of your being. Detoxification was rare, prolonged, and excruciating. It carried a high fatality rate, and relapse was almost inevitable. *I should feel all of that now. Something is different.* "Truth from the ashes." He turned from May, whose hands were a blur of motion. "Even now she seeks to pull you from these walls with magic. She will fail… for now. I need to go back to my chambers." He drifted off the wall and flew toward the spire of his chambers.

"Damn you! Wait!" Finn shouted.

"I forgot." Redmond turned back. "You do not fly."

"No, I don't." He grabbed Redmond, rubbed noses, licked his cheek, and then kissed him hard.

Nimby did a series of cartwheels, bouncing across Finn's shoulders, her song now an ancient tune about shopping for puppies in windows.

"I do this," Finn growled and in front of all transformed into the massive wolfhound. He butted his flat head against Redmond's flank.

"Get on!" Nimby shrieked.

And like mounting a horse, Redmond did.

The Hound raced down the stairs and through the Center toward Redmond's tower.

Redmond worked the locks and, unused to taking the stairs, grabbed fists of thick fur with both hands as he was carried up hundreds of steps to his chambers among the clouds.

Once in his quarters, Redmond went to the drawer that had held his stash. It smelled of neither piss nor fairy dust. "I should be sick. I should be horribly sick." He looked at the Hound and felt inside himself for any trace of dust withdrawal; there was none. "It's been over a day. And once an addict relapses," he said, as though talking to one of his classes, "it's like they'd never been sober. This makes no sense. I should be sick. Very sick. Fever, vomiting, uncontrollable diarrhea…."

The Hound licked his hand, the air shimmered, and he turned back into Finn.

Redmond stared at him. "That's it. You. You're the answer. You are the truth in the ashes."

Finn looked at the empty drawer and then at Redmond.

"Ding, ding, ding," Nimby cried. "We have a winner. Johnny, tell us what he's won."

Finn shook his head and captured Nimby in two fingers around her waist. "Please shut up for half a second."

Nimby clamped her hands over her mouth. Her eyes grew large, and her cheeks puffed out like the effort might make her explode.

"You've got to be kidding." He stared at Redmond. "So what you're saying is I need to go out there and pee on a few thousand fairies."

Redmond nodded. "Yes, that might do it."

Thirty

FINN'S LAUGH ended with a bark. *Truth from the ashes, Jesus! Let it go. Today is one hell of a different day from yesterday. And the night of a thousand fires. Stop!*

He looked at Redmond. *A day ago you didn't have him.* "I've got to get with the program."

Nimby alit on the tip of his nose. "Woof," she said and sang again about puppies in windows.

He looked past her whirly tattoos, crazed red eyes, and swallowtail wings that beat fast to keep her balanced, and focused on Redmond. "You said withdrawal from dust is bad."

"Very. It took me a year."

"You don't look sick now."

"I'm not. Not in the least."

"Maybe you didn't pick up a habit this time."

"Not how it works. Once a dusthead, always a dusthead. If you're able to withdraw, all it takes is a single bunny and it's as if you never stopped."

"Seriously?" He waggled his eyebrows and drew a tick mark in the air.

"Very funny. Clearly you never heard the story of how questions killed the questling, but yes. I should be puking my guts out at this moment."

"And nothing."

"Nope. I just have…."

"Say it."

"I want to rip that silly robe off of you and…."

"Yeah." Finn gently plucked Nimby from the air and placed her next to Redmond's stash box. "So piss. Any piss or just mine?"

"Yours." It was Redmond's turn to chuckle.

"Say it."

"Hair of the dog."

"I guess, though more like piss of the dog. Does she know this?"

"Doubtful, and as a medical doctor, you'd think this would be something I'd have run across. This is huge. An actual cure for dustheads. It's unprecedented."

"So maybe we caught a break. Then again, she was with the Hound. She might know this. She seems to be the source of dust, or at least a lot of it."

"There are others, but they are not sentient."

"Come again?"

"Dust," Redmond said. "The usual sources are volcanic. Whenever there's an eruption, the dealers harvest the drug."

"Not so different from her, now that we know a portion of the drug comes from dead fey."

"Yes." Redmond snaked his hands under Finn's robe and held him fast. Finn brushed his nose through his hair. "You smell good… clean, different."

"Tell me."

"You're not dusted. You are you. No additives. No preservatives."

Nimby chimed in with a twisted margarine lyric. "If you think it's butter, but it's snot."

Redmond ignored her. "May might know of this. In which case, it's not just your heart she's after. She'll need you dead to maintain her army of addicts."

"How much piss are we talking here?" Finn asked.

Redmond's hands drifted lower. "A few thousand gallons should suffice." A missile wailed overhead.

They held their breath and waited as it reached its apex and then hurtled down toward the Center. The explosion shook the tower. Through the window they glimpsed embers of twinkling fairy dust as they drifted down.

Finn pulled back. "What you told them back there. That these walls could withstand her. It's not true."

"It is and it's not." Redmond voiced the thing he most feared. "The walls will stand." He stared at the sparkly dust. "She is filling our streets with dust. The walls will fall from within, not from without."

"But we know what to do. I just have to pee on everyone. Shit! A few thousand gallons. Not impossible. All we have to do is analyze it. Figure out what's in it, how to synthesize it, and…. You have a lab here?"

Redmond's expression was somber. "It's a plan, Finn. A good one. But not one for this world… it's of yours."

"No chemistry here?"

"No, alchemy, it's the source of magic objects like your houndstone. But to pull apart the structure of a thing and make more of it… lots more of it, that's chemistry, and it belongs to the See, not here. When the realms were divided, you got science. We got magic."

"So we'll go to the See. We'll go together." Three fairy fire missiles screamed overhead.

"Finn. I can't go."

"I didn't break. And isn't love protective?" Finn said, misreading Redmond.

"Your fairy did." Redmond looked him in the eyes. "She knew she would."

"What?"

"Your pixie. She sacrificed herself to get you here intact. She'll do the same to get you back."

"She most certainly will not!"

Redmond gripped Finn's hand and brought it to his lips. "This is war. Finn, there have been horrible casualties, and there will be more. Too many. Your coming here was fate, and now you need to go back. Find your chemist, preferably one with a taste for alchemy, make a few thousand gallons of magic wolfhound piss, and bring it back."

"I'm not leaving you. I'm a hound, remember? You're coming with me, or I'm not—"

Redmond put a finger to Finn's lips and then kissed him. It tasted of love, lust… and loss. "My place is here. If I left, the Center would fall, and there will be no safe place left. I can't do that."

"I can't leave you."

"You must."

The pain, like losing Rory again, tore at his guts. "I can't."

Nimby circled around them. "To war, to war, we go to war."

He stared at her as Redmond's revelation sank in. "Right. This is war." And for the umpteenth time that day, he told the rational part of himself to shut up. This was not the time or place for logic. "Find what's in my piss. Make a few thousand gallons, and come on back. Piece of cake."

Redmond's expression mirrored his despair. "It's possible."

"Then it's certain," Finn said.

Nimby landed on his shoulder and marched in place. She sang, "To war, to war, we're off to war. To fight, to fight, that is our plight. To die, to die, some will die. We pay today so our children may play."

With Nimby on his shoulder, Finn ran his fingers through Redmond's hair. "I will return to you. You have my heart. I'm coming back for it, and I'm coming back for you."

Thirty-One

DOROTHEA GAZED up at the split queen. "Your Highness, you are magnificent."

From atop her salamander self, May, dressed in a golden breastplate with her jeweled hair streaming behind her, looked to the Center. "It will fall. Time, years, and centuries are irrelevant. It will fall."

"Yes, Your Highness."

"Dorothea, I have been blinded by treachery. Now I shall finally taste the fruits of what should have always been mine."

"Yes, this is your time."

May marveled at the strange sensations as her thighs straddled her other half. *I am beast and queen, creator and destroyer.* Her salamander self slurped down a family of pixies. Their magic tingled through them both as the tiny creatures screamed.

Salamander May belched and reared back. *Here it comes.* She produced a glorious fireball that arced high in the sky. It hurtled across the broad moat and over the flower-emblazoned meadows.

"Ooh," Dorothea moaned. "I have never seen such power."

May tracked her missile's flight and watched it land hard on the Center's protective wards. "They still hold."

"Perfect aim. And they won't hold long," Dorothea added. "See how the magics waver at the edges. You are almost in."

Twinkles of fairy fire rained down on her target. They sparked as they connected with Redmond Fall's protective spells.

"Look." Dorothea pointed. "Some dust falls through. Too fabulous."

May chuckled and sang, "Come and taste my fairy dust." Her gaze tracked to the right, the left, and then to the rear. *My army is strong.* "Dorothea."

"Yes, my queen."

"Tell me our numbers."

"They vary."

"Yes, I'm aware… I was hungry."

"I meant no criticism."

"Just tell me, give or take a snack or two."

"Twenty thousand."

"Good. But his magic… I should never have allowed this place to be built. Should never have let him grow so strong."

"True, and it served a purpose."

"I suppose. Back in the days when I did not want my appetites to be known. I should have just eaten them, all the deviants and the defectives. But there are concerns with such practices."

"So true, Your Highness. We are what we eat. But look, more dust falls through."

"My time approaches." May turned back and surveyed her army. "Less than half will be able to make it across his moat."

Dorothea's head cocked to the side. "Something's happening."

"Tell me." But as she spoke, she felt it. "Someone's turning a lock."

"Yes."

"Either they're letting someone in or…."

"They left a door," Dorothea said.

"Someone's trying to escape. And I know who. This is my chance, and it won't be years or centuries. I will have my heart. I will be whole." Her salamander self inhaled and exhaled and, using its lungs like bellows, produced a different form of fairy fire. She hacked it up, and as it shot through her lips, she clamped down tight and, propelled by its force and magic, took to flight.

With Dorothea and twenty thousand winged, webbed, and footed creatures at her back, she flew toward the source of the magic's breach. She clung tight to her smooth white back and willed herself higher and faster. "Hurry!" She glimpsed down and saw some of her army get pulled, screaming, into the depths of the moat. Razor-tipped jaws of rare creatures made quick work of her dusted minions as others flew by her side and at her back. Several trolls and ogres clung perilously to the legs and backs of their flying brethren. Some made it across, and some fell screaming into the depths.

She felt the warp and weave of reality glimmer. "The Hound is coming through," she shouted as she alit in the meadow and raced toward the base of the Center's wall, where a shimmering door had appeared.

"Hurry, Your Majesty," Dorothea said as her long, delicate wings flitted and clicked.

"Hound!" May screamed as a tall figure appeared. *You will not trick me again.*

With jaws wide and her legs tight around her salamander back, she leapt toward the door.

I will eat you. Her pulse rang in her ears as she flew through the air. *I will devour you. I will be whole.*

She landed jaw first in the dust, her mouth empty. The door was gone. And the portal was vanishing.

"No!" she shrieked, and the salamander howled and twisted back on itself. Its broad snout poked at the shrinking portal.

No! And as the force of Redmond Fall's magic crashed down on her, she fought back. Engorged with the life's blood of thousands of creatures, she clamped her salamander jaw onto the shimmering circle. She felt the flavor of the magic, took it inside, and with a few clicks, twists, and shimmies, she stopped it from closing. *A tickle here. A tickle there.* It sparked back to life. And what minutes earlier had looked like a siege that could last for ages, ended as she chewed a hole in the Center's defenses.

With Dorothea on her right and a battalion of flying creatures and the few trolls and ogres who'd made it across, she breached the wall and entered a courtyard filled with spear and macewielding guards.

The moment stretched before her as she made eye contact with each of her would-be attackers. "It's simple," she said. "You're either with me… or you're lunch."

Thirty-Two

WITH NIMBY tucked in a pocket of his too short robe, Finn fell out of a mirror onto the pink-and-white marble floor of a place that was strange and familiar: the foyer of the Central Park West apartment of romance novelist and ex-pat fey Katye Summer. The ravishing strawberry-blonde sister of May smiled as she waited for Finn to catch his bearings.

For his part, she was a lot to take in, dressed in pink from her cleavage-teasing camisole and tight leather mini to her red-soled Jimmy Choos. *Where the hell am I?* Because in front of Katye, standing sentinel, was a massive bullfrog that was over a foot tall and wider in the haunches.

"We've not met," she said as she offered her hand.

"I've been here." Finn tried to gather his wits while trying to cover as much of himself as he could with Redmond's robe. Through the far windows, he glimpsed the park. *This is New York. And she's not to be trusted.* His acute hearing caught distant traffic and a pond bubbler gurgling on a rooftop deck. *It smells like roses. Do not trust her.*

"Take a moment." Her smile dazzled. *She's trying that glamour thing.* It was like Liam and how just looking at the man could rob him of his senses. He scrambled to his feet, aware of the warm air on his exposed chest and legs.

From within the pocket of his—Redmond's—robe, Nimby cried, "Alex, I want my Alex."

The frog croaked and, with a great leap that doubled his length, squeezed between Finn and his mistress's feet.

"That's Lance," she offered. "He's protective. Too much at times. And we've not met because we've been away." She gave him an appraising up and down.

Lance croaked again.

"He's jealous," she said. "You've done well. You are indeed the Hound. Woof. In a different life and a different body, we had a history, you and I."

Lance bellowed.

"It was centuries before you, sweetheart." She rolled her eyes. "Men… frogs… dogs. Oh dear, what has become of my dating life?"

"A question."

"You're a quick study. But what you'll find is the rules of one world don't apply in the other. Questions are fine here, though it does take an adjustment." She chuckled. "And I will still exact a cost."

Finn held his tongue. While on the surface Katye appeared friendly, there was more to her story than he knew. Including the revelation that May was correct and her sister had indeed fooled around with the Hound. *But why?*

"I want my Alex," Nimby cried. She grabbed the edge of the pocket. Her wings spasmed out of sync and would not give her flight.

"Poor thing," Katye said. "Let me see her."

"Alex, I want my Alex."

Finn scooped her out. Her wings were torn, a large section of the lower pair was missing altogether, and a white film clouded her vivid red eyes.

"Poor, brave thing," Katye said. She stepped past her protesting frog and laid a finger on Nimby's bald head. "So broken." She made eye contact with Finn and shook her head. She whispered, "Too broken."

"Alex," Nimby whimpered. "I want my Alex."

"I didn't want her to come. I tried to stop her."

Katye cradled Nimby in her hands. Tears welled in her eyes. "She's dying. So much death. It must end."

"My Alex," Nimby moaned.

"He's on his way, love, and Jerod, and all the others."

"Please. Alex."

There was a buzz from the speaker by the door and the voice of the doorman. "Ms. Summer, Alex Nevus and company are here."

She hit the button. "Send them up."

"I already did, Ms. Summer."

She smiled. "They practically live here." Her voice drifted as she soothed circles with her forefinger on Nimby's back. Seemingly lost in reverie, she repeated herself. "And we were away. But I do forget my manners. Your clothes, while I appreciate the male form…."

Lance barked.

"Hush, you know that I am yours and yours alone." She winked at Finn. "In truth I've only ever loved one man," she said loud enough for Lance, but then lowered to a whisper that only a dog could hear, "at a time."

Finn stared from the frog to Katye. *Are they all mad?*

"I have things that will fit you better. Though as I recall, you go through outfits at an alarming rate."

Cradling Nimby and with Lance tight at her heels, she led Finn into a closet filled with men's clothing. "These are his." She glanced down. "He won't mind."

Lance's abdomen pumped like a bellows as he howled his protest.

"So you say. Look, I'm fine with what I've got on." *I don't need duds from the frog prince.*

Not one for designer clothes, even Finn recognized that the walk-in closet, larger than many a New York apartment, represented more than he made in a year, probably several years. Inside were a series of floor-to-ceiling mirrors. At first he didn't recognize the tall redheaded man who looked like he was dressed for a Renaissance-fair strip club. Redmond's tightly belted robe gaped wide across his chest and threatened to do so down below.

"Nonsense." She brushed past him, making more contact than was necessary. "Here." She grabbed a dark green shirt, a pair of drawstring black pants, and suede sandals with thick leather straps. "This should be quick to get in and out of… and no reason for smalls. Though as I recall," she said, letting her free hand drift onto his shoulder and down to his chest, "that would be the wrong word to describe—"

Lance rammed his head into Finn's shin.

"For the love of God." Finn knelt. *And this is how we get a room at Bellevue.* "Look, Lance. I'm not interested in what your… girlfriend is offering. I got a boyfriend; at least I hope I do."

Katye glared at them. "Pheh! So some things do change." She shrugged. "Ah well, c'est la vie, c'est la guerre, c'est la dreck."

Finn straightened, having appeased Lance. "You said there's been so much death. Are you referring to the fires?"

"To all of it. What's been"—and holding Nimby—"what's upon us, and what's to come."

Does no one give straight answers? He wanted to ask more when he caught the sound of an elevator and voices in the outer corridor. A key turned in the front door.

"I'll greet our guests and return this one to her Alex. We have much to do. Dress and then join us."

He watched her leave and then shut the closet door. Even so, he easily heard the greetings from rooms away. *That's Alex and Jerod. Charlie and Liam... who's not human.* He heard Flora Fitzgerald's faint Irish lilt and caught the whiff of lavender. *Hail, hail, the gang's all here.* There was a girl's voice—*Alice Nevus*—and a pair of women's voices that were identical. *But not possible if they're speaking at the same time. Unless they have two heads. Losing it.* There were others too. Some he placed names and faces to from the night of a thousand fires. He dropped Redmond's robe to the floor and stared at his body in the mirrors.

"Woof, indeed." He smiled. *All the gain with none of the pain.* His thoughts fixed on Redmond. *Is he okay? I need to get this done and get back to him.* And the craziest piece was that in the midst of something so insane, *I've fallen in love... with a fairy... and you're a dog. Don't care.* He shut down the rational part of his brain, the part that could dispassionately pull apart an arson scene, discern where and how it started, if someone was to blame, and even if someone needed to pay. "I am in love with Redmond. I love Redmond," he whispered.

He's an addict.

He snorted. *I pissed on his bunny.*

And like a lead weight, the absurdity of the task before him returned. "What the fuck?" He glanced in the mirrors, threw on the clothes, and headed toward the voices in Katye's library.

Even having been there before, the magnificent room, less pink but with views of the park and a soaring coffered ceiling inset with lavish scenes of gods and ancient allegories, was a lot to take in.

Heads turned. All quieted as he entered. He recognized Alex, who cradled Nimby in his hands. His face twisted with tears and grief.

"I'm sorry," he said. His voice boomed across the room. "I didn't know this would happen."

"It was her choice," Katye said. "She knew. She chose."

Alex was beyond words. He tried to soothe Nimby, who lay broken in his hands, as she whimpered his name over and over.

Jerod spoke. "There's got to be something we can do."

Katye shook her head. Her message was clear. "In times of war, sacrifices must be made." She looked to the two Marilyns. "Mothers send children far away to keep them safe. Lovers are torn apart, and there is death. None of this must be in vain. And yet—" Like a general rallying her troops, she turned on her heels and made eye contact with all. She acknowledged the fey, most with surgically altered ears and teeth. She smiled at Flora. Finally she turned back to Finn. "Speak. Tell them what you've learned."

Charlie interrupted. "Finn, is that really you?"

Despite the somber room, he smiled at Charlie's bewilderment. "Yeah, I've had the romance novel makeover." He flicked back his hair. He would have gone further, but seeing Alex with Nimby…. *Why did she come with me? Right, sacrifices.*

"Is that all?" Flora asked through narrowed eyes.

"No," he said without humor. "You were right. None of us are here by chance." His gaze landed on a tall auburn-haired man standing next to a waif-thin blonde with a furry red dog in her arms. *Redmond!* But no, when the guy turned, he recognized them both as fey who'd fled the Unsee and landed in Manhattan. *Frederick something and…. Lianna.* Their paths had crossed on the night of a thousand fires.

"You are the Hound," Flora stated.

"Apparently so."

She persisted. "And the contract between the Hound and May…."

"Was not written on paper but on hearts."

"So you do know," Katye said.

"Yes." He looked at her. "And I would know why you and your sister Lizbeta concealed that fact. Or the fact that you were fooling around with an earlier version of me… the Hound, despite knowing your sister May was in love with him. Not exactly sisterly."

Katye sank into a tufted red leather chair. Lance hopped onto the arm and stared at her. "None of us is without fault," she admitted. "You've learned much, and perhaps my role in this does indeed paint me a villain. We saw no other way to stop her. To end the war. But as I see now, we merely pushed things back another thousand years. And here we are again. You, me, my sisters, death."

"Please just be straight with us," Finn said.

Flora spoke. "She can't, Finn. Don't you see? That's a mistake we keep making. Fey illogic and human logic are incompatible."

"Thank you," Katye said.

Flora, no stranger to Katye's collection of rare manuscripts, unfolded the centerpiece of the beautiful work of an eleventh-century monk. She pointed at a central figure with long silver-and-red hair. "This is the Hound back then." The man sat upon a throne, a jewel around his throat and one hand covered in silver. The bottom of the picture showed another world underground.

There, on a second throne, sat a beautiful blonde queen—May—and at her side her two sisters, Katye and Lizbeta.

Finn walked over and stared at the drawing. "Around his neck, that's the houndstone. It's somehow inside of me."

"Yes," Katye said. "You gave it to May."

"Apparently I also took it back."

"Indeed," Katye said. "But more than that. It holds her heart, and you took it."

Finn glared at her. "I did what?"

"You did as you were told. You were a very good dog."

"By whom?"

She nodded and would not look either him or Lance in the eye. "By me."

"You tricked her." Finn struggled to pull the pieces together. He remembered May's anguish as she'd bared her soul and past hurts to Redmond. "What sort of sister does that?"

"Finn." Flora placed a hand on his forearm. "Stop thinking like a human."

"Right." He stared around at the others, all eyes fixed on him and Katye. *There's a reason to this insanity.*

"Don't think in straight lines," Flora said. "The fey are twisty." She looked to Katye. "I think I know why you tricked your sister May."

"Then speak," Katye said. "I cannot force my lips to do what must be done."

"Your magic is love."

"Yes," Katye said. "It is my special, as May's is power and Lizbeta's is peace."

"You used your magic to make your sister fall in love with the Hound."

Katye nodded. "I thought that by so doing we could end the war. Enemies would become lovers, and all would lay down their weapons."

"And that's not what happened. Because magic is twisty, and the three sisters are like weights and balances caught in an eternal dance. Your spell backfired."

"No," Katye corrected her. "You were correct before. It didn't backfire. It was met with an opposing force. May's special, her power, would not allow itself to be overrun. So every night she and the Hound would love and be lovers. But come the dawn's first fingers, love flew away and war returned. If anything, it made things worse."

"So you and Lizbeta came up with another plan."

"Yes."

"You broke your sister so that she could never rule the three realms."

"And this is where I came in," Finn offered. "You had me steal her heart."

"Yes, and Lizbeta wrapped your deed in her Mist so that none would or could remember what you'd done."

Finn remembered the anguish in May's voice. "She never knew. All her attempts to cross over, to steal hafflings, they were always doomed."

"Yes, and now she knows the truth."

Jerod, who'd not left Alex and Nimby, spoke through clenched teeth. "So all that crap you told us about being tricked by May, and how Lizbeta was lured into the Mist, those were all lies."

"No. Not lies. Much of it was truth. But what you see now are three broken sisters. None of us fit to rule. At best Lizbeta and I have attempted to restrain May, but she has grown too strong."

Finn looked at Katye, who had moments ago tried to seduce him. *She's supposed to be one of the good ones.* "And now she knows how to put herself back together. Rip out my heart, steal another haffling, and presto chango."

Alex's voice wavered through clenched teeth. His gaze never left Nimby. "You used us."

Nimby looked up at him with unadulterated love. "Alex." Her voice was barely audible. "I should not leave you, because you're stupid, stupid… learned nothing, nothing…."

"Of course I used you," Katye said. "But given a choice between May's brutality and what Lizbeta and I have tried to do…."

"Point taken," Jerod said, his attention riveted on Nimby.

"Nimby knew what she was doing," Katye said. "She knew that Finn had to make it through without breaking."

Nimby shut her eyes. With her final breath, she whispered, "Alex, my Alex, my Alex. Pay attention." And she died in his hands.

Jerod, who'd not left his side, wrapped an arm around his shoulder.

Katye nodded. "We all have our roles in this sad drama." Tears streamed. "Your little Nevus fairy was brave and true. Have no doubt that her sacrifice was for you… for all of you."

Alice joined her brother. She stared wide-eyed at the dead pixie and wept, as did most of the others.

Finn, the only one other than Alex who heard Nimby's last words, chewed on them. "So what didn't you learn, and what are you supposed to pay attention to?"

Liam spoke. He gave a courtly nod to Katye. "It was not from spite that Lizbeta and Katye have pulled our strings. Just as what has been done to them is a direct result of their own actions. Magic bounces and ricochets. And the big spells, the world changers, those splatter far and wide."

Finn nodded. "Like friendly fire?"

"I don't know what that is," Liam said. "But when Lizbeta and Katye used the Hound to trick May, it's a spell that came with unintended consequence."

"But expected," Katye said. "You are wise, Liam Summer."

"I have lived centuries at May's court. I learned to hold my tongue, to do her bidding, to stay alive, and above all else, to watch and to learn. Your spell bounced." Not breaking her gaze, he spoke one of the rules of magic. "What you send to me, goes back to you times three. For good or for ill."

"That," Katye said, looking away from Liam and toward Alex, now surrounded by his two mothers, Alice, Adam, and Jerod. "That is the truth. I was indeed tricked into my tragic love with Lance, the loss of most of my magic, as was Lizbeta pulled into the fabric of her own power. But it was less May's doing than our own magic bouncing off of hers and hurtling back at us."

Finn shook his head. "You didn't know what would happen. So you what? Figured, what the hell, let's roll the dice and see—"

"Hush," she interrupted. "I have tipped my hand, at least as much as I know of it. It matters not, for none of us have the ability to go back in time. And Lizbeta and I have bought a millennium where human and fey have not slaughtered one another."

Still sitting sentinel on the arm of her chair, Lance croaked.

"Yes, love. It brought me to you. But enough of this. There is work ahead of us." She turned to Finn. "I pray that your journey was not in vain. Hound, tell us what more you've learned."

And here it comes, Finn thought. Like running a case with a marshal colleague, he ran the facts before jumping into what he knew was madness. "May grows strong. She is not whole. She wants to rip out my heart because apparently hers is in here as well. Next, you should know that she has raised an army of addicts. Thousands of them. In all shapes and sizes."

"Dust," Alice whispered.

"Yes, she makes the stuff by the truckload, and it's highly addictive. Though it's not clear it does much to humans."

"We know," Charlie said. "After all the fires last month, there was fairy dust in the craters. It doesn't do much to humans, but half the expat fey in Manhattan are hooked on the stuff."

An uncomfortable silence spread as furtive glances darted around the room.

"Just say it," Alice said. "May got me hooked. She took possession of me the way she'd done with Alex. Only different, because I saw and heard, even felt every sick thing she did. I was so dusted, I didn't mind. All I cared about was more, that the supply would never end."

"Alice," Alex said, with Nimby's body cradled in his hands, "you don't have to do this."

"I do, brother, because while I know you love me, and Jerod…." Her words trailed. She stared at Nimby and then across at her real mother and the carbon copy, changeling. "Since Liam ripped May from inside of me, my life is pain. At first physical, wondering if I were going to die, though I guess we hafflings have a hardy constitution, and the occasional giant-salamander possession doesn't keep us down."

Her attempt at humor was met with silence as everyone stared at her.

"You are the girl who went down the hole," Marilyn said as she crossed to her daughter and attempted to hug her.

"Don't." Alice shrugged her off and pressed back against a wall. "If May has created an army of addicts, then it's an army that will not care if they live or die, as long as their supply is uninterrupted. A month after my last taste of dust, I truly believe that death is preferable to a life like this. And brother, despite what you said, it does not get better with time. True, the rip and tear of the first two weeks when I was withdrawing has gone. It did not kill me, though I understand that was a possibility. Maybe it's our unique constitution, half human and half fey. But now a month has passed. A month of getting up every day and wishing I was dead.

"Everything hurts. There's no color, no joy. And worse of all, I know that this will never get better." She looked around with red-rimmed eyes etched with dark circles. She looked at the floor, and like the curtain coming down, her hair hid her face.

No one spoke.

Silent seconds stretched into a minute.

Charlie's attention was pulled by a weird shimmer in the air. It hovered over Finn. "Finn, what's happening?"

Finn growled and convulsed.

"Holy mother of God," Flora gasped.

With all eyes now on him, Finn shucked off his human form, clothes and all, and was replaced with a massive Irish wolfhound, whose head and shoulders towered over the seated Katye. Unbidden, he strode with curiously dainty steps toward Alice.

He stopped in front of her and extended a paw into her hair-blocked line of sight.

"What?" she muttered and looked up. Despite the Hound's size, she appeared unafraid. "Whose dog is that?"

Flora answered. "It's the Hound, Alice."

"Oh."

The Hound lowered his head to where Alice could reach up and pet him, which she did.

"He's so soft," she said, letting her fingers play in the silk of his fur. Her expression softened as she did. "Nice doggie. Soft, like a puppy." Her voice took on a dreamy quality, free from her earlier anguish. For the first time in over a month, her mouth turned up into a smile.

The Hound moved in closer, his body next to Alice's as she let her hands roam across his broad, silky back.

"Hell no!" Jerod shouted as the Hound lifted his rear leg closest to Alice. He ran toward them.

"Don't!" Katye yelled.

He'd have been too late anyway.

A stream of dark amber pee that glittered in a shaft of light sprayed down Alice's leg. She didn't appear to mind. The expression on her face shifted from a smile to a serene daze. "Thank you," she whispered as she scratched between the Hound's ears. And with a voice of awe, "I feel better. I feel normal…."

Flora clapped her hands to the sides of her head. "We've just learned something new."

Thirty-Three

WITH SWORD in hand, battle blood raced through Redmond's veins. He stood in the Center's western courtyard and braced for what was to come. *It has fallen. All I have fought for.*

A hole had been pierced in the outer wall, and the wards had been breached. He didn't need to be told his tactical error. *When Finn left, she saw the opening and took it. But is that all? And here she comes.*

May, resplendent in her gold breastplate, sat upon her salamander self as hordes of dusted fay swarmed in behind her. At her side flew a creature half human and half praying mantis. He recognized her as May's closest confidant.

His gaze darted over the breached wall, and he searched for any sign of Finn or the Hound. *He got away.*

Behind him, students and guards trembled. The former, a small cadre of mixed fey, tried to look brave. The ogre guards did what they did: they grumbled and complained. "If you'd only let me backfill those positions, we wouldn't die so fast."

Screams filled the air.

High atop the back of her engorged salamander, May reveled in her triumph. "Your great center has fallen, Doctor, as I knew it would. Your pathetic attempts to confine me, to keep my kingdoms from me, have failed. You have failed. And now there's just one thing left before I put you out of your miserable existence. Tell me the location of the Hound. He has something that does not belong to him."

Schooling his features over a gut roiling with terror, Redmond knew *This is where I die.*

However, just as May had said, it was a day he had anticipated. So while he and several dozen beloved students and well-compensated guards remained to fight and to die, a thousand others now raced for their lives through a network of warded tunnels. Yes, she might hunt them down later, but at least for today, *Every second I buy will give safety to some. And maybe Finn...* the thought of him raised the ghost of hope. *No, he must stay away. Be safe, Finn. Be safe, my Hound.*

He held his ground and his sword as May, flanked by her dusted minions, advanced. He pictured Finn, the way he first met him and in his other forms. It kept his hand steady and his knees stable. He replayed that first kiss, their night together, and the morning after.

The air reeked of fairy fire. *Buy time.* "You lead an army of addicts," he shouted.

Her eyes narrowed, and she did not stop. "You could join them, Doctor."

"No, I got over that. I'm cured."

Her head cocked, the salamander, unconcerned by his sword and those of his quivering and grumbling backers, stomped toward him. Her broad head darted forward, and she bit his sword in half.

"This is not possible," Dorothea spat out. "Once dusted...."

Redmond thought to run but instead looked the salamander in the eye. *Here it comes.*

Its head darted about his own. She sniffed him from top to bottom and then back again.

The two Mays appeared perplexed. "Not possible. You're not dusted, and yet you were. You should be sick. There is no sign of that. Tell me the way of it."

"He lies," Dorothea chattered. "Bite off his head. He buys time and stalls the inevitable."

"No," May purred. "I will know of this."

So now I have two things that you want. Frightened as he was, it was hard to hide the smile, remembering how the Hound had peed on his stash and how over the course of a night's lovemaking he'd woken free from his addiction. *Every second, more get away.* "It is a process, my queen. A fusion of mortal chemistry and fey alchemy." *Every second....* "I can show you."

"Your Highness," Dorothea said.

"Yes, he buys time, but it will not matter. For I will end him. This is of use. Show me here. Show me now."

"The proof is in my chambers."

The salamander sniffed him again.

"I smell trickery, Doctor." May pointed to two pixies, Luluba and Seamus. Redmond stiffened.

"Excellent, those two will do," she said, and then to a pair of her dusted ogres, "I will snack on them… slowly. I will do it before your eyes, Doctor, if you do not give me what I want. So yes, let us go to your chambers for proof, and then you will quick quick like a bunny show me how to do this thing, how to undust the dusted. Then you will give me the Hound, and we will end this farce. It has gone on too long. It is time to take back what is mine. And it is time for others"—her gaze fixed on Redmond—"to be my just desserts."

Thirty-Four

FROM OUTSIDE New York University's Chemical Sciences Building, Finn, Alex, Jerod, Alice, Charlie, Lianna, and Frederick Flowers watched Liam approach the weekend guard. The blue-uniformed security officer, a paunchy guy in his midfifties, stared slack-jawed into Liam's eyes.

Alice whispered to her brother, "So that's the thing I do… he's way better at it."

Charlie growled under his breath. "Yeah, he's real good at it."

"Jealous much?" Finn asked.

"Can't help it. Though I know there's no reason for it. Makes me feel like a shit."

"With a dude that hot, you'd be crazy not to feel it."

"It's not just that's he's hot," Charlie said.

"I get it… got it. I was there. I saw him deliberately throw himself in front of her."

"He's good, Finn. I really love him."

A smile played across Finn's lips. Standing there with Charlie, who looked a lot like Rory, he realized that the ache in his chest was gone. In its place was a soft sadness at the loss of his best friend, but that other piece, that hole inside of him… gone. "Redmond."

"What'd you say?" Charlie asked.

Finn grinned. "I met someone."

"Really? And by the way, like the changes. I always thought of you as Rory's hot friend. But now… if I wasn't spoken for…."

"Thanks."

"So tell me about Redmond."

Before he could, Liam turned from the starry-eyed guard, who handed over his ID badge. "Come on," Liam said. "He'll be dazed for a couple hours, then good as new."

"Tell you later," Finn said as they pushed through the revolving glass door, bypassed the befuddled security man, and piled into an elevator.

"Is he going to be okay?" Alice asked Liam.

"Yeah, no permanent damage done."

"Teach me."

He looked at her. "You're stronger than you look."

"Tell me," she said as the others listened in.

"I've seen what dust does," Liam said. "Few recover. Those that do often walk like ghosts through the Unsee. You're well and truly better. Your eyes are clear. Tell me if you still crave."

She shook her head. "I got peed on. That seemed to do the trick."

"No symptoms at all?" her brother asked.

"No, Alex, though at some point we should talk about what it's like playing host to May. She's not really mad, you know."

"Are you kidding?" Alex replied as the elevator coasted to a stop, a bell dinged, and the door whooshed open.

"I'm not," she said as they followed Alex down the deserted corridor toward the labs. "I think we make the same stupid mistakes over and over. Maybe she's mad, but before we start saying that, we have to remember she's not human. She doesn't think like us. She's as close to a god as exists. And our rules and our silly sense of fairness, it's nothing to her. Why should it be?"

Alex stopped. "What happened to my sister? She's been replaced with—"

"You," Alice replied. "You think I don't listen. I saw what you had to do all those years to keep us out of another nightmare foster home. I'm grateful. But Alex, even you couldn't stop the worst of it."

He held her gaze. "I know. I'm sorry."

The others hung back, still in hearing range but knowing to give the brother and sister a moment amid the danger, loss, and chaos.

"You have nothing to be sorry for. I suppose in my case, being a dusthead, being possessed by May, even the stuff that happened all those years ago." With a sweep of her hand, she pushed the hair from her eyes and looked at him. "Alex, there's something I've always wanted to know and have never asked."

"I think I know."

"Did you kill Sean McGuire?" Referring to the foster father who had molested her and dozens of other children before falling to his death down the basement stairs.

Alex hesitated.

"It's okay if you don't want to tell me. No, on second thought, it's not. Because if you did, you shouldn't have to carry that alone."

He swallowed. "It was both of us. Nimby helped." Unable to speak through his tears, he led them to the end of the hall and a door marked Organic Lab II.

Lianna approached Finn as Liam used the guard's ID over the keypad. "Katye said we didn't have much time. What's happening back there? In the Unsee?"

All listened as they entered the massive room with its rows of narrow stainless-steel tables outfitted with alcohol burners and metal stools. Through the tall windows, they glimpsed Washington Square Park and the south-facing buildings.

"It's war. May has either eaten or addicted much of the population. The one safe place, the Center, is under siege. But here's the thing, and I'm not one for raining on parades… though apparently I might be pissing on one, if we're able to synthesize hound urine. How the hell do we get it back there? We're going to need a few thousand gallons of the stuff."

Alex walked over to them, his eyes moist. "Maybe yes, maybe no. Shit!" He gritted his teeth. Jerod put a hand on his shoulder as Alice rested her head against his side. He nodded, but the grief was too much. "I was given a pixie, and most of the time I was fucking mean to her."

Jerod smoothed circles on Alex's back. "She could be a pain in the ass," he said as his own tears fell.

Alex took a deep breath. "Yeah, she could." He looked to Finn. "Urine is mostly water. We need to find what yours is made of. It's going to be a crystal, like uric acid or something. Though I doubt we'll be that lucky. From there we can rehydrate when we get to the Unsee." He grabbed a Pyrex beaker and handed it to Finn. "Here. The restroom's down the hall."

"Be right back."

"You know," Charlie said to Liam. "We traveled to the Unsee in Engine Twenty-Five. It holds three thousand gallons. And talk about something designed to spray, 'cause that is what we're talking about. Pissing on the masses."

"What? But how?" Jerod asked. "We know the rules…. Nimby gave her life for them. And who the fuck set those twisted things up?"

"I think we now know," Liam said.

"And?" Charlie asked.

"While we don't lie, the fey certainly twist and conceal. The rules, the Mist, the separation of the realms, this is all the doings of Lizbeta and Katye. All part of their efforts to contain May. That it backfired on them both, trapping Lizbeta in the Mist and Katye to the See, was not deliberate. Katye was telling the truth."

"Or some fraction of it," Alex blurted. "While I can't believe I'm saying this, it almost makes you feel bad for May."

"I told you, brother," Alice said. "She's not as crazy as everyone says. This is payback. But more." She looked at Alex and Jerod, Charlie and Liam. "She had her heart broken. What they did to her was cruel, like pig's blood at the prom cruel."

"I get that," Alex said. "Do you want me to feel sorry for her?"

"I don't know, Alex. I'm glad she's out of me. And for the first time in over a month, I don't wish I was dead. But when May was in control, it wasn't all bad, and I haven't sorted that out. But something about the way she approached the world, and not the 'let's eat everyone we can' part, but her confidence, her absolute belief that she was meant to rule, it felt natural. It fit. You know, like the best pair of sneakers you've ever had."

Lianna spoke. "Truth. Some are born to rule. Those are the shoes that fit." She and Frederick nodded in unison.

"That's just strange," Jerod said. "So bouncing from freak show to freak show.... Charlie, your turn. I still don't understand how you got a fire truck into the Unsee."

"No clue. I was asleep. It was in a dream, or so I thought."

Liam interjected, "We were both dusted, and...." A shy smile spread across his beautiful face. "It was in that first bit of love. So there was lots of magic, fey and human at the same time. Don't know if that's the solution, but...."

"It had to have been the dust," Charlie said. "And that neither one of us broke was because of love." He broke into a grin. "And that's kind of the proof right there that you didn't glamour me into loving you."

Liam was about to speak when Finn returned with a beaker full of golden pee. Alice giggled. "There's glitter in it."

Alex took it and held it up in a shaft of light that streamed through the window. "It does sparkle. Did you put something in it?"

"Just get on with this," Finn said. "So I have twinkly pee. We already figured there's something different about it."

Alex put the beaker on a lab table, flicked on a burner, poured Finn's piss into an Erlenmeyer flask, and hooked that up to a clear reflux chimney.

The liquid started to boil, and a dense fog climbed up the Pyrex tubes. A colorless liquid trickled out as Finn's sample shrank.

"It really sparkles," Alice remarked as the sample diminished and darkened.

"I've never seen anything like that," Alex agreed as whatever was in the flask caught the light and refracted it back in brilliant golden bursts.

Finally, when all the liquid had separated out, what remained was a dark gold crystal that crackled with light and energy.

"Pretty… and weird," Alice said. "Now what?"

"This way," Alex said, and he led them through the maze of workbenches toward a locked door with a sign—Authorized Personnel Only.

Alex waved the guard's badge over the keypad. Nothing happened.

"I got this," Finn said, and with his bare hands he twisted the handle and broke the lock.

"Big and strong," Charlie remarked.

"Do not flirt, Charles Michael Fitzgerald," Liam said.

Charlie cracked a smile and grabbed Liam's hand. "Now you know what it feels like." Before Liam could respond, Charlie kissed him.

"Woof," Finn said, and he threw open the door.

"What is all this stuff?" Alice asked as they took in the computer equipment that looked a bit like an industrial copier.

"It's a mass spectrometer," Alex said as he carefully spooned a tiny bit of the crystal into the sample chamber. "Every compound resonates with a unique frequency. It's like a fingerprint. If it exists, this machine will tell us what it is."

Finn muttered, "And if it doesn't exist?"

"We're screwed." Alex pressed Start.

Within seconds the LED displayed a bar graph with several spikes. An integrated printer spat out the hard copy.

Alex took that and fed a series of related numbers into a computer next to the spectrometer. "Crap!"

"What?" Jerod asked.

"No match. Either there's a contaminant, or—" He stared at the screen and then at the printout. "Wait a minute." He grabbed the flask with the remaining golden crystal and ran back to the lab. The others trailed behind. He dissolved the crystal into a second solvent and again attached the refluxer. He looked back. "I think I know what it is."

"You going to tell us?" Finn asked.

"I need some dust to be sure," Alex said.

"Sadly," Lianna said, "I know where we can find some."

"I'll go with you," Jerod said. He looked to Charlie. "Okay if we borrow Liam for a bit? We might need his special talents."

"Great," Charlie replied.

"It's my pleasure," Liam said.

"You think there's dust in my pee," Finn stated as he helped Alex set up the apparatus.

"We'll find out."

They stared as fluid bubbled up the chimney, only instead of clear, this time the fluid was gold, and what remained at the bottom of the flask sparkled like diamonds with a bit of a red-silver goo that clung to the original fluid line in the flask.

"Damn," Alice said. Her expression clouded as the familiar smell of baking cookies wafted out.

"You're right, definitely dust," Finn said as he and Alex took the golden liquor, set up a second chimney, removed the solvent, and were left with a smaller mound of a metallic substance the color of gold. There was also a bit of the rust-red goo. Its molecular structure, altered by the solvent, had clumped into a ball about half the size of a pencil eraser.

"Now we're getting somewhere," Alex said as he took the three products back into the analytics room. One by one he put them through the spectrometer. The metallic white powder had no matches in the catalog of known substances. The gold turned out to be gold. And the goo was organic with a strong peak for keratin and a bit of noise that was probably the red pigment.

Alex looked from the readout to Finn. "Give me a piece of your hair."

Finn gripped a couple of strands on his chest and plucked them out. No stranger to the lab or the equipment, he looked over Alex's shoulder. "It's a match. I have hair in my pee."

"Apparently."

"That can't be good."

Not even ten minutes later, Liam, Lianna, and Jerod returned with two dust bunnies they'd purchased in Washington Square Park. Even on visual inspection, it was clear they were a match for the white powder. To be certain, Alex ran a sample through the machine.

Jerod placed a hand on his back as if reading his thoughts. "It was her choice to do it, Alex."

Alex tried to focus as tears streamed. "She loved coming to the lab, would make me crazy and write stuff in my log books that I'd have to try and explain to the TA."

"I know."

"Why?" Alex said. "Why did she do it?"

Jerod paused. "For you, for me, for all of us. She knew what she was doing."

"She's really gone."

"Yeah."

Finn quietly ran a finger through the two substances. "Fairy dust and gold. A marriage of magic and mortal. It's symmetry. One has the power to enslave humans and the other fey. Combined…."

"It cured me of my addiction," Alice said.

"So now"—Finn looked over their tiny band—"all we need is to mix up a couple thousand gallons of the stuff, get it into a truck, and drive said fire engine into another dimension."

Alex pulled up the calculator on his cell. He punched in figures on the pad and quickly guesstimated the amounts of the three ingredients. "On the plus side, it's mostly water. From there we're looking at three parts of fairy dust to one pound of gold dust. So." He groaned. "Let's say five pounds of 24K gold dust and fifteen pounds of fairy dust."

Charlie's phone rang. It was Gran. "Charlie, Katye thinks she knows how you and Liam made it through. It was the dust, and you must have attracted a nightmare."

He put it on speaker. "Come again."

"A puka, Charlie, so it wasn't a real engine that can carry thousands of gallons of whatever you hope to mix up."

"This doesn't sound like good news."

"It's not."

Katye got on the line. "Charlie, tell me if Finn and the others can hear."

"They can."

"I believe there is a way, Finn. Pukas are strong, they are ancient, and they are deadly. There will be a cost, and we haven't much time. But like you, they are two-natured. The puka will come if the Hound… if you… call him. Tell me the answer to the riddle of your piss."

"Fairy dust, gold, and a bit of hound hair. All together they neutralize the dust and the addiction. Problem is we need a lot of all three."

"Gold I have, Finn. And the dust is out there. May left more than enough when she ravaged our city. And you seem perplexed by the bit of fur."

"I'm not," Liam interjected. "It's a magic joke."

"Exactly," Katye said.

"Confused human here," Charlie replied.

Alice groaned. "That's just cheesy…. Hair of the dog that bit you, Charlie."

"Yes," Katye explained. "It's a principal both magic and scientific; a thing may be both cause and cure. We cannot delay. And now we know what must happen. The faster the better. I sense horrible things are happening… have happened in the Unsee. I pray we're not too late."

Finn narrowed his gaze and pictured Katye. Like Liam, and Alice too, he saw the effect she had on the others as they hung on her every word. He wasn't buying it. "What aren't you telling us?"

There was a pause. "I'm sorry, Finn. But I believe the Center has fallen. I'm truly sorry." She hung up.

Finn stood slack-jawed. He pictured Redmond, and then Nimby who'd given her life to save others. Rage pulsed through his chest and down to his clenched fists. He threw back his head and howled and howled and howled.

Thirty-Five

REDMOND LED the two halves of May and her entourage up to his chambers. He dragged his feet, and his knees shook. *Buy time. Just buy time. Every second buys a life.*

Her dusted ogres, some who had once been members of his own security force, restrained his two pupils. Luluba's lip trembled as she struggled to hold back tears. Seamus, unable to take his eyes off the white salamander, seemed frozen, like an animal who knew it was doomed.

"This is where I kept my dust." He led them to the small chest.

Both Mays sniffed its contents. Her humanoid half ran a finger through the interior and brought it to her nose. She turned to Redmond, and her costume shifted from a gold battle breastplate and riding britches to army camo. "Tell me." She stood inches from his face and stared into his eyes.

He could not move. *Every second I keep her here, more go free.* The thought brought small comfort.

"Hmm." She appeared perplexed. "You are truly free from the dust."

"Yes, my queen." He searched his memory for the hours he'd spent with her, hunting for anything that might buy another minute. He pictured the tunnels under the Center. She would not know of those. *Is there a way I can save Luluba and Seamus?* He could not turn his head to see, but his other senses were riveted on the terrified sprites. *What do I know of her? What can I use?* He stared into her amber eyes as a stiff gold collar of lace formed around her neck and her long hair braided itself into an intricate woven do. *She is driven. She is the most powerful creature in the three realms. None of that matters.*

"Oh, Doctor, I can almost hear your thoughts. You know that when I eat you, for the briefest time, I will share your emotions, your memories… your love."

Her mouth twisted as if she'd tasted something bitter. "Tell me where he has gone. Tell me where my little dog has scampered to."

And this is the heart of things... literally. The Hound has her heart... my heart. Stay away, Finn. She will gut you like a fish. Be safe.

"So silent," she whispered, her lips inches from his own. She held a finger before his eyes and grew the nail into a two-inch talon. She placed it at the notch of his neck. "But no, you're the snack that's saved for later. These two, on the other hand—"

Like a vise had been removed from around his neck, he could move. He followed her with his eyes.

"So tender." She sauntered toward Luluba and Seamus. "You can't imagine the food I had to endure in my sister's mist. Too much troll and ogre. All so brutish... but powerful."

"You are all powerful," he said, his tone the most soothing he could muster. His hope fixed on a desperate gambit. *Her ego. Play to her ego.* Through pursed lips, his words flowed on the currents of his ability to comfort and soothe. "I see where so many have horribly underestimated you. They betrayed you in the most cruel manner imaginable."

"Yes." With talon extended, she turned as the salamander joined her, and like a monstrous puppy, it settled on the ground around her.

"You are magnificent," he said without guile as he beheld her, now in a glittering gold gown, her hair laced with jewels, surrounded by a throne of the white monster. She sat on the beast's accommodating hide.

"I will say this, Doctor. You may be the only one in all these many centuries who understands. The stories of me, how I am painted. It is not fair. It is not true."

"I do see that. None of this was your fault. And now you seek to undo wrongs of the past. To restore an earlier balance. To regain what should be yours. It is horrible, unforgivable, what they did to you."

She winced.

"I'm sorry." His words like honey to a bear. "I did not mean to remind you of your sorrow."

"But you did, Doctor." She braced a hand on the salamander's flank. "There are so many layers to my sisters' betrayal. But worse, they thought to fool me. They thought me stupid. That Lizbeta presumed to wrap me in a fog, and the other.... you know of what I speak."

"Yes. They worked potent magics on you. They made you forget how magnificent you are. They made you forget"—and as the words left his mouth, he knew he had to say them, and he regretted them—"your heart and the Hound."

She gasped. "I should have known it was him. It was always the Hound." She glared at him. "Seriously, Doctor. Now is not the time for your tricky tricky."

Crap!

"Tell me his location."

He fell onto bended knee. "He traveled into the Mist."

"Tell me his purpose."

While not a lie, Redmond shaded the truth and colored his voice with magic. "To return a dying pixie to her family in the See."

"Tell me how. There are few ways to travel without breakage, whether human or fey. It's only the haffling, the puka, the true lovers, the sacrificial lamb… and…. Oh, Doctor, it's all Lizbeta's mist. It clears before my eyes. These are all her magics that she has set against me."

She stood up from her fleshy throne and glared at him. "You hide something from me." The salamander rose at her side as she crossed back to him. With death-tipped fingers, she stroked his cheek.

He stared at the floor and smelled the salamander's fetid breath. He heard its jaw unhinge.

"I am, my queen, and I will tell you all, but—"

"No buts, Doctor. Tell me."

"I hesitate, because to tell you all, I will reveal things you've shared with me in private. If it is your wish that I lay all bare, I will do so, but there may be things you'd not want others to hear."

The Mays looked around the room, dusted ogres, the restrained students… Dorothea. "A couple good meals and all who hear will be dead. But not you, Dorothea. Of all, you are the only one who has stayed true."

"I am that, Your Highness."

"As you wish," Redmond said. "Then I will start with the time when you and the Hound were joined in the bliss of bodily union. When his flesh and your flesh—"

"Wait! Leave us." She turned to the guards. "Empty the room. I would be alone with this one. You too," she said to Dorothea.

Redmond caught Luluba's eye. He gave her the briefest of nods. Out of the queen's sight, she'd soon be out of mind… and with that came hope for her and Seamus.

He returned his gaze to the floor. And drawing on his magic, he launched into a retelling of May's story, with her as a shimmering heroine. *Buy time.* "Those who should have followed and loved you tricked and betrayed you, and still…." His voice filled the room and brought her a sense of peace. He painted her sorrows with broad strokes. "You have overcome tremendous obstacles and enemies. And still, your greatness is not appreciated."

"They were mean to me," she stated, lulled by the drift of his voice and the warmth of his compassion, like a mother's kiss.

"They were, and in the cruelest way imaginable."

"I could eat them."

"You could. Though you did get some revenge, as their magic bounced off of your own."

"Yes, what goes around." She smiled. "I know what you're doing, Doctor. I allow it… for now. But stop with the prevarications." Her tone lost its dreamy lilt. Her amber eyes and the salamander's flame-red ones bore into him. "Tell me of the Hound."

Redmond grasped just how weak his abilities were in the face of hers. "He took back the houndstone. Lizbeta gave it to me. She told me it would protect me as I looked after you."

"Apparently my sister was wrong. Though it raises the question of how she got it."

"From your other sister."

"I will eat them both. Tell me his location."

"The See."

"Of course. Tell me his intent."

Every second and more go free. Redmond gauged May's responses. He played out his vocal magic but hid it in a more conversational tone. "He seeks out the haffling children."

"Vile creatures. But useful."

"Yes." His words again washed over queen and salamander. "They are of use, for they represent safe passage."

"I've ridden two of the three," she offered. "Pity that the last is a boy. Tell me what you know of him."

"I don't know anything," Redmond admitted but added, "I'll tell you what I suspect."

"Do."

"That if I were his parents. I'd hide him well."

"They did," she said. "They nearly succeeded. But I huffed and I puffed and I—" She stopped in midsentence.

Redmond observed the shift in both sets of her features. The salamander shivered.

"Something went sideways," he offered.

"Yes. The boy and his parents fled from me. As you are clever, Doctor, speculate. Tell me where you think they'd flee."

"To the See," he said without pause. "It makes sense. The boy can travel unbroken. I cannot speak to the parents. But in desperate times…."

"Yes," she sighed. "It is tiresome."

"You have done so much, my queen. Surely, you deserve a rest."

Outside, day had darkened to dusk. Redmond did not stop. He helped May recall her greatest victories and let her know that she was not to blame for any misfortunes. He played priest and cheerleader. And while she never totally let down her guard and fully intended to eat him, his words were like a balm; they lulled and soothed. "I will save you for later," she muttered, close to sleep.

"As you wish, my queen."

The salamander had curled up by the fire. Its hide reflected the orange and reds of the flame as May in her glittery gold frock rocked in Redmond's favorite chair.

They have escaped, he thought and felt a sense of accomplishment. *I will die before the next sun, but it was not in vain. And Finn, my beautiful hound, be safe, and be free. You brought me love, and I will die without regret.*

May's head nodded forward, though one of the salamander's eyes stayed fixed on him. *She is nearly asleep; perhaps….* Set to change the tone of his voice and the tune of his magic to that which would lull her further, a scream unlike any he'd heard shredded the night.

The two Mays startled. The beast's tongue flicked the air to try to taste the cacophonous intrusion.

Redmond ran to the window, not caring that the Mays were right at his side. They all stared out toward the Western Sea as the horrible noise grew. And with it, in the distance, spinning red, white, and yellow lights flashed from atop an unfathomable metal beast that raced on round black feet.

"Tell me!" she shrieked and grabbed Redmond by the shoulders. "Tell me."

"I do not know," he said. *Here it comes.* He did not feel fear or even resignation. He closed his eyes and waited for the kiss of death.

"Tell me," she repeated.

He opened his eyes. His ears filled with the wail of the creature that approached. "It is not a banshee."

"Obviously."

"It is not of this world." And while he had no illusion about his imminent death, an idea sparked as the flashing lights found their way into his chamber. *Finn.*

Thirty-Six

AT THE wheel of the submerged Engine Twenty-Five, Finn breathed through the respirator as the fabled black mare with a chain yoked around its powerful neck did the impossible—tugged a tenton vehicle from one world into another. His breath rasped in his ears as he held the neck of the breather tight to keep the water from rushing in and drowning him. He imagined the footage that had been shot through cell phones as they'd hurtled across the barriers of Riverside Park and plunged into the depths of the Hudson. He opened his eyes. There was nothing to see, just murky black. But that was nothing compared to the ice-cold terror as the frigid, algae-rich water had filled the cab. *Too late now*, he'd thought, his last clear image of the crazy horse thing that might drag them to their death.

Next to him sat Charlie and Liam. But his thoughts were on Redmond. Raised Catholic but not religious, Finn prayed. *Dear God, I know it's a cliché to call on you when the chips are down, and to be fair, I don't know if you exist or not. But please take care of those I love. Please help those who should not have come. Don't let Flora be broken by this trip. Let Charlie and Liam go on to have a happy life. Protect Alex and Jerod.* And like a child saying his prayers, he took inventory of all those who were in the back for this ill-advised trip. *Protect Alice, who has known too much suffering for someone so young.* He again thought of Gran. *I should never have let her come, Lord. She won't survive this. Why did I let her come?* But she'd insisted, against his protests and those of her grandson, Charlie. *Is she trying to do what Nimby did? Fuck! What have I done? I'm sorry for the F word, Lord. Don't let her be a sacrifice. And Lord, I know the Catholic gay thing and all, but please keep Redmond safe. And if I'm going to die and have my heart ripped out, if I could have one thing, let me see him again.* And because his own gran had taught and overtaught the words, they came unbidden. *Now I lay me down to sleep….* It helped, some. *Why did I let Flora come?*

There had been no time to argue, and short of physically restraining her, she'd been adamant. "I will have this adventure," she'd insisted. Alex's changeling mother agreed to care for her brood of cats.

He, Charlie, and most of the others had tried to dissuade her. "Your family, Flora, how can you just leave them?"

"Gran, you're needed here," Charlie argued.

"I am truly blessed," she'd said as she'd taken her still steady hands to the clippers and shaved Finn's head and torso to provide the needed fur for the magic mix. "Yes, I have a beautiful family who loves me and I them. But when I was a little girl, I played with pixies like Nimby." Not stopping from her task, she'd cried. Her tears cut him deep. "As I approach the end of my life, I would be with them again. If just to see them. To know I was not mad. No, that's not it. I did see them. I want to be with them. It's that simple. And forgive me for the words that are about to leave my mouth, because, Charlie, I do love you, and my children and my grandchildren and… I have buried too many. I have learned to not think about the pain I carry and to focus on those I love. But when I was a little girl, living in poverty I did not understand. I'd follow the pixie tune as they called to me to come and play. I knew joy and happiness unlike anything before, or anything since. I am coming with, and unless you plan to chain me up and lock me in a closet, you will not stop me."

Katye made matters worse as she appeared from her closet with pillow-sized bags of pure gold dust. "Time moves different in the Unsee, Flora Fitzgerald. The few years you have here will be multiplied. And we have no time to argue."

With the raw ingredients of gold, fairy dust, and hound hair, they'd piled into Finn's Bureau of Fire Investigation SUV and driven to Charlie's station.

Liam and Alice glamoured the firefighters.

"Of course you can take it for a spin," Charlie's probie mate Kyle had said as he'd gazed into Liam's eyes and wondered why for the first time in his life he found a guy hot… really, really hot. *Charlie's a lucky man.*

In under fifteen minutes they'd mixed a slurry of gold, fairy dust, and hair, introduced it into the engine's three-thousand-gallon tank, and with lights and sirens ablaze, stolen a piece of FDNY equipment worth two-and-a-half-million dollars.

Charlie instructed the passengers in how to use the respirators. And as Finn's rational mind pointed out the insanity of what they intended to do, he'd driven toward the river. *At some point I'll wake up.* But what played foremost in his thoughts was *Redmond, I'm coming. Be okay. Be safe. Please.*

As he turned north onto the Henry Hudson, he rolled down his window and did as Katye instructed. He thought of the puka, a creature he'd glimpsed only in the pages of her ancient texts, and howled. The noise soared over the sirens. The passengers clapped hands to the sides of their heads, as even with the respirator hoods, it hurt. His call was answered by tens of thousands of dogs, the wolves and coyotes in Central Park Zoo, and one other beast, which like him was two-natured.

The connection with the puka hit him hard and fast. Like someone had picked up the phone. Wordless impressions and images flooded Finn. They came with threat, warning, and a reek of rotten eggs and algae. *Great, olfactory GPS. Just follow the stench.*

"What's happening, Finn?" Charlie asked.

"Our ride's here. Everybody hang on!" And he floored it.

Cars, cabs, and Uber did their best to veer out of his way as he raced north. They flew past the fifties and sixties, Finn's nose fixed on the puka's call.

"I can see what he sees," he said as he gripped the wheel and, with the practice born of decades, played the air horn to get sluggish motorists out of the way. One recalcitrant Lexus got the addition of the high-volume speaker. "FDNY, move over now!" And under his breath, "Fucking Jersey."

"Tell us what you see through the puka's eyes," Liam said.

"Water, and when he looks up, he sees the Cloisters."

"What is it about that place?" Charlie asked.

"No clue," Finn said as he calculated the blocks that remained. "Roll up your window." And then into the intercom for those in the back, "Respirators on tight. Windows shut. Pray."

They raced beneath the span of the George Washington Bridge to the lowest point in the highway, where joggers, skateboarders, and families with strollers enjoyed the beauty of the park and paths that lined the river.

Finn's heightened senses fixed on a disturbance in the water. *I'm really going to do this.*

"Here we go." He howled again, and with air horn and speakers on full, he searched for an opening in the Sunday traffic hurtling south. *Not good.* He cut the wheel to the left. The engine tore through the steel guardrails. Horns blared, and brakes shrieked as the fire engine did the unthinkable and barreled across three lanes of south-headed traffic. But it was a Sunday, and while he heard the scrape and crash of steel and plastic, *No one's dying... here.*

Hurtling toward the river, he caught his first glance of the great black puka as it arose from the river. Far larger than any horse he'd ever seen, its eyes like burning coals. The Hound took over. *Bye-bye brain,* he surrendered to whatever the Hound was, and with his foot heavy on the gas, they bounced across the dainty park at seventy miles an hour. They ripped limbs from ornamental trees, flattened flowerbeds, and then hurtled into the chill waters of the Hudson.

Now submerged and with all sense of time gone, Finn sensed a blush of light.

Water streamed off the windshield, and like a curtain being raised, a world appeared.

Conscious thought returned, but so too the part of him that was the Hound stayed connected with the puka. Like a tennis volley, rational thought and animal sensation bounced back and forth.

Just ride it. He don't smell so bad. Got to pee.

His breath caught as he stared past the puka's powerful head and neck while he pulled them forward with barely a ripple. He focused on the distant shore, to a citadel of white. *Redmond, I am coming.* He observed his connection to the puka. *It's both leash and lead. There is no malice toward us. There is...* he searched for words to equal the emotions that roiled off the puka.

Like a connoisseur with a fine wine, he caught hints of resignation, of weariness, and of hope.

He wondered about his passengers as he cautiously let go of the respirator and slid it off his head. *How many are still alive? And Gran, with nothing or no one protecting her. We should not have let her come.*

He pressed the intercom. *No way any of the electronics are still good.* But it crackled and clicked, and sure enough, it was loud and clear. "Head count."

Like in gym class, those in the back identified themselves.

"Flora."

"Alex."

"Marilyn."

"Alice."

"Jerod."

"Adam."

He glanced from the tugboat puka to Charlie and Liam. If not for their dire circumstances, he would have commented on how cute they looked holding one another, Liam held tight in Charlie's arms. *What must that be like? Get through this alive, you moron, and find out.*

What if it's too late? If he's already dead? Like an elephant had stomped on his chest, Finn gasped. "Nine against an army," he muttered, *and two too young and one too old.* He caught strong whiffs of fairy fire and sea air.

He stared at the spires of Redmond's beloved Center. Plumes of smoke rose from within.

His wards failed.

"She has breached the Center," Liam said. "This is bad."

Cold and wet, Finn struggled to hold back despair. *What will we find?* His thoughts reached out to the puka. There was no answer, only urgency as the creature pressed toward the shore.

Finn smelled the others' fear, and he heard the sounds of panic and destruction from the shore. "I will not give in. Redmond could still be alive." His words rang false and triggered echoes from years back, wondering if Rory would rise from the ashes of 9/11. He did not, and now he stared at another tower, in another world, under attack and likely to fall.

Charlie spoke. "So what's the Center? You said you tried to seek asylum there."

Liam flicked his nose. "No questions, love. Please."

"Right."

"So?"

Finn held his breath as the puka tugged Engine Twenty-Five toward a flat white-sand beach. Its front hooves sought purchase in the sand, and the truck's tires connected with the sandy bottom of the Western Sea.

The puka, for the first time in the crazy voyage, strained to drag the front tires onto where the waves gently lapped the shore. Its shoulders sagged. It stopped and turned back. Its red eyes sparked in the sun.

Finn sensed the connection with the beast break like a tow chain letting go.

"What the hell. Here goes nothing." With a lump in his throat, he pressed the ignition button.

There was a silence that warped and expanded.

His gut clenched. He heard a click. *It's flooded. Of course it's flooded.* And then the impossible. The engine roared to life. "Thank you." *Thank you, God.* His eyes fixed on the beach. His body attuned to the thrum of the engine, he answered Charlie's question. "The Center was the last safe place in this world. It's Redmond's."

"Your guy?"

Finn hit the gas. He both felt and heard the churn of sand and shell beneath the tires. "Charlie, you stop asking questions or—Crap!" The front of the vehicle rose up as the rear wheels dug deep into the sea floor.

"We're not moving," Liam stated. "Not in the way we—"

The truck lurched. Finn braced his feet into the floor as his hand shot out to keep Charlie and Liam from smashing into the windshield.

In the rear camera, dotted with water, Finn spotted the puka, its head braced against the back of Engine Twenty-Five. As it pushed, Finn again felt the connection. It was ancient and had nothing to do with his human self and everything to do with the Hound. Unbidden thoughts flashed through his mind. *We're connected, you and I. And this Hound thing is old as fuck... as are you, my friend.*

The puka snorted, the fire engine's rear tires found enough purchase on the slick rock, and being careful not to spin out, Finn eased on the gas.

Riveted on the Center and the portion of its outer walls that had crumbled, he felt guilt and urgency. He gritted his teeth. "She came through just where I left. She sensed when Redmond lowered the wards. This is my fault."

"Don't do that, Finn," Charlie warned.

"The past cannot be undone," Liam added. "But it can be redeemed. Wrongs can be righted, and heroes sometimes save the day. This is war, Finn Hulain. You may not have fought one, but the Hound has."

"Right," Finn said as the truck gained momentum. Its broad tires churned over beach and dune. *Come on, doggy, let's see what we got.* A growl rose from his belly, and with it came an image of a massive dog with its jaws clamped around a wide-eyed and heavily armed foe. "Sounds good," Finn said, *throw them off-balance*. He flicked on the lights and sirens and gunned the engine.

We are Finn, and we are the Hound. He thought of the stories Gran read to him and Rory. Tales that always insisted they were true but invariably led to the theft of forty thousand cattle. Or those where his namesake, Coohulain, single-handedly defeated twelve thousand soldiers. *We are Hulain, and we are the Hound. And we will save Redmond. And we will lick his face.* "What the—"

"No questions," Liam warned.

Finn grinned.

"Tell us what is funny," Liam stated, his own gaze glued to the rapidly changing scenery through the windshield.

"I think I broke this time."

Liam turned and eyed him, from his booted feet to his peach-fuzz shorn head. "You are not broken, Finn Hulain. You are merely more of the creature you were meant to be."

Aiming the truck through copses of trees and broad flower-filled meadows, Finn smelled and tasted the changing air. "Yes." He chuckled. "I want to lick Redmond."

"He will enjoy that," Liam replied.

The roar of the engine and the wail of the sirens pulsed through him. He steered the truck over level meadow toward a gravel road atop an embankment. It led straight to the Center and ended at the broad moat that surrounded the vast fields that encircled Redmond's city. The bridge across had been retracted. It was literally the end of the road.

"There's got to be a way across." He remembered how Redmond had just lifted into the air and flown without effort.

"There is not," Liam replied. "Not if they don't want to let you in."

He started to brake, not wanting to send them all hurtling into the water. His gaze caught on something keeping pace with the truck. "We're not alone." In the side mirror his eyes met the puka's. A shiver trickled down his spine and brought a certainty of action. "The hound and the horse," he murmured. *This feels familiar.* He shifted his foot from the brake and slammed on the gas. "Respirators on," he shouted into the intercom. "Brace yourselves." And like a team of synchronized divers, the puka and Engine Twenty-Five shot off the road, arced briefly into the air, and then plunged into the moat's deep and critter-filled waters.

Thirty-Seven

As the two Mays, who were seconds from biting off Redmond's head, startled at the unfamiliar wail coming from the shores of the Western Sea, he bolted for his closet. While he'd believed the wards around the Center were impenetrable, he'd also worked in contingencies. He locked the door behind him, grabbed a sword from the wall, and pressed a panel to reveal an arched window with a balcony.

Behind him, the salamander ripped at the door. Her talons dug deep.

No time! he thought as the panel slid shut behind him. With his breath fast and his heart pounding, he looked down. *No.* The devastation below tore at him. The horrible scream that had startled them all was a fitting background for this apocalypse. Bodies lay everywhere, and hordes of addicted fey shattered windows and broke down doors. They stole or destroyed anything of value. An ogre with a battle-ax, who had been an inmate levels above May, spun circles in the square below. Every few twirls he'd stop and viciously lop off the arms and heads of ancient statues.

"This is now in the past. It cannot be undone." He took to the air.

He knew it was a temporizing measure. *She may be broken, but she will find me. Do I stay or do I go?* He searched for the source of the horrible noise, *like a hound out of hell.*

What his eyes landed on forced his hand. For in the alley next to his tower, the ogres that had escorted the wing-shackled Seamus and Luluba from his chamber were high on dust and had backed the two sprites against a wall. Their intent was clear. They had the munchies, and his two brilliant pupils were nothing more to them than a savory blue-and-green snack.

With sword outstretched, he flew toward them.

He alit in a concealed alcove behind the lumbering trio, two who had begun the day as members of his security force. Their uniforms were in tatters, and the chomping of their jaws added a grinding percussion to the wail that grew even louder. The third was another freed sociopath. This one—Snark—had the gluttonous eating disorder, BED. He had been incarcerated after wiping out entire colonies of brownies.

One against three he knew was hopeless. But the determination on Luluba's face and Seamus's wide-eyed panic gave him no choice. He heard his own words rattle in his head: *"Sometimes, in the face of death, we either fight or bow down to the will of tyrants. The price of freedom is not free."*

The murderous inmate who had gorged repeatedly on defenseless brownies swung his ax and sang in a deep baritone. The words were barely audible over the siren's roar. "Chop you into bits and nibble on your bones. Grind you into paste and spread you on my scones."

The hell you will! Redmond gripped his sword, swung out of his hidey-hole, and shouted at the ogre, "Hey, fatso, the last thing you need is scones!"

The ogre roared and turned. "Don't call me fat!"

Redmond widened his stance as recognition lit in the ogre's dust-glazed eyes.

"I know you," he roared. His two compatriots stood by his side, their focus split between their quavering snack at the alley's dead end and their ex-boss wielding a sword. "You locked me up. You made me hungry."

"He's puny," one remarked.

Their escaped leader cocked his head. "He's got more meat than they."

"That's for sure," Redmond said. He ripped the top of his robe open and ran a hand across his chest. "Much more meat." He hazarded the briefest glance at Luluba, who unlike the frozen Seamus could act in a crisis. "And you're hungry, Snark. Always so hungry. It's never enough." He nuanced his voice, but with the chaos and the alien roar, his magic barely carried the few yards that separated them.

"Hungry, so hungry," the ogre replied, and he advanced on Redmond, who matched his each step forward with two steps back. His goal was to draw the three of them from the alley mouth and give Luluba and Seamus a chance to escape. His mind skittered over possibilities as he tugged with his words at the three dusted ogres. In quieter times, he'd used Snark's fascinating case to teach his students about esoteric eating disorders. *"It's the hunger,"* he'd instruct. *"Food for them has become nearly as strong a narcotic as dust. Tragic if you think about it. Because it's possible, though not easy, to become free from a dust addiction. But one has to eat, and so abstinence from the substance of your addiction is never possible."* The other two were pure followers. They'd attached to Snark as they had to his head of security, Gark. *He must be dead.*

With sword in hand, he continued his backward walk. His senses drank in fresh dangers: the crash of broken glass from homes and businesses being looted, the screams of those who had not been able to flee as they defended their families. *Luluba and Seamus know of the tunnels. Just a bit more and they can flee.*

"I'm hungry," Snark whined.

Before Redmond could toss back a scrap of soothing magic, the eight-foot ogre squatted on his powerful thighs and sprang into the air. He landed a yard from Redmond, who reflexively raised his sword.

Snark spun his ax in easy loops as saliva dribbled from the corners of his fleshy lips. "Hungry."

Redmond tracked the rhythm of the ax. He darted to the side, which brought him within arm's reach of another ogre. He slashed up and cut deep into the howling beast's forearm just as the third ogre jumped overhead and landed at his back, cutting off his escape.

But as he did, Luluba grabbed a piece of wood, and with Seamus at her back, she headed toward him.

"No," Redmond shouted. "Run!"

"No," Luluba yelled back as she headed toward Snark with the intent of beaning him with the board. With her bound wings and shackled feet, her movements were slow and awkward.

"Run," Redmond cried as he tried to spin free from the tightening trio of ogres, one who howled in pain, and Snark, who was in the throes of his hunger lust.

Luluba gritted her teeth and slammed the board down on Snark's head. He threw back his arm and sent her flying into a heap against a wall.

She got back up, but now Seamus grabbed the same board and swung it with all he had at the back of Snark's legs.

The ogre's knees barely shook as his ax picked up speed and he stared at Redmond.

Just as Snark revved into the final rotation, a drop of rain fell in his right eye. He blinked, and his arm faltered.

Redmond caught the glitter of something falling from the cloudless sky as he seized the opening and pivoted. The ax whistled by his side and slammed to the ground.

Snark grunted. His comrades closed in for the kill.

Redmond felt a faint breeze and used it to sweep through an opening between his attackers. It gained him a good thirty feet, and if he'd chosen to run, he could have. He glared at Luluba and Seamus, now both armed with boards. He knew their behavior was due to his teachings. It gave him no comfort. *But if they die, it is with free will. And so we fight.* Drawing on his encyclopedic knowledge of ogre psychopathology—*If I can take out the alpha, the two followers will be left adrift*—he taunted Snark. "In the daylight, I can see how fat you really are. Though fat doesn't cover it. You're beyond obese." He remembered sessions with Snark, where the origins of his disorder were laid bare from a childhood filled with deprivation, parental neglect, and frequent bullying. "Your poor mother. I can see why she abandoned you." And while it went against all his professional ethics, Redmond retrieved the most painful memory that Snark had divulged in a tear-filled session. "She burned all of your toys before she left. She held Jang Jang, your favorite cuddle creature, the one you'd cry into every night, she held it over the fire, and she dropped it in." He modulated his voice to that of a female ogre's. "No one will love you. No one will ever love you."

Redmond's words had their desired effect.

Snark roared. He lowered his head and, in a blind rage, closed the yards that separated them.

Redmond kept his sword down and his eyes and ears focused on Snark's charge as raindrops tickled his cheek. The ground trembled. He quieted his thoughts, slowed his breath, and kept his grip loose.

With barely two yards between them, Redmond feinted to the right. Snark had too much forward momentum and couldn't make the correction. He turned his head as Redmond brought down the sword and sliced it clean off.

Blood spurted high into the air.

Luluba and Seamus looked from him to the decapitated Snark and his twitching torso to the remaining ogres.

While Redmond's earlier assessment of them being followers was accurate, what he had not calculated was dust munchies.

"More for me," one muttered as he turned and advanced on Seamus.

The other looked at Redmond with his bloodied sword. "That one's too much trouble. I call green."

"I got blue."

But before either could make good on their threats, a female voice cut through the incessant noise. "There you are, you tiresome little man."

All heads turned and beheld Queen May, resplendent in a bloodred gown astride the back of the great white salamander.

And that's when the rain, a twinkly golden one fueled by swirling winds, began to fall hard and fast.

Thirty-Eight

FOR THE second time that day, Finn watched the puka pull, and then, through the rear camera, push Engine Twenty-Five onto dry land. With lights and sirens twirling and wailing, they made land twenty yards back from where May and her hordes had breached the Center. Bloodied bodies and broken fey were everywhere.

"It is war," Liam said, his words drowned in the siren's roar.

"This better work," Finn replied as he and Charlie hustled to unroll two hoses. Without words, they stuck them both into the moat and sucked in three thousand gallons of water to mix with pure gold, fairy dust, and hound hair.

"Tell us what to do," Alex said as they watched and waited.

"Two teams," Finn instructed. "Charlie's going to turn these on full and hard. Alex, you take the head of one, and I'll get the other. Jerod, Marilyn, Adam, you're with him." He smiled. "Gran, get behind me, Alice, Liam, you too. Charlie, tell us when."

"Aim high," Charlie added, his fingers poised to flip the switches. Finn widened his stance. "Brace yourselves."

The others followed his lead as Charlie turned on the flow and cranked it to full. The thick hoses filled and pulsed to life.

"High," Finn yelled above the siren as pressurized and reconstituted wolfhound pee shot up and out.

At their side, the puka stomped the ground. It caused two waterspouts to form on the moat's surface. They danced and twisted and jumped from the broad lake and attached like dervishes to the liquid being shot from the hoses.

"Holy crap!" Charlie shouted as he grabbed a section of hose behind Alice and tried to steady it. He yelled to Alex, "Hold tight."

"I'm trying."

"Keep your weight low," Finn instructed. "Dig in with your legs and feet."

"Got it."

With hearts pounding, they watched the golden storm engulf the Center. Time stretched, and what seemed like hours took less than fifteen minutes to drain the truck.

The puka's water cyclones shrank and then died away as they lost fuel. The hoses flattened, and deafened by the siren, the band of travelers stood frozen.

Finn moved first. He laid down his hose, and not taking his gaze off the crumbled wall, he climbed into the engine's cabin and flicked off the siren and then the lights.

The silence echoed as they stared into the breached citadel.

Finn hopped down from the truck. The puka snorted, and almost as one they bounded toward the boulders of the destroyed wall.

"I've got to find Redmond," he shouted. His words fell away, along with his clothes and his human form. He sniffed the air. His broad shaved head darted back and forth, desperate to find the scent of his love. He snarled as they passed creatures wakening from dust lust with eyes filled with bewilderment.

Ogres with blood-covered swords and axes dropped their weapons as shameful memories of what they'd done intruded.

The reek of blood and death made it difficult for Finn to focus.

The puka too seemed out of her element, or so he thought as she leapt into the badly damaged fountain in the central square. She snorted in the Hound's direction and pawed at the shallow waters.

He followed her lead and leapt into the body-strewn pond, where sparkly sharp-toothed fish feasted on their unexpected banquet.

The puka lowered her head, and the Hound hopped upon her back. He was not graceful and did not care as he slunk low and held fast.

The water swirled beneath the puka's hooves. It picked up speed as it spun ever faster, and like an elevator, a water cyclone grew and carried hound and horse high into the sky.

And he caught the scent. *Redmond.* He smelled his love's fear and courage, but all that mattered, as the Hound grinned and his tongue lolled, was that *Redmond.* He howled and barked with joy. *He's alive!*

Thirty-Nine

THROUGH THE oscillating wail of the alien noise, May sensed threat as she raced on the back of her salamander self down the circular stairs. She was furious and frightened and determined to hunt down and eat her fleeing doctor. In truth, he had brought her clarity. It helped and it didn't. *I have lost so much. Even this and even now*, assessing her current divided state and the fact that somewhere in all of this travel between realms she had been robbed of the most basic ability to fly. *One more thing for which they will pay.*

Her salamander self was less reflective. She lapped the air with her tongue. The taste of the doctor was clear and near. She bounded sure-footedly down the hundreds of stairs with her other self queen-like upon her back.

They hit the ground and, without stopping, charged through the door.

Something is wrong, May thought, unable to appreciate the chaos and bloodshed that was all around. Red, green, blue, and lavender blood spattered against the Center's glittering white cobbled streets and marble walls brought her no joy. Even her hunger, while never slaked, was more of a dull pit. *Something is wrong. And what makes that scream?* Having glimpsed the red metal beast from the balcony where her doctor had taken flight, she realized *It is obviously from the See. But how did it come to be here?*

Her salamander self, driven by scent, turned into one of the Center's once-tidy tree-filled squares.

"There you are. You tiresome little man." Her words rang false in her ears as she stared at her handsome doctor, with a bloodied sword in his hand and an ogre's head and twitching body before him. His pair of wing-bound pixies and dusted ogre guards completed the tableau.

Her entrance surprised them, but then something warm and wet landed on her cheek. She gazed up as a powerful wind whipped through her hair.

The salamander's tongue caught the strange liquid. It squealed and bucked as the rain came down.

May held tight to her other self, but a sick malaise blossomed in her gut, and her gown grew heavy and wet, the threat she'd sensed earlier blossoming into panic.

The salamander screamed as the water hissed on its now slick skin. Flames sparked as rivulets of gold tore at the creature's hide.

One of the ogres shouted, "Doctor. She's behind you. Run!"

"Traitor!" May gasped. "You will die!" she screamed as the salamander writhed and shrank. Her feet touched the ground, and she felt for the magic that would unhinge her jaw. It would not come. There was nothing.

The air filled with the crackle and pop of flames that seemed to devour her salamander, which shrank, now the size of a large pig. She stared. *What is happening? Where is my power? Where is my special?*

Searing pain tore through her gut. She stared across at her doctor, half expecting to find he'd planted his sword in her belly. But no, her hand covered her middle. *Not again.* She searched for her salamander, now the size of a rat. It circled her ankles and attempted to spit fairy fire. Not even a wisp of smoke came from its tiny mouth.

To Redmond, the warp and weave of time had expanded. Where every day he wasted seconds, minutes, and hours, this one sword-gripping moment was a universe to itself. He stared at May, felt the vulnerability of his back and the two ogres who had seconds earlier wanted to kill him and eat his students, and prepared for battle with a creature whom he suspected was immortal.

"I will not live in a world of your making," he shouted through the rain.

May's hair tumbled and covered her face as her salamander self, now the size of a mole, ran frantic circles around her legs.

Behind him, one of the ogres cleared his throat. "Doctor, tell us what to do."

That's a good thing, he thought. As ogres were not subtle. What came out of their mouth was bankable. "Stay at my back till I tell you otherwise. One of you unshackle the sprites."

"Yes, Doctor," they replied in unison.

"Luluba and Seamus, you are both to flee the Center and find safety."

They too answered as one. "No."

Luluba continued, "This is our fight as much as yours. This is our world."

To which Seamus blurted out, "And I love you, Luluba. If we have to die, I need you to know that."

In the midst of all, there was a heavy pause. And then Luluba spoke, "I love you, Seamus."

Redmond made the connection as May threw back her head and searched the sky for the tempest's source.

"You will all die!" she shrieked.

"Not today." He remembered how Finn had pissed on his dust bunnies and how just his presence had freed him from the drug's enslavement. *How the hell did you do this?* Despite all, it was impossible not to smile. *He's pissing on all of us.*

"How dare you! I am May, queen of the Fey," she screamed. Her gown was soaked and was an unstable hodgepodge of chintz and tutti-frutti spangles.

He realized that the Hound's pee had robbed her of most, possibly all, of her power. But he would not risk another life. With sword drawn, he advanced on May.

"Doctor, stop. I am your queen."

"Take her to the cells," he ordered the ogres. "We have work to do."

He clenched the sword's hilt. Having just separated Snark's head from his body, he knew he could do it again.

"You wouldn't," she shrieked as she backed away, her escape thwarted by a clear-eyed ogre.

A tiny movement caught Redmond's eye. He looked down, and without thought, he stomped his booted foot onto the tiny salamander version of May. Its blood squished ichor green.

"No! It is forbidden!" she shrieked and fell to the ground.

He halted, half expecting a bolt of lightning to strike or a sinkhole to swallow him. For yes, a physical assault on royalty was treason.

May sobbed, her gaze riveted to the squished portion of her own flesh. Luluba and Seamus, their wings and feet unbound, flitted to his side.

"No." May crumpled to her knees. "You can't have done this."

"And I did," he said as the weight of his action pushed back the rage. "This is the end. For now you are irrevocably and truly broken. You will never rule."

Her head shot back, and she sprang to her feet.

He had no time to back away but did not strike her as she tried to claw at his face. The ogres intervened and gripped her arms and shackled her hands behind her back.

"Lock her away," Redmond instructed. He watched as she tried to gather her magic, her clothes and hair now a fluid mess, leaving her naked in parts and dressed in a patchwork of fabrics and fashions.

"Tell us what we're seeing," Luluba said.

"That which cannot, and should not, be fixed. We shall lock her up, for there are those who would still follow her, though I don't think our prior precautions will be necessary."

He looked to the ogres. "But take no risks. If you come upon any fairy dust, do not touch it. Seal it up tight so that we may dispose of it. Now get her out of here."

"You can't do this," May protested as one ogre gripped her by her bound wrists and the other laid a guiding hand on her shoulder. "You will pay. You will all pay."

"We already have," Redmond said. "You are not to leave her side until I come," he shouted after the ogres as they led her away. While things might never return to business as usual, ogres needed clear instructions. It was best to leave nothing to interpretation. He wondered if his grumpy captain of the guard had survived.

"There are so many dead," Seamus murmured.

His words sparked a swirl of emotion within Redmond. A stranger to committing cruel acts, he stared at the tiny creature he'd killed. Its blood had turned from green to an acid yellow, its innards laid bare. He took his sword, and knowing that salamanders were creatures of resurrection, he crouched and methodically chopped it like a prep chef into smaller and smaller pieces. His work was interrupted by something hot and wet on the nape of his neck.

Startled, he whipped his head around to find his beautiful hound, albeit hairless. It lapped at his face. "Finn!" He nearly fell backward as he dropped his sword and struggled to his feet. "Finn!"

The massive dog wrapped his front legs around Redmond's shoulders.

"Finn!" His fingers played over the silken stubble as they embraced. He breathed in the warm musk of his two-natured lover. "You came back. You came back to me," he whispered into the Hound's strong neck. "You are the hero of this tale, and I love you."

Braced on his hind legs and Redmond's shoulders, the Hound's focus shifted to the dismembered salamander. He barked and freed himself from Finn.

His back arched as he circled the mangled salamander remains. He sniffed the ground and then positioned himself over the once-great monster. He raised his right hind leg and pissed on it. As the stream met blood and guts, there was a loud sizzle, and flashes of sharp white light cut apart what remained. Magic rippled in the air as all that was left vanished.

At a distance, a crowd of fey several deep stood or hovered around the spectacle in the square. The rain had stopped. The sirens had gone silent.

"We have no queen," someone whispered. The words carried as though he'd shouted.

"She is not dead," someone responded.

"She will come back."

"She will want blood."

"She will eat us all."

"No." Redmond picked up his sword, and with soothing magic and honeyed words, he brought comfort through the fear. "May is not fit to rule. Here or anywhere. She is forever broken. She will not and cannot come back. And you have my word that she will never harm another soul." The last words he wondered at. But he mused, *The fey don't lie, so that must be the truth.*

Forty

LIGHTNING STRIKES and thunderclaps exploded from the Mist. Finn, still in the form of the Hound, stuck close to Redmond. Having been separated once, he vowed it would not happen again.

Redmond was his for now and forever. He sniffed the air. The cloying sweet stench of fairy fire was gone. *Good.* Something new approached, a blend of ozone, metal, and an emotion that made his limbs feel heavy. He pressed his flank against Redmond's legs and shook his snout. *The Mist comes.* He looked up as it rolled across the Western Sea and onto dry land.

Screams of fear arose from the Center. "We are doomed!"

"She was all that kept the Mist at bay. This is her revenge."

"It will devour us!"

"We should not have betrayed our queen."

Redmond groaned. His voice warmed the Hound, who wanted to say *I love you* but barked instead. *Close enough.*

Redmond whispered in his ear. "This is the curse of we fey. Freed from a despot and they already see the next terror."

The Hound shivered and shook off his animal form. Finn, albeit hairless and naked, wrapped Redmond tight and looked around at the hundreds of fey in varying shapes, colors, species, and sizes. Where he'd peed on the salamander remains, the marble cobblestone glistened as though freshly washed.

"Come," he told Redmond. "Let's face this new adventure together."

Redmond turned into him and stroked his shaved head. "Your hair." He slid his hand down to Finn's now smooth chest.

Unconcerned by his nakedness, Finn cocked an eyebrow as another part of his anatomy rose. "I'll explain it all. Apparently, there's a bit of fur in my pee."

Redmond smacked the side of his head. "Of course. I should have known."

"Do tell," Finn replied, savoring each moment with Redmond.

"You are the catalyst. The thing that changes everything but unto itself remains the same."

Finn chuckled. "I thought you guys didn't know chemistry."

"We don't. It's alchemy."

"It's the same where I come from. A catalyst can be used over and over to make a reaction occur."

"And that is what you are." He gripped Finn's hand tight. "You are mine, at least for this life. You have changed me. But when my life or your human life has run its course, you, the Hound, go on." He chuckled.

"Tell me," Finn said.

"I see the joke in it."

"I wondered if you would."

Redmond flicked Finn's nose with thumb and forefinger. "You think me dim."

"Never. I just thought it was a human thing."

"Hair of the dog," Redmond groaned. "It's obvious once you see the thing. When… if… we come through this next adventure, tell me how it was done."

"Of course, but you've got the gist of it."

"And more," Redmond whispered, one hand on Finn's broad chest, the other wrapped around the nape of his neck.

"Everything. We will have time for everything."

"One hopes," Redmond said as lightning cracked the sky.

Finn turned toward the sea and the rapidly approaching wall of mist. His breath caught. "It's just one thing after another."

"Yes."

The Mist, which had rolled like a juggernaut toward the Center, now halted and spread against the distant edge of the broad moat. Behind it, all was concealed.

Its advancing arm, like an amoeba's pseudopod, rose up hundreds of feet. At its base an opening the size of a door appeared, and a broad, wispy tongue formed a bridge across the water.

"We are doomed," an elf muttered as she gathered her brood and hid them in her skirts.

Luluba approached Redmond. She appeared torn between this new danger and the curiosity of her professor's naked and human boyfriend.

Finn smiled at her. "I don't bite… much." But he too was riveted by the tiny speck at the base of the Mist, where something solid waited, like an actor behind a curtain.

Finn looked through the breached wall toward Engine Twenty-Five, now parked and silent.

Someone had turned its flashers back on. Next to it stood the group he'd crossed over with, and a few yards away from them, its focus on the Mist, was the puka. He trained his hound senses, ever more accessible, onto the puka. Who he'd come to realize, like May's salamander, was not necessarily in its true form. The black mare was more like a shell or comfortable costume. She had no fear, but other emotions caught in Finn's ears and his nostrils—excitement, anticipation… and even. She's *aroused*.

"Tell me," Redmond said.

"I think we're okay. Whatever is about to happen, I think we're okay."

Charlie jogged over to Finn and Redmond. He stopped every few yards to glance back at the wall of milky blue that rose from the distant meadow and obliterated much of the sky.

He gave Finn an appreciative nod. "I cannot get over how buff you got."

Before Finn could respond, Charlie held out a hand to Redmond. "I'm Charlie Fitzgerald. Finn and I go way back."

The two shook. Finn smiled at the gesture, and as he often did, inventoried the similarities between Charlie and Rory. Only now, this was pure Charlie and everything he loved about him and what he represented. A guy who ran into buildings on fire for a living. Sure, they might all be facing death… again, but what mattered to him was coming over to meet Redmond.

Charlie whispered, "I'm glad you found each other. Love is awesome! Finn, we'd all but given up on you."

"'Tis true," Redmond replied as two female figures appeared before the mist bridge.

Katye, all in pink with her strawberry-blonde hair falling below her waist, and Lizbeta in a shimmery blue-black gown comprised of fairies no larger than pinheads, each of them holding a thin strand of mist that trailed behind her like a wedding train.

Gasps filled the square. "The Sisters."

"It's the Sisters. We are doomed."

"They will take revenge. They will eat us all!"

"For the love of God," Finn muttered. "You are a gloomy lot."

"Yes and no," Redmond replied. "It's a basic fey defense. If you expect the worst, you're never disappointed, and sometimes you get a good surprise."

"Not just fey," Charlie replied. "Lots of humans are like that. But not me." He stared at Katye and Lizbeta, both of whom he'd met. "Something big is about to happen." He glanced toward Liam, who met his gaze. He beckoned with his head for him to join them. Liam shook his head.

"Oh, for Pete's sake!" Charlie shouted. "Liam, get over here."

"I can't," Liam replied. "I am not invited."

Redmond's gaze narrowed as he turned from the approaching fairy queens, who daintily glided across the bridge. "I know that creature."

"Watch it, buddy. His name is Liam. He's my boyfriend."

"He is changed."

"He is brave, and he is sweet," Charlie replied.

"You know his past."

"I do, and don't you dare throw that in his face. You don't know what he's been through and why he did the things he did."

"True." Redmond looked from Charlie to the approaching queens to Liam and the others by the flashing red beast. "Liam Summer," he shouted. "You are welcome here, as are all of your companions." His gaze strayed to the puka, a creature he had studied at length but never once seen. "I extend my hospitality to all of you. Be my guests, and stay for a day or stay forever."

Before Gran, Liam, or any of them could take him up on the offer, the two sisters floated past them and stopped before the crumbling wall.

Lizbeta raised a hand that seemed tethered to the mist. Silence and calm washed over all.

It was like fairy dust, minus the drug. Both she and Katye turned in unison, stopping to give a little nod to each of those by the fire engine, to the puka, to Redmond and Finn, and even to Luluba and Seamus.

Katye pointed at Alice. She whispered to Lizbeta, who in turn nodded and then spoke. "You have done well. Now bring us our sister. Bring us May."

Forty-One

REDMOND TURNED to Gark, who to his great relief had escaped the dust and helped hundreds of inhabitants flee through the tunnels. "Do as Lizbeta asks. But take no risks."

"Yes, Doctor."

As they waited, Lizbeta and Katye wandered outside the walls of the Center. "You are welcome to enter," Redmond offered.

"Thank you, but no," Katye said as she stood next to the puka and stroked its broad back.

"They're not really here," Finn told him.

"Tell me."

"I can smell it, and look how Lizbeta is still covered in mist. She's here, but she's also elsewhere. As for Katye, observe how the light around her is not of this realm. Her scent is not of here but of my world. Though I don't think she's there either."

While he'd not intended for his words to carry, Katye responded. "You have grown into the Hound." She gave his naked form a slow once-over. "You suit one another." She smiled as she caught the glances between him and Redmond. She nodded. "May this life of yours be long and filled with happiness. It is possible. Love makes everything possible."

A loud belch emanated from within Engine Twenty-Five. It was followed by three more. "What the hell—" Jerod started to say before Alex clamped a hand on his mouth.

He licked Alex's fingers as a sustained baritone cry came from under one of the benches in the back of the fire engine.

"Stop that." Alex pulled back his hand and wiped it on his pants.

"No questions." He climbed back into the fire engine and searched in the cubbies and under the seats for the source of the noise. "We had a stowaway," he yelled back as a giant blueandgreen African bullfrog hopped into the doorway and then leapt to the ground.

"Lance!" Katye cried out and would have come to his side if not for her sister's restraining hand.

"We cannot. He cannot," Lizbeta said. "We must be resolute."

"Yes." Tears popped in the corners of Katye's eyes as Lance bounded toward her. He made as if to leap into her arms, but where he should have connected with something solid, he passed through as if she were not there. He landed on the ground, shook his head, and tried a second and third time. With each try, he croaked, thumped his meaty hind legs, and wailed.

Katye crumpled to the ground, her gaze torn between her frog lover and her sister. "Please," she implored Lizbeta.

"It cannot be. You know this."

Katye crouched on the ground at eye level with Lance. "I am sorry, my love. So sorry." Her words choked in her throat. "We end here." She clutched her belly as Lance howled and hopped toward her, his every effort to make contact thwarted by her lack of substance.

Gark returned with May and the two ogres who'd escorted her away. At a cautious distance, a parade of fey followed.

The restrained May appeared old. Her skin hung from her bones, and deep bags were etched beneath her amber eyes. Her clothes were like something a child might throw together when playing dress-up in her mother's closet, only they continued to change with mismatched shoes and pants and dresses that were sometimes on her body and would then twist and shift to become turbans and scarves on her head and around her neck. She strained against the shackles that confined her hands and immobilized her fingers from working magic.

The crowd gasped. She sneered and shouted at them. "You are nothing without a ruler. The Mist will devour you all."

A pixie cried, "It is a curse. She is cursing us!"

"She cannot," Lizbeta said as she approached May and the guards. "Sister." She placed a restraining but gentle hand on May's shoulder. Strands of mist wafted from her fingers and wrapped around May. It calmed the disarray of her clothes as a tidy little black dress, complete with kitten-heel pumps and an updo, arranged themselves. "Our time has run its course, sister." Lizbeta's gaze landed on Alex, Adam, and Alice Nevus. She raised a mist-trailing arm and pointed to them. "There. You… Marilyn Nevus. You are the mother of kings and of the girl who went down the hole."

"Yes. That is true," Marilyn said with caution in her voice.

Lizbeta's extended hand moved like a compass pointer. It passed over Marilyn, Alex, and Adam, and rested on Alice.

"Yes," Katye said, still crouched near Lance. "It is for that one."

"Agreed," Lizbeta replied.

Alice did not move as the sisters studied her. Free from her previous dust addiction, her eyes were blue and clear as a summer sky. "Tell me," she said.

"Alice, it is for you to take the throne, as it was intended. Learn from May's mistakes… and from ours. Choose your court wisely, though I think much of that is done." She made eye contact with each of those who had come through.

As her gaze landed on Flora, a tiny silver pixie shrieked, "It's Flora Fitzgerald! It's our Flora!"

Flora's head whipped around. "I know that voice."

Before the words had left her mouth, a flock of tiny pixies, most of them silver but a few with skin of copper and gold, swarmed around her. "Flora Flora Flora. It's you we adore-ah. Flora Flora Flora, you never could conform-ah. Flora Flora Flora, it is you we shall transform-ah."

Flora's eyes were bright as she held out her fingers like perches and whispered forgotten names to the tiny creatures who alit. "Hyacinth. Melba. Spring Grass. Frog Toe."

Around her silver-haired head, the pixies sang. Their words blurred together as the beating of their wings cast a milky opal haze. Strands of colored silk flew between their tiny fingers, and like a macramé project gone mad, fabric formed.

Despite her heartache, Katye pointed and clapped. "A pixie cocoon. They weave a cocoon."

"Gran!" Charlie shouted. "Get out of there." He raced to her side, but the whirr of wings created a solid wall he could not penetrate. "Gran. Get out!"

"No, Charlie," she shouted from inside the thickening wall of multicolored silk. "It's beautiful, Charlie." Her voice grew soft. She giggled.

Liam came to Charlie's side. "It's okay… I think."

"Gran." Charlie pawed at the dense fabric, his fingers tangled in the limbs and wings of manic pixies, who'd stop for a millisecond, waggle a finger, and then get back to their weaving. "Gran."

She stopped answering. She giggled.

Frantic, Charlie looked around but found that all eyes were trained on the magnificent structure the pixies wove. He looked to Katye. "Help her."

"Charlie, the thing is done. Look."

He turned back to find a couple dozen pixies smiling at him from midair. Between them was a six-foot-tall banana-shaped woven sculpture that glistened with rainbows.

"Go ahead, Charlie," one of them said. "Give it a whack. Break it open."

"I've heard of this," Liam said. "I've never seen one."

"Nor I," said Redmond. "This is fascinating. Do as she says, Charlie. Open it."

"Gran." Charlie gently touched the brilliant fabric. It was hard to the touch. He pressed harder, and it cracked like an egg.

"Go for it!" a pixie urged, his pink-and-black wings atwitter with excitement. "Give it a smack and whack."

Charlie rapped his knuckles hard and created a hole at the top of the structure. He saw only air inside. "What…."

Liam jabbed his shoulder. "No questions."

Frantic, Charlie broke off hunks of the brilliant construction. Halfway down, he stumbled back. For there inside the cocoon was a little girl with auburn hair, cornflower-blue eyes, and silver wings held fast by the remnants of her shell.

The pixies could not contain their excitement. "Get the rest, Charlie. Big and strong. Get the rest. We want Flora. We want Flora."

The girl made eye contact with Charlie. "Set me free, Charlie."

"Sure… Gran." And with Liam and Redmond to help, they cracked and peeled away the last of the beautiful casing.

She whispered so that only they, and of course the Hound, could hear. "I think you better start calling me Flora."

The previously grumbling crowds stood and gaped in silence. Flora, with the aid of several pixies, spread out her dove-white wings to dry. She shrugged her shoulders, and the wings twitched. She looked at one of the pixies. "Okay, it's more in the back." She began to beat a rhythm. A gust of wind sent her six feet up. She threw back her head and laughed. "I can fly, Charlie. I can fly!"

The puka whinnied with impatience, turned, and made for the misty bridge that spanned the moat.

Katye smiled, though her cheek was still stained with tears. "Perhaps we've managed one good thing this day. Flora had to break, and that's not always bad." She knelt on all fours next to Lance. And while their flesh could not connect, she kissed him on the mouth.

As they separated, the air around him sputtered and sparked. And where there had hopped and wailed a giant blue-green bullfrog now crouched a tall, beautiful man with flowing raven curls, and like Finn, he was naked. He attempted to embrace Katye. His arms found only air.

"No." She held a hand to her chest. "We end here. We follow in the steps of our parents, and for any with even a whiff of the mortal, this passage would mean death. There are no exceptions, no haffling or true-love codicils. Not even a willing sacrifice, like tragic Nimby or lovely Flora, will give safe passage to anyone mortal."

"Then stay, Katye. Stay with me," Lance pleaded.

Lizbeta, with one hand clasped in May's, which had been freed from her shackles, gave Katye her other. With a sigh and sad smile, they followed the puka back across the moat and through the opening in the Mist, which closed behind them.

As rapidly as the Mist had appeared, it retreated. Where it had curtained the edge of the Unsee, it flew back farther and farther still, and then it vanished from sight.

Forty-Two

A HUSH spread over the several thousand fey in the field and clustered in the square. They watched the Mist retreat to leave the glittering expanse of the Western Sea.

"It's gone. The Mist is gone. That cannot be."

"May's gone. She will return. She always returns."

The crowd's numbers swelled as those who'd hidden in basements, tunnels, and attics came out.

A circle formed around Redmond, Finn, Alice, the transformed Flora, and the others.

It grew tighter, and there was no mincing of words as seeds of discontent found the fertile soil of fear and uncertainty.

"A girl. That is no queen. Queen Alice. That's not a queen's name."

"And a haffling at that. She will flee between worlds and leave us to war. Or worse, she will cause a human invasion."

"You must give her a chance."

"They will steal our lands."

Dorothea, grief-stricken and furious, fanned their fears. "It will all fall to chaos. We must bring Queen May back. Sure, she ate some of you, but she kept order. She was a true queen. This puny mortalette, she is nothing."

Finn ran a hand across his shorn head. He looked to Redmond and around at the others, which included the ex-frog Lance, who like himself didn't have on a stitch as he stared out at the sea where his true love had vanished.

"I am sorry for you," Finn offered.

"We had centuries together, and now…. I am Lancelot, by the way. Those two I've met." He nodded toward Alex and Jerod. "The others I've seen through different eyes. The world is quite different when you're green and hoppy."

"I can relate."

A fight erupted in the crowd as an ungraceful troll accidentally disturbed a platter of brownies. The tiny creatures screamed in protest and jabbed needle-sharp swords into the troll's feet and ankles. The lumbering creature tried to flee, but in so doing knocked over a pram of baby elves, whose mother joined the brownies in their attack.

Liam turned to Charlie. "This is how and who we are. Without a ruler, no matter how despotic, we fall into turmoil. This, more than anything, was the cause and need for the Mist. I see that well. It's no mistake that the war between our kind had no end."

"Enough!" Alice shouted. Her voice, like a clarion, soared over the crowd. As though born to it, her feet floated off the ground. She rose to a height that brought her level with Lance and Finn, who came to her sides like a pair of naked sentinels.

Taking their cue, Redmond, Alex, Jerod, Liam, Charlie, Marilyn, Adam, and Flora with her battalion of pixies followed suit.

Alice nodded to Finn.

He smiled back at her. "You will do." He raised his chin and howled. The sound carried beyond the walls of the Center. Like the waves from a nuclear blast, it roared across the meadow, the moat, and the forests beyond. It sailed out over the Western Sea in one direction and to the eastern borders in the other. It carried to the north and to the south. It brought silence and caused all who heard it to stop, to wait, and to listen.

Alice raised her arms. Her palms faced upward as she floated higher than the tallest ogre or troll. Her blonde hair floated behind, and while dressed in jeans, a Ramones tee, and scuffed red high-tops, all eyes fixed on her. Her graceful arms drew symbols in the air. She again looked toward Finn, held up three fingers, and nodded.

He howled in strong bursts. From all sides, even from within the earth, it was answered by thousands. The roar was deafening.

New fear appeared on the faces of the mob. Whispers stirred.

"She calls an army."

"She will force us to her will."

"She will be worse than May."

"Yay!"

Alice floated and danced upon the wind. She appeared unfazed and unafraid. With clear blue eyes, she gazed out over the kingdom she'd been handed. She wafted higher. She looked from the mumbling crowds to her brothers and mother. She spoke as the first of the massive dogs she and Finn had summoned appeared.

He looked up at her. "We are an army. We are your army, my lady."

"Yes, and so our reign begins." She assumed the posture of the statue of Mary that stood atop her elementary school in Chinatown in New York City, and with arms wide open, she declared, "I am Alice. I am the girl who went down the hole. I am a haffling, and I am whole. I will be your queen."

CALEB JAMES is an author, member of the Yale volunteer faculty, practicing psychiatrist, and clinical trainer. He writes both fiction and nonfiction and has published books in multiple genres and under different names. Writing as Charles Atkins, he has been a Lambda Literary finalist. He lives in Connecticut with his partner and four cats.

Website: charlesatkins.com
Blog: calebjamesblog.wordpress.com
Facebook: www.facebook.com/Caleb-James-536765356387453

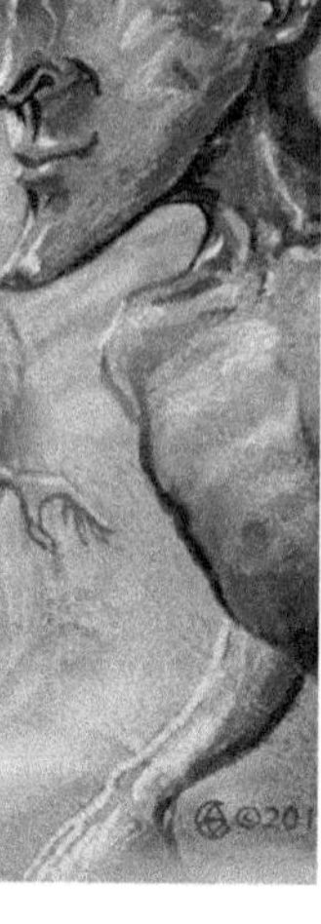

Haffling

CALEB JAMES

The Haffling: Book One

All sixteen-year-old Alex Nevus wants is to be two years older and become his sister Alice's legal guardian. That, and he'd like his first kiss, preferably with Jerod Haynes, the straight boy with the beautiful girlfriend and the perfect life. Sadly, wanting something and getting it are very different. Strapped with a mentally ill mother, Alex fears for his own sanity. Having a fairy on his shoulder only he can see doesn't help, and his mom's schizophrenia places him and Alice in constant jeopardy of being carted back into foster care.

When Alex's mother goes missing, everything falls apart. Frantic, he tracks her to a remote corner of Manhattan and is transported to another dimension—the land of the Unsee, the realm of the Fey. There he finds his mother held captive by the power-mad Queen May and learns he is half-human and half-fey—a Haffling.

As Alex's human world is being destroyed, the Unsee is being devoured by a ravenous mist. Fey are vanishing, and May needs to cross into the human world. She needs something only Alex can provide, and she will stop at nothing to possess it… to possess him.

www.dsppublications.com

THE HAFFLING:
BOOK TWO
Exile
CALEB JAMES

The Haffling: Book Two

Liam Summer, with the face of an angel and the body of an underwear model, has done bad things. Raised as the whore and cat's paw of a murderous fairy queen, he has ruined many with his beauty. When Queen May's plot to unite and rule the fairy and human realms fails, Liam wakes naked and alone in a Manhattan building on fire. Unaware the blaze is arson, and he's its intended victim, he prepares to die.

Enter ax-wielding FDNY firefighter Charlie Fitzgerald, who Liam mistakes for an ogre assassin. As Charlie rescues Liam, he realizes the handsome blond has nowhere to go. So he does what he and his family have always done—he helps.

As for Queen May, trapped in the body of a flame-throwing salamander, she may be down, but she's not out. Yes, she failed the last time, but Liam— and others—will pay. She knows what must be done: possess a haffling, cross into the human world engorged with magic, and become queen and Goddess over all.

As Liam realizes the danger they all face, he discovers unexpected truths. That even the most wicked are not beyond redemption, and that love—true love—is a gift even he can receive.

www.dsppublications.com